SoulShares
Gale Force
Book Two

Rory Ni Coileain

Gale Force© 2015 by Rory Ni Coileain
SoulShares Book 2.

For more information contact:
Riverdale Avenue Books
5676 Riverdale Avenue
Riverdale, NY 10471.

www.riverdaleavebooks.com

Design by www.formatting4U.com
Cover by Insatiable Fantasy Designs Inc.

Digital ISBN 9781626012004
Print ISBN 9781626012011

Second Edition, June, 2015

First Edition May 2013 Ravenous Romance.

Dedication

To my son. *Allons-y!*

To my sisters. One for all, all for one!

And to Triunity — One Love, thrice expressed.

Prologue

The Realm
June 24, 2012 (human reckoning)

Surely there was a way to explain this. *"Your Grace, I have certain moral objections to ending the world as our race knows it"*? Well, no… nice drama, but not strictly true, and it was those little inconsistencies that ended up coming back to bite you in the ass. "Yes, I could. No, I won't."

Liadan had begun to smile with Conall's first pronouncement, but her smile quickly faded. Liadan Mavelle was evidently not a Fae accustomed to hearing the word 'no.' Most Nobles weren't. When one could channel the element of one's Demesne, one got used to everyone—well, everyone who wasn't a Royal—dancing to one's tune. "Somehow, I don't think I heard that correctly."

Of course, if there was one thing a Noble of Air could be sure of doing, it was hearing correctly. Even a commoner such as himself could hardly claim to have missed anything the air might have brought to him. "Then allow me to repeat myself, your Grace." He bowed slightly, letting his mildness carry the weight of his sarcasm. "No."

1

"Perhaps you misunderstand. This is not a request."

Conall closed his eyes. Maybe the Noble would mistake it for a commoner's subservience. But it actually was discovering there was a point at which inane clichés gave him a headache. "I understand perfectly. But no vendetta is worth the cost of what you're asking me to do."

The Noble lady scoffed. "Cost? To the most powerful mage since the Loremasters? Don't make me laugh."

""I wouldn't dream of it." *Because it might break your face. And come to think of it... No, Conall. Don't go there. Bad Fae.* "Not to me, your Grace. To the Realm." Was it even worthwhile to try to make her understand? He'd given up hope of driving away the greedy, the righteous, and the merely curious; it was almost as if Fae were willfully blind to what the unchecked use of magick did to the world around them. Especially *his* magick.

But maybe this time... "Magick isn't infinite, your Grace.

Whether you channel the elements, as you and your fellow Nobles do, or play with the raw stuff of magick itself, after the manner of us common folk—"

Liadan snorted, a very unladylike sound. "There's nothing at all common about what you do, Conall Dary."

Conall plowed a hand through his hair, until the copper mane stuck out every which way. Maybe if he just looked a little more imposing, a little more impressive, his words and his observations would carry some weight. It didn't help that he'd stopped aging, physically, somewhere short of the mid—to late twenties, the norm for a Fae. He just didn't *look* like what he was, and even a people accustomed to looking youthful for centuries seemed disinclined to listen to him. Even when they could see perfectly well what he was capable of doing.

"Look, your Grace." He glanced around, then up; an apple tree shaded them from the late afternoon sun, blossoms and fruit of every color apples knew hanging just over their heads. He reached up and plucked a perfect golden orb from a low-hanging branch and held it out on his palm. "It's in the prime of life, wouldn't you say? And yet, in the course of things, it ages. Unlike, say, the luckless female who has her eye on your *bragan a lae*." Liadan's intense green eyes narrowed—well, perhaps 'toy of the day' hadn't been the best choice of words. "Your pardon, her eye on Lord Declan. Yet watch what happens, when I age this fruit, the way you ask me to age her."

Conall closed his eyes, cupping the apple in his palms. The barriers he had to keep between himself and his magick were formidable, in necessary proportion to his gift, and taking them down even for so small a thing as this was not something he did lightly, or easily. But if it worked, if he could make her understand, it would be worth it. He sighed, and breathed deeply, and reached within.

And the magick leaped up, as it always did. Swirled within and around him, ecstatically. It gloried in freedom, the way a caged bird did, once released. One of the definitions of magick—one of the best— was that it was the essence of wildness, of untameability. And though it lay quietly enough, stored in every living thing in the Realm, it was never

3

meant to *remain* quiet. It was meant to be set free, channeled, by one with Conall Dary's gift.

Set free. And spent. Irrevocably. He focused, turning his will to the apple in his hand. He filled it with the torrent that poured through him, and shaped it with a whispered word, Air, sculpting power. Pictured the fruit softening, withering. Beginning to die.

"Yes." The Noble lady's voice was a hushed whisper, almost reverent. "Exactly that."

Conall's eyes snapped open. The apple was what he had expected, a moldering heap of skin and slime that made his skin crawl. Dead petals brushed his skin as they fell from the branch over his head; he looked up and shuddered at the sight of the dull wood of the branch, the mottled fruit, the leaves hanging limply. This was what the branch looked like, with most of the magick sustaining it drawn from it by the demands of his channeling.

"Perfect." Liadan smiled, a very cat-in-cream expression. More a bird-in-cat, actually, anticipatorily sated. "Why would you be unable to do the same to a Fae?"

For a moment, all Conall could do was stare. "Don't you *see*?" He gestured sharply upward with a curt nod.

The female shrugged lazily. "It's a branch. It will recover eventually."

Conall's jaw muscles worked as his teeth ground together. "That's not the damned *point*." If he watched carefully, he might be able to see the power gradually suffusing the branch again, the leaves trembling as if in a breeze, the colors gradually intensifying, the apples filling out, flowers budding once again. But recovery would take time, and the branch would never be exactly as it had been. Everything in the Realm was formed of magick, and every use of magick drained it. Usually the drain was barely perceptible, even to the exquisitely honed senses of a Fae. But Conall Dary, the greatest mage since the Loremasters, left a swath of destruction in his wake every time he tapped his powers. Which left him with no choice but to lock them away, as often and as securely as he could.

"A fruit is meant to age and die. A Fae is not." He fought the urge to speak more slowly, more loudly; to act as if an Air Fae was unable to understand you was the worst insult imaginable. And he had a feeling he was going to need some insults left to fall back on, no sense wasting them all now. "As much power as it took to do this, it would take a thousand times more to age an immortal Fae."

"And you lack the power?" The Lady Liadan pouted, with all the sullen charm of a thwarted toddler. "I wouldn't have thought so, after all the tales I've heard about you. Do you save your powers for those who bed you, so they'll spread nothing but glowing reports?"

Conall's lip curled in a snarl. "Some of us have no need to enhance our abilities, your Grace." There was no way, of course, he was going to tell this supercilious twat he had never dared risk the magical power surge that overwhelmed every Fae during sex. Never dared so much as friendship, not since just after he came into his birthright of power, and learned in the hardest way possible the only thing anyone ever wanted from him was that power. Present company included. "And provoke me as much as you like, I'm not going to damage the very fabric of the Realm so you can have the satisfaction of the shrieks of a wrinkled, toothless courtesan!"

Liadan's hands balled into fists, catching up the pale blue silk of her gown. But her voice was calm, even cool. "You will do as I command, because I command it. You need no other reason, and you will not speculate as to mine." Her dark hair stirred in a wind that seemed to cling to her. "And you will not speak to me in this way."

"I will not waste my breath speaking to you at all." Conall turned on his heel. "As well speak to a stone, it has better chance of understanding."

Conall stopped short, without time for so much as a cry, as the air became solid in his lungs. Caught by surprise, choking, he clutched at his throat, struggled in vain to draw breath. His vision went white around the edges, and began to dance, stars exploding all around him. His chest heaved, without result; he fell to his knees. And in his panic, he reached within for magick. But he stopped. *No—not even to save my life, no—*

—something struck the back of his head, hard, and white went black.

***

There was something warm and wet under Conall's cheek. He looked up, and was seized with a wave of dizziness and nausea so severe that his head hit the floor hard. When it did, the warm wetness splashed; drops fell within his line of sight, and he saw that it was blood. His own, presumably.

6

What the hell...? He pushed himself up. Well, no, he didn't. His hands were chained behind his back, and the chains were burning him. He sucked in a breath, and damped down his magickal abilities with everything in him. The searing heat told him he was bound with truesilver; truesilver burned at the touch of magick, and chains forged from it burned more fiercely with every use of magickal power by or near the one chained. Unfortunately for him, unless he kept his own abilities under rigid control, he channeled enough magickal energy as a matter of course to burn his hands off at the wrists. Even the small trickle of magick it had taken, and was still taking, to heal the wound that had only just stopped trickling red down the back of his neck was raising blisters. Throw in the way his gut roiled every time he even thought about actively using magick, and no, he was most definitely disincentivized to use any kind of magick.

Where the hell was he? He managed to turn his head a little, and saw a curved gray stone wall limned in moonlight. A bare room, with a polished floor that reflected the moonlight like a flawless mirror.

No, not quite flawless. There was light within it, the faintest traces of it. Points, slivers, arcs. His vision blurred the traces at first; they almost seemed to dance, to shift. But slowly, as he focused, it came clear. Light, like the finest wire imaginable, set in a floor of midnight black, in a pattern of...

Bile rose in Conall's throat, burned at the back of his throat. Not *a* pattern. *The* Pattern. The bitch had stopped the air in his lungs, bashed him over the head with something—probably the tree branch he had so thoughtfully killed for her—and then, somehow, had

7

him truechained and dragged to the Pattern's portal, here to await the proper alignment of the moon to trigger its magick. Disposing of a witness? Or simply mortally offended by his refusal to tear a hole in the magickal essence of the Realm for the sake of her jealousy? If he had to guess, he'd go with the latter; the Lady Liadan didn't seem bright enough to be worrying about the former.

No amount of blithering was helping him ignore the deadly danger just below his face, or doing anything to relieve his growing panic. Gathering all his strength, he pushed against the floor with his legs, and rolled onto his back, away from the lethal gleaming black surface beneath him. Once his head stopped spinning, though, he saw the last confirmation of his suspicions, the round window set into the wall, the circle of the full moon nearly filling it. And when the window was full…

As he watched, shivering, a black shape passed between him and the moon's disk, wheeled, and passed again. A hunting night-hawk, by the look of it, and a *savac-dui*, a black-hooded hawk, his own House-guardian, by the piercing call carried to him by the wind. An Air Fae could understand any language carried by the air, and legend had it that there was a spark of Fae soul in every bird. They understood. Especially the predators, closest kin to a Fae. In their language that was not a language he heard:

fREE yOURSELF

He shook his head, despairing. Small wonder the hawk saw his predicament; nothing escaped the eyes of the night hunters. But as perceptive as it was, he dared not take its advice.

Not that he couldn't. The portal chamber was warded from within by the mightiest magicks of a score of scores of the ancient Loremasters—he could feel the wards, sense the intricacy and the sheer power of the channelings—but if any Fae since the Sundering had any chance at all to break through those wards, it was he.

But, as he had tried to tell Liadan, the cost was too great. Not to him—although he would surely lose his hands to the truesilver, channeling magick so intense. No, the loss of his hands paled beside the toll that would be taken by the magick itself. Magick strong enough to shatter the wards around this place would leave everything for hectares around blasted and devastated, never to recover. It could damage the Pattern itself—even destroy it.

tOO lATE

As the cry reached Conall's ears, the full moon filled the window. A cold light flooded in, and it was as if the floor fell away beneath him, the smooth, unyielding blackness giving way to the brilliant, cold tracing of the lines of the Pattern. A wind began to swirl around him, fierce, battering, and for one heart-stopping moment it seemed he hovered above the cruel edges. He looked down... down... it went on forever, there was no bottom; he hung suspended over nothing but the glittering wires. Panic was a metallic taste in his mouth, a sick fire in his veins. He *could* be free; the magick was surging in him, itself desperate, trying to get away from the yawning chasm below. All he had to do, it gibbered at him, was close his eyes, block out the stomach-twisting sight, and whisper a word. One word.

"No."

And on the word, all fury broke loose. The wind slammed him against the wall, wrenching his shoulders in their sockets; sucking the very air from his lungs, silencing him utterly. His own element, turned traitor.

And then the wind came for Conall Dary.

Chapter One

Greenwich Village
New York City

"What?"

"I said, I can't thank you enough for doing this." Terry laughed softly. "You aren't going to tell me you can't hear me over the needle, are you?"

"Sorry." Josh felt himself blushing a little, and let up on the foot pedal. "What do you mean, 'this'?—giving you a couple of days off, or inking your Firebird?"

"Both. And no apologies necessary, we both know how wrapped up you get in your work." Terry took advantage of the pause to tilt his leg so he could look down his calf and see the bird's brilliant plumage. "That is absolutely exquisite."

"So is the bird." Josh grinned, and turned to dip the needle once again in the bright red ink, stepping on the foot pedal a few times to fill the reservoir. Just because he and Terry hadn't succeeded as a couple was no reason not to appreciate the other tat artist's incredible dancer's body. "You sure you don't want to take a break, here? We've been at this for what, two hours now? And we have to start lining up for the march in a couple of hours."

11

"You think you can finish in an hour?"

"Well, I could, but—"

"But nothing." Terry's jaw firmed. "I want you to be the one to do this, and if we put off finishing it till tomorrow, Bryce will be back, and—"

Terry's voice shut down, but Josh easily finished the sentence for him. *And he's not going to want my hands all over your leg.* "All right, baby, I'll take care of you." He gently patted the hard-muscled leg propped on the table before him, and stepped on the foot pedal again. "Though you could do this last bit yourself, just as easily."

Dark curls swung and bobbed as Terry shook his head. "Nope. Your ink is special, you know that. It always has been. Why do you think my appointment book filled up within half an hour after I sent out the e-mail blast that you'd be here for a few days before the march?"

Josh cleared his throat and bent to study his work more closely. "Probably just a coincidence. I haven't worked in Greenwich Village in what, five years? Six?" Carefully, he filled in a tail feather, the vibrant color seeming almost to glow.

"Six sounds about right. But you're magic, I tell you. People don't forget that."

Josh chuckled, wiping away excess ink with a soft white cloth and moving on to the next feather. Magic? The Village had been magic, for a while, sharing Terry's tattoo parlor by day and his bed by night, whatever nights the other man hadn't been out pursuing his avocation at dance rehearsals, or performances, or meeting rich patrons of the fine arts.

He bit back a growl, gradually etching the finely-

grained pattern into his ex's flesh. Their breakup
hadn't been Terry's fault, the man was as innocent as a
kitten, for God's sake. He lived for ink and ballet, and
Bryce had been passionate about both and willing to
help bankroll Terry's second life, his trockadero
company, something Josh had never been able to
manage. And then he'd found out about the
opportunity in D.C.... and it had just seemed like the
time to go. You lived, you learned, you cried, and you
moved on.

And every once in a while, you came full circle.
Even if only for a couple of days. "That does it, baby.
Take good care of it." He patted Terry's thigh. "I'm
clocking out, as soon as I clean up here. See you
uptown."

***

Josh's shoulders ached—the careful padding of
the Mother Ginger puppet's light pine frame wasn't
much help, this late in the Pride march. Mother Ginger
needed to make some serious time with Jenny Craig,
in his humble opinion.

Helping Terry out like this was still more fun than
just about anything legal, though. The dancers of
Terry's trock company were marching in costumes
from the *Nutcracker*, and of course all the 'little
children' who occasionally scurried to hide under
Mother Ginger's voluminous skirts were in fact large,
sweaty men in nothing but tights and overstuffed
jockstraps. Emphasis on the 'sweaty'—even the
swamps of D.C. had nothing on dear old New York
City in late June.

Almost done. The last glimpse he'd gotten from under the skirts had been of Grove Street just branching off Christopher. Just a few blocks from Terry's apartment, and not all that far from the end of the route, either. Then he could shed his burden and head over to Rose's Turn for a cold one, assuming he could get in the door on Pride Day—oh, no, wait, Rose's had closed, the year after he left the city. *Wonder what that hot bartender's doing now—*

Josh stumbled, nearly fell headlong, and barely caught himself as Mother Ginger teetered precariously. *What the hell—*

There was a man under his feet. A gorgeous, chained man.

He stopped dead, convinced for one awful moment he'd somehow knocked the guy down, that he was responsible for the dead weight not responding to the accidental nudge of his foot. But that didn't make sense, he hadn't been walking fast enough for that even with the big wooden frame he was carrying. Whoever this was, he must have been down already, and rolled under the puppet.

Carefully, Josh lifted the frame off his shoulders and set it down, kneeling under it, letting it shelter the two of them as he took the other man by the shoulder. At the contact, all the air left him in a rush, and a tingling sensation swept across his skin. But before he could finish sucking in a breath, it was past. *It's the heat. Must be.*

There was a bit of dried blood on the man's shirt, worst toward the back, so Josh rolled him gently. There wasn't much swelling, and no bleeding at all, though there was a long, mostly-healed-over cut barely visible through the short red hair. And the back of the man's head was flecked with what looked like—but surely couldn't be—shreds of bark. *What did he do, back into a tree at a dead run? A week ago?*

"Josh? What is it? You okay under there?"

Terry's voice, God bless him. "Got a man down, baby. Get this thing off me, will you?"

As Terry awkwardly moved the heavy puppet off the two of them, Josh rolled the stranger to face him. And found himself short of breath again. The guy was beautiful. There was no other word for it. Thick, wavy, copper-colored hair, fine straight brows, cheekbones that could probably cut paper, and the most perfectly shaped mouth Josh had ever seen outside of a few dreams he'd never admitted even to his boyfriends. Totally compelling.

"Hey—" He didn't want to shake the guy, not with a chance of a head injury, so he did the best he could with just his voice, as he reached down and cradled his head in the crook of his arm. "You with me? We need to get you out of here, get you to a doctor." Because the march wasn't stopping, at least not for long; the columns of the marching band just behind them were parting like a river around them.

Long eyelashes fluttered; eyes of a startling green opened; gazes met, locked. *Damn, I could look into those eyes forever.* And the odd thing about the thought was, it didn't feel odd. Not at all. In fact, the eyes were as hauntingly familiar as the mouth, and were giving him thoughts that he had absolutely *no* business entertaining at the moment.

The perfect brows furrowed in concentration. "Doctor?" The redhead shook his head, ever so

15

slightly, even that movement making him gasp. "Out of here... me, with you." His voice was soft and halting, his accent thick, musical.

Terry appeared beside Josh, the Sugar Plum Fairy's tiara askew in his riot of dark curls, the front of his tutu oddly crushed from carrying Mother Ginger over to the sidewalk. "I'll run ahead and get Bill or Jaquon to come back for Big Mama—you need help?" He nodded toward the redhead, obviously trying to keep his eyes averted; for a tattoo and piercing artist, Terrence Miller had a not entirely comfortable relationship with blood.

Josh opened his mouth, intending to tell Terry to find a doctor in the crowd, or even call an ambulance, though how long it would take one to get here through the parade was anyone's guess. But the redhead's gaze caught his again, held it.

"Help. You."

The words were barely audible, but as far as Josh was concerned, the din of the parade didn't exist, and the quiet plea dropped straight into his ears. "You need a doctor." Where the words were coming from, he had no idea—it sure as hell wasn't his brain. *That* had left the picture as soon as they'd locked gazes.

The redhead shook his head again, more emphatically. "You." His voice caught on the single word; he groaned softly, and his head fell back against Josh's arm.

What the hell am I supposed to do? Josh swallowed hard. *Maybe if I take him to Terry's place, I can call a doctor from there—an ambulance would have an easier time getting to someplace off the parade route, anyway. If he even needs one.* "All right," he whispered back, impulsively reaching to move a lock of hair out of the other man's eyes with the tip of a finger.

At the delicate touch, the other man nodded slightly, and the amazing eyes closed again, leaving Josh feeling as if some kind of current had been cut off. He blinked, shaking his head as he became aware of the clamor around the three of them once more, startled, almost deafened after the strange silence.

Without turning his head, he pitched his voice to carry to where Terry was hovering. "I got this, baby. Is it okay if I take him back to your place?"

"Not a problem. See you in a couple of hours." And Terry was gone, racing to catch up with the rest of the dancers.

Wasting no time, Josh gathered the redhead into his arms, and cursed, softly, as he noticed for the first time the other man's hands were chained behind his back. *Who the fuck did that?* Growling low in his throat, he lurched awkwardly to his feet, the stranger in his arms; the other man was an unwieldy burden, but Josh was reluctant to leave the slight form in the street, even for the moment it would have taken to stand, bend, and pick him up. He staggered to the sidewalk; by the time he cleared the curb, he'd gotten his balance, and people moved aside for him to let him hurry off.

The breathtaking eyes didn't open again on the way home. The man hardly moved, except when jostled. Although… well, Josh had to be imagining it, but it felt as if the redhead was nestling against him. And damn, he liked the feeling. He more than liked it.

I want him. The thought was startling, both in its clarity and its urgency. He'd had his share of brief encounters, sure, but he'd never felt anything like this, the need to be closer to a man than the man's own skin. Not even with Terry.

There was another awkward moment when they made it back to Terry's building; fortunately, Terry and Bryce lived on the ground floor, so there weren't stairs involved, but getting out his keys without dropping the injured man was still a neat trick. He managed, though, and carried the other man straight through the tiny apartment to the bedroom, setting him down carefully on the neatly-made bed before turning for the bathroom.

"Need... you... with me."

The whisper reached into him, brought him up short. Slowly, he turned, almost believing he'd imagined it. No one said that sort of thing to him. Ever.

The redhead lay where Josh had left him, in the middle of the bed. He wore a linen shirt, of a strange, old-fashioned cut, stained with dried blood, and trousers of the same, with what looked like—but in lower Manhattan couldn't possibly be—grass stains. But he only had a moment to notice all that, because those eyes were on him, the green of them washed out with pain, but so intense, he felt as if he were falling.

"I need you." The voice was of a piece with the rest of him, hauntingly beautiful. And then the slight body jerked, and he gave a soft cry—almost reluctant, as if admitting to pain, or to need, was worse than the pain itself. And those *eyes*...

Josh slid into the bed beside the redhead, his arms going carefully around him, gathering him close. He started out being gentle, as gentle as he could be, but another long, intense shiver ran through him as he wrapped himself around the other man; his whole body was caught up in the need to be close to this man. To protect him, to shelter him. Possess him? *Hell, yes.* "I'm here," he whispered. "Don't be afraid. Please, don't."

Green eyes met brown, speaking even more eloquently than the stranger's musical voice. "Not afraid of you."

I want to kiss him. Josh felt dizzy, for all that he was lying down. *Shit, I need to…*

"Please." There was desperation in the single word, and confusion, and pain, and need. And then there was a kiss, and arms that held tightly, a faint cry of pure longing.

Cry? Or cries?

Chapter Two

One of these days, I'm going to figure out how to thank my husband properly for this wedding gift. Tiernan straightened up from behind the bar, scrubbing at his streaming eyes with the heels of his hands and wishing to hell he had something to tie his hair back with. Fae and full-strength industrial bleach did not coexist happily. Well, maybe humans didn't exactly love the shit either, but this was a royal pain in the ass.

But the health inspectors were due any day now, and he couldn't *always* bribe them. It looked bad. And he couldn't leave this for the setup crew, not with Mac's lungs in the shape they were in. Fucking shame the healing magicks of Earth only worked on other Fae. Not that Mac McAllan, or any of the other human staff, had a clue what their boss was.

Tiernan grimaced and bent to inspect the space under the bar. Two more shelves, and then he could probably leave the rest of the cleaning to Mac—

"What the *fuck!*"

A bolt of pain shot through the Fae's head, directly behind and between his eyes, in the spot his

20

husband insisted on calling his "third eye." *Humans are strange. DAMN*. He pinched the bridge of his nose in a futile attempt to dull the pain, as he cast out with his magickal sense. Something was fucking with the wards he'd set up around the building, and if he were just a little more competent at warding, he might be able to guess exactly where it was happening.

Though what was doing the fucking was a very poorly kept secret, and Tiernan had to work to keep from shuddering. *Shit*. Six months of expecting exactly what he was sensing was making it no easier to deal with. He took a deep breath, and carefully 'felt' around the perimeter of the club, not letting his breath out until he was damned sure the breach wasn't anywhere below ground. There was no telling what might happen if the *Marfach* got anywhere near the ley nexus that was buried under Purgatory, but the odds were against it being anything even remotely good. But the club's wards were solid, and the extra protections around what had once been the back half of the sub-basement storeroom were even more so. No, the trouble was above ground.

Son of a bitch. In broad daylight. Not that the fucker needed the cover of darkness, any more than he himself did, but Tiernan might have felt just a little better if his race's ancient enemy had seemed even slightly more intimidated by the defenses he'd managed to jury-rig. His hand curled around a paring knife as he eased himself out from behind the bar; a ridiculous weapon, but better in the hand of a seasoned knife-fighter than nothing at all.

He started for the stairs that led up to street level, but thought better of it halfway there and Faded upstairs instead. He'd seen the 'closed' sign in the window of Raging Art-On these past few days, and remembered Kevin mentioning something about Josh LaFontaine having gone to New York for the Pride festivities there. So there would be no one there to see him materialize out of nothing, or do whatever he might have to do after that.

He Faded into a small, spotless room in the back of the tattoo and piercing parlor; it helped for him to have been to his destination the old-fashioned way before he tried to materialize there magickally, and he remembered the padded table in the little room very well, having spent several memorable minutes there two months ago while the human gave him a Prince Albert. *Some of the best money I ever spent.*

Tiernan eased himself off the table and into a fighter's crouch, all six senses fully alert. There was no sound in the little storefront, though early Sunday afternoon traffic in the Adams Morgan neighborhood came through in a muffled sort of way from the street outside.

I'd hear it if it was still here, wouldn't I? The *Marfach*, the closest thing to a devil the Fae had ever known, couldn't survive without some form of magickal substance to warp into an abode for itself; it preferred the living magick of which everything in the Realm was formed, but after that form of sustenance was lost to it in the Sundering, it had made do for over two millennia in the ley lines of the human realm. Until, like a fucking idiot, Tiernan Guaire had used magick to kill an asshole who was holding a knife to his SoulShare's throat, and in so doing had left enough of the substance of magick in the corpse to enable the *Marfach* to reanimate it and take up residence. *It won't Fade, not in a human body.* He shuddered, remembering all too well what it had felt like to Fade with Kevin, in the supercharged aftermath of the assault and the killing. *It has to be here physically if it's here at all. And it's not.*

The sharp pain in his head had eased to a throbbing ache. Quietly, he made his way out of the piercing salon, into the narrow hallway that led back to the exit to the alley on the one side—*oh, fuck me sideways.* The frame of the back door was splintered, in the area of the lock, though it didn't show as much as it might have, since someone had attempted to pull the door closed. In a way, that was a relief; he'd been worried for a while that the *Marfach*'s human host, Janek O'Halloran, might somehow have come into possession of a copy of the master key, during his former tenure as Purgatory's bouncer.

Tiernan pulled his gloves off and worked them into the back pockets of his jeans, then knelt to examine the wreckage of the door more closely, with his magickal sense as well as his others, and cursed under his breath. Tread marks on the outside of the door bespoke a boot; not surprising, O'Halloran's feet were large enough for each to need its own zip code. What was seriously troubling was the fact that the magickal ward that should have been part of the fabric of the door wasn't there. It hadn't been broken; if that had been the case, his pain would have been a lot worse. It just wasn't there.

So where was it? He stood and ran his fingertips lightly over the door, and the clean, white-painted walls to either side of it, searching for the telltale glissade of energy left behind when he had traced

Earth magick through the outer walls and the door. Nothing.

No. There. On the inner wall, where the door led back into the piercing room; he picked up the trace just past that door, and followed the tingle to the door that gave into the slightly larger room that housed Josh's tattoo studio proper. He made a long arm across the narrow hallway and brushed his fingertips against the opposite wall, just long enough to satisfy himself there was no magick there either; frowning, he rested his palms, crystal and flesh, against the closed studio door. *It's as if the wards wrapped themselves around this one room, when they were forced. What the hell?* He pushed gently against the door with his open hands.

And something pushed back. Something magickal.

Shit. Tiernan yanked the door open, and stared in disbelief at nothing whatsoever. Oh, there were what he supposed were the usual accoutrements of the tattoo trade, a pneumatic tattoo machine with a foot pedal, an autoclave, rows of drawers, a glass front cabinet full of clean white cloths and boxes of gloves, a sink, biohazard containers. But nothing that should have pushed back at him.

There has to be something here. His palms were still tingling with the unmistakable residue of pure magick. Not that it was something he made use of often; being a Noble, he generally channeled the magick of his element rather than tapping into the raw stuff commoners favored. He'd had no choice but to use it during his battle with the *Marfach*, of course; Earth magick had been his physical weapon, but without the near-lethal supercharge from the great nexus, his Noble magick would have been about as effective as trying to stop a bullet with a used Kleenex.

Puzzled, he rested his crystal hand on the tattoo gun, sitting in its rest next to the padded table. And jerked it back, as magick sizzled along his palm. *What the fuck? Not possible.* He worked his fingers, his hand, until the tingling subsided, then reached out again, this time with two fingertips.

He was ready for it this time, and let the tingle flow up into his hand, up his arm. It didn't feel like a channeling, there was no pattern to it, no purpose. Just latent energy. *Maybe it just absorbs energy from the nexus.* Tiernan scratched his head, staring down at the floor between his feet. The source of the ley energy *was* right under his shitkickers, more or less. That had to be it. And the wards, being his own half-assed creation, probably hadn't been able to share space with any kind of non-elemental magick in any concentration, and had stopped contracting when they met it.

Tiernan shook himself; glancing around the rest of the room, he reached into his pocket and pulled out his phone. Josh LaFontaine was in his contacts, of course, along with the real estate agent responsible for the vacant clubwear boutique and massage parlor that took up the rest of the ground floor. It was going to suck for Josh to get called back from a vacation to deal with this, but life was what it was. He touched the number and put the phone to his ear, all the while walking around the room, touching the walls.

"Hello, you've reached Josh LaFontaine, proud owner and operator of Raging Art-On. The shop is closed until the 26th of June, but if you'd like to leave a message..."

Tiernan grimaced, waiting for the message to finish playing out. Best not to try to explain the whole thing in a voice mail. "Josh, Tiernan Guaire. Call me back when you get this. It's urgent."

Touching the phone off, he debated with himself for a few seconds, then placed a second call.

"*Lanan*." Kevin's low voice, with its undertone of delighted laughter, was instantly calming. In some ways, anyhow. "Coming home early?"

"I wish." Tiernan shook his free hand to free it from the needle-like tingling sensation. "The *Marfach's* paid us a visit, it broke into the tattoo parlor. I'm up there now."

"Oh, fuck." The laughter was gone in an instant. "What was it after?"

"Beats the shit out of me. But it bent the wards all out of shape, they seem to be surrounding the tattoo studio proper now." Tiernan sat down slowly on the adjustable padded table, looking at nothing, his magickal sense still extended, checking the integrity of the remaining wards.

"Maybe it thought there was a way into the club through the parlor?"

Tiernan cursed softly. The whole reason for warding the club, and the building in general, was to keep that particular crawling horror the hell out of Purgatory, and away from the ley nexus that would probably serve to feed its power at least as easily as it fed Tiernan's own. "Let's hope there isn't. I'd better get the wards back up, though. Stronger than before, if I can manage it."

"You need me to come down there and deal with the cops?"

Tiernan chuckled. His issues with law enforcement might have started with the Realm's Royal Defense, but they hadn't ended there, and his husband had resigned himself some time ago to being Purgatory's liaison with Washington, D.C.'s finest. "Not yet, *lanan*. I want to get the wards back up first, and I can't do that when the place is crawling with uniforms and attitude. I'll call them when I'm done. Shouldn't be more than a few hours, I want to do a better job this time." He shook his head, grimacing. If only he wasn't so dependent on elemental magick, he could put up a *proper* ward. There were times when being a commoner, rather than a Noble, would come in very handy. "I might need you to come down here later, though. If it turns out I need to tap into the nexus for the power to finish the job properly."

He could almost hear Kevin's grin. In order to handle the unimaginable energies of the ley nexus that lay below the floor of what used to be the storeroom in Purgatory without frying every nerve in his body, Tiernan had to be in a state of intense sexual arousal, and his husband was more than adept at getting him there. "Not that I have any doubts as to your abilities, my Fae, but I find myself hoping you'll need help." A pause. "Have you called Josh yet?"

"Yeah, I got his voice mail. I'll try him again after I get done with the wards and before the cops." He left the tattoo studio, and returned to the ruined back door, carefully fingering the large splinters. "I'd better get my ass in gear. Talk to you soon, *lanan*."

Touching the phone off, he sank to the floor, sitting cross-legged with his back to the door. He held up his hands and took a deep, theoretically calming breath, the clear-as-crystal living Stone of his left hand catching the light that filtered back from the storefront and fracturing it into rainbows that skittered around the hallway. He closed his eyes, letting out that breath on a sigh, and rested his hands palms up on his knees, reaching within for the energy of Earth. Trying to weave the stuff of living Stone into an invisible, intangible barrier strong enough to at least slow down a being of ultimate evil.

Slowly, the shards of light began to coalesce, following the magickal energy, painting the plain white walls with colors invisible to human eyes. Hopefully the fucker would last this time.

Maybe the *Marfach* had turned up here looking for a way down into Purgatory. But Tiernan was willing to bet it had at least been willing to stop to sample the magick to be had in Josh LaFontaine's tattoo studio.

Chapter Three

Greenwich Village
New York City

What the hell was that?

The Fae stared into the warm brown eyes just inches from his own, his own eyes wide, his heart racing, his lips still throbbing from the force of the kiss that just ended. His head ached, spun; pain chased itself down every nerve, yet somehow it was less where their bodies touched, where this male's hands wandered over his body. There would be time enough later to be astonished that he was letting the dark-haired one do this—no one *ever* touched him.

The worst of the purely physical pain had subsided as he had been carried through the crowded streets; his only actual injury, as far as he could tell, was what was left of the lump on the back of his head, which had surely healed as quickly as any other injury not mortal. But the agony of being sieved through the Pattern was another matter. He sucked in a breath through clenched teeth, the memory still both raw and untouchable.

A gentle finger touched his lips. "Are you hurting?"

"Yes… no…" Damn this gift of Air, that let him repeat back like a moderately intelligent parrot only that which he had already heard. He needed more words. Specifically, he needed *kiss me again and don't stop until I quit shaking.* Which made no sense. This male's touch eased him, yes, but it also aroused him. And arousal brought magick; arousal was dangerous, deadly. Letting anyone get close to him was even more so. Yet this stranger's touch eased the pain, like the hands of a Water Fae sculpting Fire. He should push this human away. He would.

Just not right now. He needed him too much.

Conall pulled at the truesilver chains that bound his hands; there was no burning now, no nausea. They were only chains now, on this side of the Pattern, with no power to do him harm even if he drew on the store of magick bound within his body. Truesilver knew its purpose, and the purpose of these chains had been to keep him from channeling until the Pattern could take him.

But even ordinary chains were enough to prevent him from doing the astonishing thing his body told him he needed to do, which was fit this male to him, carefully and deliberately. His gaze played almost reverently over the vividly colored designs that covered the smooth hard flesh of the other male's arms. *Do all humans look like this?* For a moment he was torn between fears; fear of the rising clamor of the sensations he had never dared allow himself, and fear the dark-eyed one would pull away before anything more could happen. But then a shiver ran through the other's frame, and one hard-muscled thigh slowly insinuated itself between Conall's. Not demanding, not forcing; merely inexorable.

And, incredibly, with that touch he felt the faint caress of what could only be magick. That shouldn't be possible, not in the human world. Every Fae knew that all living magick had been withdrawn from the human world and sealed into the Realm with the Fae at the time of the Sundering. So what was he sensing? Not magick, surely, not from a human. But then what was he feeling, washing over him in gentle, sensual waves? His own wishful thinking?

"What the hell am I doing?" the other male murmured. His voice was hesitant, his dark gaze confused; his body, though, showed no sign of either hesitation or confusion, taking gentle possession of Conall. Awkwardly, he yielded to the larger male's weight, the force that rolled him onto his back and pressed down into the cradle of his hips. As unfamiliar as the position was, his memory of the pain of the Pattern's sieve still yielded to the promise of an unknown pleasure; he gasped for breath, his tongue stroking over his parched lips.

Yes… The word whispered itself in his head in two languages at once, Fae and human. *Yes. Arouse me. Let the magick build, my own or this strange newness.* He shivered, and whether it was from fear or need, he had no idea. *Just long enough to let me finish healing.*

"Oh, *shit*." The other male rolled slightly, the sweet weight leaving Conall as a hand slipped behind his back and ran down his arm to his wrist, feeling at the chains. "We have to get these off you."

The human surged up, off the bed, disappearing almost instantly through an open doorway, leaving Conall slack-jawed. *How could he just stop?—but I*

*wanted him to stop, didn't I? I can't let him make me
feel like that—I can't let anyone make me feel like that.
King's arse, my head is spinning.* With the human out
of his arms, and out of sight, the pain and the
sluggishness were closing back in, along with the
confusion that made it difficult to track the muttering
that drifted back in through the doorway.

"I know Terry used to have a pair of bolt cutters.
Where the hell did he... oh, under the sink. Right." A
clattering sound followed, and the dark-haired male
returned, bearing a red-handled implement and
wearing a triumphant grin. And also wearing, Conall
now saw, an odd sleeveless doublet and short leggings
of heavy blue fabric that had seen better days. Both of
which clung to his body in a most enticing manner.
"Can you roll over for me?"

*Please ask me that again in a few minutes. And
use some of those words I need.* The relief the human's
presence brought was intoxicating; even with his body
and his mind once again at war with themselves and
each other, he smiled as he rolled onto his stomach.
Hands worked at his chains, and then there was the
cold kiss of metal and a sharp *ping!* He felt the cool
weight of the chains fall away, and his hands dropped
away from each other, his arm muscles screaming
pleasantly at the release he hadn't realized he needed.
And there was a hand on his arm, running up and
down the length of it; he closed his eyes with the
pleasure of the gentle touch, letting it drive away the
pain and the murky haze of the aftermath of transition,
and start the sweet slow arc of arousal all over again.
So strange, to be touched. So strange, to enjoy it.

Weight shifted beside him; a knee, planted on the

bed. And the soft caress of a mouth, on his cheek, his temple. Warm breath in his ear; a kiss, shaped into the shell of it. "This has to be a goddamned dream." The whisper was hoarse in his ear, the breath it rode hot and urgent. "I've never seen such a beautiful man in my life. And you're letting me do this. Touch you like this." The tip of a tongue slid into his ear, probing gently and intimately. "I don't even know your name."

For this, at least, he had the words. "My name is Conall." He drew a deep, unsteady breath. "And I am not a dream."

"Yes, you are." Teeth closed gently over the top of Conall's ear. "You're every dream I've ever had since I first wondered why girls did nothing for me. And I'm Josh."

Conall's eyes closed, as a shiver chased itself down his body. This felt like a dream. If only because dreams had always been his only safety, his arousal's sole refuge. Dreams were the only place where he could safely allow the kind of feelings this male, this Josh, was awakening in him. Surely here in the human realm, he could allow this; when he became fully aroused and channeled magick, in instinctive response to the pleasure this male was so insistently coaxing from him, it wouldn't suck the life from his surroundings. It couldn't, because here in the human world there was no living magick in the things around him, to be drawn on. And a human male couldn't possibly be intending to play him, use him. He groaned softly as a hand slipped under his shirt, and a broad, callused palm glided up his body. His back arched and twisted, cat-like, following the demanding hand. *Better than a dream.*

"Shit." The word was barely audible, reverent. "How do you like it? I want to make it good for you." Josh's tongue traced his ear again. "Better than good."

"How?" Conall bit his lip, hard. Something was happening to him. Something beyond arousal. Maybe even beyond magick. Delight; a bright gleam of pure, sweet joy that pierced the murk of transition and made his abused body feel as if it glowed. "I don't know." *Show me*, he wanted to say, but the words weren't there. *Show me how I like it. Show me how good it can be.*

"What do you mean, you don't... oh, sweet fuck." Conall felt the body against his stiffen. "Have you ever... been with a man?"

Conall shook his head, twisting to face Josh, his hand resting lightly on one brightly-colored shoulder, his palm tingling, his heart suddenly racing. He needed arousal, needed to draw the magick out of himself so he could heal. But even more, he needed this male's touch. Needed something breathtaking that was hanging just out of his reach. Before the fear returned, before he closed off this wonder and forced it away. "Please. Josh." He cupped one unshaven cheek in his hand, his eyes closing in pleasure at the brush of whiskers against his palm. "Please."

Lips brushed his palm; a tongue-tip flickered out, traced, tasted. "I'm out of my mind." Josh's voice was hoarse, his breath warm against Conall's hand. "But I don't care." The human caught at his hand, held it tightly as he leaned in and took Conall's mouth. The Fae moaned, his mouth opening to a driving, questing tongue; Josh's weight shifted over him, freeing him to move, and he rolled to lie on his back, his legs curling loosely around the other male's flat, hard hips. He felt and heard the human's breath catch, sensed heat flaring and an exquisite hardness grinding against him.

And the dizzying rush, as the way opened in him for power, for magick. Yes. He would heal, completely, both his physical injuries and what the Pattern had done to him. And then he would take what the human was so eager to offer. He reached up and buried his fingers in Josh's thick dark hair and drew him closer still, reaching within himself and seizing the magick—

The pain was blinding. He cried out with it, and Josh recoiled. *No!—no, I need him!* Instinctively, he gripped the human more tightly, with hands and legs, as he struggled to master the crawling agony that consumed him. Surely the Pattern itself could not have been worse than this.

There was a treasure of magickal force within him, as within any Fae, pure power bound up in him, to be drawn on for any use of magick that went beyond the natural birthrights of all Fae. Most Fae had only a taste of the talent, and drew on the Realm's own latent store of power for the small channelings they could manage, or replenished from that store afterward. His own capacity was a freak of nature, greater than any since the days of the lost Loremasters. And that trove, that power, was still there. Alive and vital, humming within him as it had since the day he first came into his powers over two hundred years ago. But trying to touch it, channel it, to shape it, as he had done as easily and as naturally as breathing within the Realm, was pain beyond imagining.

"Conall! Christ, what's wrong?"

Sweat broke out on Conall's brow, stung in his

eyes as he struggled to master himself. His arousal was causing the pain; sexual energy instinctively called to magickal energy. But he still needed Josh, needed him close, needed him in a way that had little to do with sex and almost everything to do with that glissade of joy that had driven away the darkness of transition, and eased the burning rawness left by the passage through the Pattern, the severing of his soul.

"Stay with me…"

Chapter Four

"Well, if that wasn't a clusterfuck, I've never seen one."

Janek ignored the throbbing pain in his temples as he opened the refrigerator and palmed a carton of yogurt. The *Marfach* hated yogurt. And it hated to be talked to. Especially by the guy who was really nothing more than its meat carriage. So whenever he felt up to it, which wasn't nearly often enough, he sucked down shit that tasted like glue and talked to himself.

The kinslayer's wards should not have been enough to keep me out.

Janek barked out a laugh. "Aw, are we pouting today?" Throwing himself into the only chair in his pathetic efficiency apartment, and hearing a rat, or something larger, scurrying away behind it, he ripped the top off the little carton and tipped it up, not bothering with a spoon. He barely had enough feeling in his fingers to get the top off the thing, never mind hold a utensil. "And that 'kinslayer' shit stopped impressing me months ago. The pretty boy has balls. We know that. You promised me I could feed them to him, remember?"

Only after I have finished with him.

"Yeah, what the fuck ever." He slammed down the last of the slimy shit, and then licked the white plastic clean, just for fun. He felt the creature that lived in what was left of his brain cringe, and grinned. "And the wards didn't keep us out, that back door caved in nice as you please." With the help of iron-soled shitkickers, and ankles and shins that didn't really feel pain any more.

Yet they stopped us at the inner door.

"News flash—whatever they were, they didn't stop *me*." No, he'd strolled in calm as you please, and opened the door to the room where LaFontaine did piercings. He'd idly thought about trashing the place, the industrial the guy had given him while he sat on that table had hurt like a son of a bitch. But his brain-sucking master, or mistress, or whatever else it felt like being, had yanked on his leash and made him go on to the next door.

He kind of remembered what had happened next. His hand had tingled as he opened the unlocked door, just for an instant as he yanked it open. Then he'd tried to step through, and it was like a flash grenade had gone off in his face. He hadn't felt the pain, of course, but his driver had screamed until Janek's throat had gone raw. He guessed that the *Marfach* had taken full control at that point, because the next thing he remembered was fumbling with the key to his apartment door.

Something inside that room kept us out.

The voice in Janek's head sounded female now, the way it did when it wanted to wheedle something out of him. As if sexing things up had any effect on him any more. The bitch had tried to jerk him off once, as a reward for good behavior. Numb hands and a dead dick and a supernatural evil being who didn't know when or how to quit. Yeah, close enough to hell as to make no difference.

What was in there?

For all its raw power, the *Marfach* had not one fucking clue about how things worked in the human world. So it wasn't any real surprise that it couldn't identify tattoo equipment, especially not from the quick look Janek had gotten before whatever had happened, happened. "It was just machinery. For tattooing. Putting ink on skin." He held out his own hands, so the voice in his head could use his eye to see the garish decorations that ran up and down his forearms.

Something about it reinforced the wards.

Janek got the impression that the *Marfach* wasn't really paying attention to him any more, and he grimaced. When his passenger's focus strayed, it was usually a sign that what was left of his own mind was about to go switch-off for lack of maintenance. *Anyone who thinks the zombie apocalypse is going to be fun is full of shit.* "That's bullshit." His voice came out much too loud, as he tried to get the attention of the thing in his head. "You said the wards are magick, and only more magick can reinforce them. There's nothing magickal about tattoo equipment. And the ley lines are in the basement."

One of your premises is faulty.

The voice was even more distant, now.

But which?

Janek opened his mouth to reply, but everything

went cold and grey before a thought could form; he slumped in his chair, mouth gone slack and eyes half-open, as the *Marfach*'s mind raced.

Which?

Chapter Five

Greenwich Village
New York City

"Stay with me…"

Josh took his weight on his hands, staring wide-eyed at the breathtaking face below him that was twisted into a mask of pain. "Conall, Jesus Christ, what is it? Did I hurt you?"

The ginger gasped for breath; his eyes flew open, and the fear in their electric depths made Josh's heart pound. *Is it his head? But that's healed!*

He tried to roll away, intending to get the cell phone he'd left in the bathroom before the march and do what he should have done in the first place, namely call a fucking ambulance, but the other man's grip in his hair and around his waist tightened; one hand released his hair and caught at his arm, gripping with a strength Conall's slender frame didn't even hint at.

"You don't hurt me." The whisper was strained, urgent. "You make it good. Please."

Conall's words came slowly, haltingly, as if he had to stop and think before each one. *God, what if he's had a stroke?* "What's wrong? Are you in pain?" *Stupid-ass question.*

41

Yet as he watched, the other man slowly mastered himself, mastered his pain. Conall's breathing slowed, his eyes no longer showed white around the beautiful, gemlike green, his body gradually relaxed until the hard arch left his back and he settled to the bed. But the grip on Josh's arm never slackened, and the compelling gaze never left his, not for an instant. "Just... be with me." The words were gentle, but the tone, the gaze, was not. They held him, transfixed.

"I'm with you." He reached out a hesitant hand—hesitant, where just a minute ago he'd been ready to lose himself in those eyes, let those hands do whatever they wanted. As insane as that was. Men only fell this hard in books, the kinds of books he never read. But he had to be with this man; time enough later to figure out why. He ran the backs of his fingers along one cheekbone, traced the bow of Conall's upper lip with his smallest finger. It felt as if some strange, subtle current left him through that fingertip, to flow into the other man; he winced as Conall's eyes closed again. "I *am* causing you pain. Somehow."

Conall's eyes didn't open, but he shook his head. Only a little, but firmly. And he whispered... something. No language Josh had ever heard before. *"Fai dara tú pian beag. Ach tú'a sabail dom ó pian i bfad nís mo."* One hand curled around his, raised it.

Josh shook his head, his eyes stinging. "I don't understand." And yet he almost did. That whisper was in the back of his mind, its meaning hanging just out of reach. Something about pain. And causing it. And helping with it. *I am out of my effing mind.*

Gently, he moved a strand of hair off Conall's

forehead. "Maybe we should get you a shower. You might feel a little better."

"Shower, yes." The redhead smiled, the lines of pain around his eyes vanishing; he rolled, as if trying to get up, then fell back, chuckling softly. "Help, please?"

If it'll light up your face like that? Hell yes. "Here, let's get you up."

With only a little awkwardness, the two of them working together managed to get the smaller man out of bed and on his feet; Josh put an arm around him, and guided him to the tiny bathroom. Well, big for New York City, but tiny by any other standards. Most of the floor space was taken up by the jeans Josh had discarded in favor of the shorts he'd had to wear in order to survive an entire parade under Mother Ginger's skirts; hastily he kicked them under the sink, grimacing as his cell phone fell out of the pocket and skittered across the floor. *I'll worry about that later.* Some other time when he wasn't sharing a confined space with a man whose hotness defied all known physical laws and who was about to get naked. "Um, Conall, how much help do you think you're going to need?"

Some clichés were actually true; this man's laugh sounded like music. "How much help do you have?"

Jesus, I'm blushing. How long has it been since that happened? "Here, let me get you out of this shirt. Does this untie?" Josh fumbled at the laces at Conall's throat with fingers that were suddenly as dexterous as sausages, carefully easing the shirt up over his head and dropping it to the floor. And trying not to gawk. *So this is perfection. Good to know.* Conall wasn't musclebound, not at all—he was slight, if anything—

43

but every muscle on his lean torso was cut with a chisel and beautifully outlined.

And then the other man turned, just a little, and Josh's breath caught again, this time in purely artistic appreciation. Ink. Exquisite ink. Gently, he turned Conall until he could see all of what he'd just gotten a glimpse of; an elaborate pattern of something that seemed equal parts Celtic knotwork and tribal design, done in a shade of silver-blue that seemed to gleam even in the harsh fluorescent light of the bathroom, spread out between his shoulder blades and rising almost to his neck. "You have to tell me who did your tat work." *So I can have my tombstone done properly. "Here lies Josh LaFontaine, dead from sheer fucking envy of..."*

"Tat work?" Conall paused, his expression obviously puzzled, bent slightly at the waist, his trousers halfway down his thighs.

Josh waited for the rush of heat that washed over him to subside before even trying to answer. *Merry fucking Christmas, if he's that size soft, do I even want to think about... oh, hell yes I do.*

"Yeah." He cleared his throat and tried again. "Your ink." A pause. "On your back."

"I have ink on my back?"

Already twitching with the effort of keeping his hands to himself as the other man disrobed, Josh reached out and traced a finger along the intricate pattern, following an endless loop over and under, around and through. A soft groan called him out of what was almost a reverie; looking up, his gaze met Conall's in the mirror, and he bit his lip at the sight of the other man's widely dilated pupils, the chest rising and falling with rapid panting breaths.

Conall turned suddenly, and caught at Josh's wrist. Pain glinted in the depths of his amazing eyes, but so did arousal. And determination. "Touch me." The other man's soft lips caressed the inside of his wrist. "And tell me."

"Tell you?" Josh blinked, shook his head. His cock was giving him hell against the zipper of his shorts, but it was the very best kind of hell, and it only got worse as Conall's trousers slid the rest of the way down his legs, revealing thighs that went perfectly with the chest, and, well, yes, that cock was definitely something to write home about. While you were still laid up and unable to walk and had nothing else to do. "Tell you what?"

"Tell *to* me." Conall obviously noted where Josh's gaze had gone, and Josh could swear he saw a faint blush creep into the other man's cheeks. "In the shower. With me. Tell."

"With you?" *Someone tell me why I'm asking stupid questions.*

Reaching over his head, Josh grabbed the back of his muscle shirt and hauled it off, then toed off his sneakers and made quick work of his shorts. His own face heated slightly as his semi-erect cock fell free, but he made no move to cover himself. *It's not as if he can't tell what he does to me.*

Strangely, Conall had made no move to turn on the water, so Josh reached past him and started the shower running. As he pulled back, Conall's hand shot out and clasped him hard around the wrist; Josh turned, puzzled, just as the other man raised his hand and used Josh's hand to cup his own cheek. Swallowing hard, Josh stroked the other man's face with his thumb, and together they stepped under the rush of the water, drawing the frosted glass of the sliding door closed behind themselves.

Josh groaned as Conall's arms went around his waist; he bent and took the redhead's searching mouth as he groped blindly for the shampoo he knew Terry kept in the shower somewhere. Compared to the hands that stroked his back, the water was coarse, and stung. He stumbled as his hand just missed closing around the plastic bottle, and pushed Conall against the wall; he felt and heard soft laughter, even tasted it, as the other man's tongue tentatively parted his lips.

"Tell to me." Josh felt Conall's lips moving against his, as a hand curved around his ass cheek and drew him closer, bringing his cock to rigid attention. Teeth caught gently at his lower lip, followed by a caressing tongue; water spilled over both their faces, trickled between their bodies. He braced his hands against the shower wall, one on either side of Conall's head, the water gleaming on the colorful tattoos that covered his powerful biceps.

"What do you want me to talk about?" His shaft was pinned against Conall's abs, and every slight movement of the redhead's hips was sweet agony. "How much I need you? Because when you're close like this, there's only one thing on my mind—oh, sweet Jesus." Conall's mouth was working its way down his throat, licking, nibbling. "I can't even think when you do that, your mouth is fucking magic."

Was he only imagining he felt Conall stiffen at that word? Probably, because the kisses and the stroking barely slowed. "Do you feel how much you excite me? Arouse me?" He couldn't help rocking his hips against Conall's, gently pumping.

And he frowned, because the other man's penis was completely flaccid, for all that his breath was coming in gasping moans against Josh's skin. "What am I doing wrong?"

Conall's head jerked up at this, and damn if that copper hair wasn't just as sexy plastered to his head. "Wrong?" That vivid green gaze pierced the steam and held Josh transfixed. "I need you," Conall whispered, barely audible over the water. "I need your touch. But to arouse me, to excite me, is pain."

"I can touch you without..." The roll of Josh's eyes, the tilt of his chin, took in their whole situation, two wet naked bodies in deliciously intimate contact, one of them rampantly aroused.

"I know you can." Conall leaned in again, his mouth working its way once again down the side of Josh's neck. "But I want you to touch me *with*."

"Christ." Josh's voice was a harsh rasp; his hips shifted, driving his aching shaft hard against Conall's slippery wet abs. Shivers raced across the skin of his arms, his thighs, his back. "I don't want to hurt you."

"I am not letting you hurt me." Teeth nipped at his earlobe. "Please, let me make it good for you, *lanan*."

Josh groaned; the softness of Conall's whisper, the warmth of the tongue that probed his ear were all the translation he needed for that word. *This can't be happening. He wants to give me a pleasure he can't let himself have?* He turned his head, and caught the other man's brilliant green gaze. And those eyes spoke. They promised. They pleaded. "Do whatever you want. Whatever pleases you."

When was the last time I ever let anyone do anything for me?

47

A shudder rippled through Josh's flesh as, with a final nip to his ear, Conall slowly sank to his knees. No fucking way was he going to stop leaning on the wall—he'd need all the help he could get to stay standing for the next few minutes.

Conall started with kisses. Soft, exploring kisses, as water streamed from Josh's body, down over the face that tilted up, into the mouth that opened to engulf one of his balls. Josh sucked in a breath through pursed lips, stifling a groan as the redhead's tongue swirled around the hot folds of flesh that encased his heavy globe. "Shit, yes." And the process was repeated on the other side, this time with the addition of gentle strokes of Conall's fingertips,
up and down the insides of thighs that were already starting to tremble.

"Tell me how to do this." Conall's tongue stroked the underside of his cock, broad and flat, all the way to the head in a single stroke. "Please. Tell me how to make it good for you."

"You don't need me to tell you." Josh's voice came out strangled, almost unrecognizable. "Fuck, there aren't words anyway." His head fell back as Conall's lips closed all too briefly around the head of his cock, and the hardened tip of the other man's tongue probed his slit, coaxing out a few drops of fluid before withdrawing.

"But I've never…" Conall's teeth grazed lightly over the bundle of nerves under the head of Josh's rigid organ.

Josh couldn't control the jerking of his hips, or the way one hand shot down to fist in thick ginger hair. "*Virgin* doesn't mean *ignorant*. You must have thought about what you like. Do that." He couldn't meet those eyes any longer; if he did, he was going to come. Hell, he was going to fucking explode. He stared at his hand, fingers splayed out over the worn black and white checkered tiles of the shower, and moaned low in his throat as Conall took him deep, cupping his balls in one hand and stroking a fingertip across his tight puckered entrance. He could feel a familiar heavy heat rolling down his spine, building at the base of it, his sac starting to draw up in anticipation.

But there was nothing familiar about the hammering of his heart, the dizzying rush of delight that was slowly suffusing him from his core outward. It was sex and lust and need gone insane, and it was so much more. Joy, something pure and rich and so different from anything he had ever known. And just out of his reach, visible but untouchable, closer with every gasping breath. "Conall... oh, fuck, oh Jesus *please...*"

The head of his cock grazed the back of Conall's throat; the other man choked, and Josh tried to pull back, but Conall lunged forward, and swallowed hard. Josh cursed ecstatically as his shaft went rock-hard and curved; the curses changed to prayers, and yet somehow never changed at all, when Conall's cheeks hollowed and he sucked hard, one finger sliding deep into Josh's ass. "*Conall* — "

Josh threw his head back, a cry erupting from deep within him as blinding pleasure met consuming joy and threatened to buckle his knees under him. His cock pulsed, his seed shooting from him in thick, potent jets, splashing against the back of Conall's eager throat, as that other sensation, delight so intense it was nearly tangible, destroyed the invisible barrier and flooded him from within. He could feel the other man swallowing, hear him gulping, choking, but taking in everything Josh gave him. Everything. *So good... so damned good.*

Josh leaned forward, his forehead coming to rest against the tile with a solid thump. He stared down, and damned if his cock didn't start twitching and jerking all over again at the expression of bliss on the other man's face. Conall's mouth still worked against his softening shaft; slowly, his beautiful green eyes opened, his gaze locked with Josh's. Fingertips stroked the insides of Josh's thighs; Conall let Josh's cock slide free of his mouth, and turned his head to rest his cheek against Josh's thick, dark bush of curls. A quiet sigh slipped from him as a corner of his mouth curved up, the water tracing paths down his face.

Releasing the thick shock of hair his hand was curled around, Josh cupped Conall's cheek in his unsteady hand, and shivered as the other man turned his head a little, to make the gesture into a caress still more tender. And then he staggered, as all of Conall's weight leaned against his legs; eyelashes brushed his palm, and he saw that the amazing eyes were half-closed.

"Are you hurt? Tired?" *Oh, shit, was it too much for him?* Josh's hand wandered to the back of Conall's head, fingertips exploring; he could hardly find where he thought the injury had been, though, and the other man didn't so much as wince, thank God.

"Just tired." Conall smiled, a slow, lazy smile that warmed Josh all the way to his toes from the inside, as the water sluiced down.

"Back to bed?"

"Only if you come with me."

Chapter Six

The wind whipped Conall's face, and snatched the breath from him; he struggled to raise his head, blinking blood from his eyes, his heartbeat hammering in his ears almost loud enough to drown out the howling wind. Overhead, on the far side of the round stone cell, the hawk wheeled and dipped against the face of the full moon, untouched by the tempest that was for this little room alone.

What the hell? Conall struggled, felt the truesilver chains biting into his wrists, smoldering as the magick flared up to heal the last of the hurts he'd been dealt. *I'm in bed. In the human world. I'm asleep. With a human curled around me like a second skin.* Yet the skin of his wrists was sizzling, the pain undeniably raw and real.

The floor was fading away under him, translucent now, the whorls of silver-blue wire humming with barely leashed power. It wasn't possible, but that didn't matter. He was about to be sieved through the Pattern again, reliving the eternal moment of agony he had blocked from his memory just hours before.

I could stop it. The thought shimmered in his mind with the trembling clarity of a drugged vision. *I could stop it, this time.* Whether it was real or not. The magick leaped in him, battered at him from within, desperate to be free, and to drag him free along with it. All he had to do was summon up the power within him, let it do what it needed to do.

Let it unravel the Pattern. Because it would.

Unravel the Pattern. Bring the Realm and the human world back together, after two millennia. Save himself measureless agony—probably at the cost of his hands, but small matter, measured against that half-remembered pain. At the cost of destroying the greatest work of magick the Fae had ever wrought.

No.

There was only one answer, one way to endure what was coming, whether it was yet another cruelty visited on him by the Pattern or a figment of his own imagination. Shivering in anticipation of the imminent agony, he retreated within himself. There was no locking away his magick, no putting it out of reach. No, it was himself that he locked away. Huddled within himself, curled into a tight ball, utterly devoid of the magick that was the life of a Fae, he waited, as he had waited the first time. And the wind howled.

The floor fell away beneath him, leaving only the wires, finer and keener than the edge of any knife. The wind sucked him down, the wires ignored flesh to bite through soul; a scream welled up from deep within him, clawing at his throat from the inside.

"Shh, lover, I have you."

It was Josh's voice, Josh's arms warm around him, holding him tightly as the Pattern faded away. Josh's lips pressed to the back of his neck. Josh's hands wandering slowly over his torso, exploring, stroking. Conall sucked in one deep breath after another, trying to still his trembling, fighting an insane urge to lash out against all this touching. Not entirely successfully; his elbow drove deep into a hard-muscled abdomen, and there was a warm rush of startled breath against his neck.

"You're stronger than you look." The soft laughter in his ear was rueful. "But damned if I'm going to let go of you."

"Why are you holding me in the first place…Oh, hell, that feels wonderful." More of the terrible tension drained from him as Josh's tongue found his ear. But then he frowned. *Hell* was not a word in *Faen*, it had been borrowed by the Fae from humans, back in the time before the Sundering. Fae worshiped no gods, and gods that didn't exist certainly had no special places for reward or punishment. So he had used the human word. But the rest, he had spoken *as'Faein*. And Josh was laughing softly, rimming Conall's ear with the tip of his tongue, as if he'd understood every word.

"I'm holding you because you need it." A leg wrapped around Conall from behind, covered with the same beautiful, vibrant designs as most of the rest of Josh's body. "As relaxed as you were when we got out of the shower, I noticed you were shaking when I put you to bed, so I figured I'd curl up with you, be there for you. Which seems to have been a good idea." Another soft kiss fell on the back of Conall's neck.

Conall rolled, in the circle of Josh's arms; he needed to see, to meet his rescuer's gaze. Josh's eyes were dark, and as breathtaking as the rest of the male; only a handful of Fae had eyes like these, and those who did were often greeted with the taunt *sule-d'ainmi*, 'animal-eyes'. But Josh's eyes were deep, and welcoming, filled with a compassion barely recognizable to a Fae. *"Cein fa buil tu ag'eachain' orm ar-seo?"* *Why do you look at me this way?* The whisper was awed — and very carefully, deliberately *as'Faein*.

"I don't know why." Josh's hand came up to cup Conall's cheek, as it had in the shower. "Do I have to know?" The human leaned in and brushed his lips across Conall's; his breath was warm, rapid, slightly hoarse.

We're both dreaming. We must be. "No." His hand curled around Josh's, held it loosely, feeling the warmth of it. *And in a dream, I can do as I will.* Tentatively, he took Josh's full lower lip between his teeth, worried it gently. *We both can.*

Josh groaned; his arm tightened around Conall and he rolled, drawing Conall with him to lie atop him, easing his thighs apart to make space for him. The Fae felt the human's shaft twitch, stir, and begin to grow, pinned between two shifting bodies.

And his own began to rise to meet it, hot flesh caressing hot flesh; Conall's heart raced, his whole body tensed in anticipation of the pain that had accompanied his initial arousal. But this time there was nothing, nothing but a swelling wave of pleasure robbing him of breath. His hips started to rise and fall, a slow, instinctive motion.

Josh smiled, a curve of the lips joyous and teasingly sensual. "No pain, this time?" The human's free hand slid down Conall's back, fingertips tracing the dimple at the base of his spine before palming one flexed-hard ass cheek.

Conall shook his head. "None." He gasped as one of Josh's fingertips teased at his tight entrance; his hips jerked, and his hand clutched at Josh's.

"Good." The human's smile flashed white in his tanned face, for just a moment before a heated kiss made Conall's eyes close in bliss. Josh rolled, pinning Conall beneath him, continuing the kiss, his hands sliding up the Fae's arms to pin them over his head. "Because I owe you one world-rocking blow job."

"No." Conall tested the strength of the human's grip, and a delicious shudder ran through his body when he found it tight. "Please, *lanan*." 'Lover,' a word he had never thought to be able to use; how easily it fell from his lips now. A dream would never hurt him, never use him. "This may never be safe for me again... please, I want you to... to..."

Even in dream his face reddened; the Fae language was replete with words to describe every sexual act and position that might occur to the members of an essentially immortal race, seeking diversion in one body after another without involving the heart. But there were no words that would let him ask for what he found himself wanting from this male. No, *with* this male.

"Where did you come from?" Josh's amazing eyes were wide, wonder writ plainly in their dark depths; the kiss he gave Conall was tender, yet profoundly hungry in its self-restraint. "How did you find me?" He thrust down, into the cradle Conall clumsily made of his hips, his erection gliding against Conall's abs.

"I'm almost sure *you* found *me*." Conall's back arched, as his body sought more contact with Josh's; his legs curled around the human's, his bare feet running experimentally up and down the superbly muscled lengths. "In the middle of that black stone path."

"Black stone…" One of Josh's brows quirked up; he shook his head, as if setting aside a puzzle for later, laughed softly, and fitted his mouth to Conall's again.

This kiss the human drew out, the heat and the hunger increasing until Conall moaned and Josh wrenched his head up. "Christ." Josh's tongue flicked out, ran around his full lips, fuller now from the intense kiss. "Everything about you makes me need you."

"Then take what you need, *dar'cion*." *Brilliantly-colored. Yes.*

"You're sure?" Josh released Conall's wrists, and took his weight on his hands, pushing up just far enough to let Conall see the top of the designs that patterned his well-muscled chest. "You want me to make love to you? That *was* what you were going to ask, wasn't it?" The human's smile was totally captivating. There was none of the reserve, the guardedness that shadowed even the warmest of Fae smiles; Josh's delight in what he was being asked to do was writ plain in that smile, and it warmed Conall to the depths of his battered soul, a balm more profound than any magick.

"It was." *And now I have the words.* "Will you?"

"Ask me again."

Conall opened his mouth, the newly-learned words ready on his lips. But Josh's finger lay across his lips, and the human's smile curved several shades toward the sensual. "With your body. Ask me without words, let your body do it."

Christ. Whoever that was, his borrowed name seemed almost adequate to the sense of awe bordering on fear Conall felt, looking up into Josh's deep brown eyes. *He has no idea just how virginal I am*. Fae were typically sexually dormant until their powers manifested, at age twenty-oneor so; Conall's own magick had come on him early, and it had become almost immediately apparent that his pleasures would be had solely from his own hands, or—as now—from his dreams.

How was it they shared a dream? It felt so natural, it almost seemed foolish to ask, but this was something he'd only heard of in stories. Something shared between Fae, born of magick.

But then Josh's weight shifted over him, and Conall felt hot moisture streak his abs, weeping from the head of the other male's shaft, and old tales were forgotten. He swallowed, hard, tasting the remembered salt and sweetness of that fluid in the back of his throat. The memory of his well-thumbed copy of the *Ninety-Six Pleasures*, now a world away and untouchable, had stood by him well enough in the shower; hopefully, it had taught him the language he needed now, the language of touch.

He eased his thighs apart, groaning softly as Josh picked up the cue and pushed them further apart with his own. The other male raised up on his hands, letting Conall look down between them, to where two heads emerged from the joining of bodies, Josh's broad and flat and a fevered brick red, his own rounder and darker, nearly purple, and both weeping copiously. He reached down, his hand curling around Josh's thick cock, and bit his lip as the other male thrust into his hand. "Oh, God... this is a dream, right? I can bareback you." Josh's voice dropped to an unsteady whisper. "And if I'm *really* dreaming, then there will be oil—hell, yes." He reached out, palming a small cut crystal bottle that appeared in the tangled black silk sheets on which they lay.

"You don't need that either—"

"But I want it." Josh's voice was low, and firm; he knelt between Conall's legs, his cock now standing up tall and curved, just as it had in the shower before Conall had done his best to take the whole thick length of it down his throat. "I want to give it to you."

With his free hand, Josh shifted Conall so the Fae's ass rested on the human's thighs; again Conall's tip wept, but this time the clear drops fell onto his own stomach, effervescing, glistening, Fae. A thrill raced through Conall at the sight, and the sensation, a frisson that brought his eyes wide open for an instant, like nothing he had ever felt before. Pure delight, like a sunbeam scattered over a waterfall.

Josh pulled the stopper out of the little bottle, setting it carefully to one side; a floral scent filled the air. "Honeysuckle. Perfect." He started to pour the oil into his own palm, then paused, and reached for Conall's hand. "Here, you do it." Carefully, he drizzled a pale golden spill into Conall's palm. "I want to feel you touching me." His hand closed around Conall's wrist and drew it toward his shaft. "I want to watch you enjoy me."

With unsteady strokes, Conall spread the oil up and down the hot, iron-hard length. *Why does he want to do this?* Yes, this was a dream, but it was no dream he would ever have known how to have; this human male took Fae notions of sex and stood them on their heads. A

Fae might care for a partner's pleasure, but only after his own was assured; and none of the myriad concepts that had flooded his mind in connection with the word "bareback" could matter to a Fae, immune from disease and quick to heal from any injury not mortal. No, this was as much Josh's dream as it was his own, and why did the human want to please a stranger so?

Josh's head fell back as Conall caressed him; the human poured more of the oil into his own hand, and smoothed it slowly, with open palm and splayed fingers, over his vibrantly patterned chest. The scented oil brought out the colors and the crisp lines of elaborate vines, flowers, and a single magnificent bird, and sent tiny rivulets of oil running down to trickle over rock-hard abs and disappear into the thick wiry curls that surrounded the base of his cock.

Conall curled up, slightly, so he could use both hands; both were needed, to take Josh's full length. The play of the human's hand over smooth, patterned flesh was fascinating, and arousing; Conall watched, riveted, as fingertips traced the softness of a flower's petals, dancing flames that all but gave off heat and light and smoke, the glint in the eyes of a hawk—

A black-hooded hawk. Conall's own House-guardian. *#fREE yOURSELF#*, he heard it cry in memory, wheeling before the full moon that had served to banish him, just hours before. And now here it was, its proud visage etched into the flesh of a human, a world away.

"*Scair-anam*," he whispered. *Soul-share*. It had to be. The Pattern had torn him asunder, ripped his very soul in two, and hurled him into the human world, flinging him directly at the feet of the one human who could make him whole. The human who bore the other half of his sundered soul.

"Please. Josh." Conall gripped the base of the thick organ more tightly with one hand, cupping the human's heavy sac with the other. "Please. I need you. In me. *Now*." Because he needed. Ached. Longed. Part of him knew he was being driven by pure instinct, the SoulShare compulsion forcing him into a closeness his waking self would never dare. But the part of him being driven didn't care. He needed this, in case the slice of paradise they'd shared in the shower hadn't been enough to start the Sharing. Then it would be his turn. Closing the circle, taking his first lover, finding his own pleasure. That joy, the ripple of sunlight, multiplied a thousand-fold. "*Please.*"

Josh's shaft throbbed in Conall's grip, twitched, jerked, spraying clear drops in a fan over his stomach. "Raise up," Josh rasped, his dark eyes seeming to glow.

Conall did his best, and his human lover managed the rest, lifting his ass long enough to press the smooth moist tip of his cock to his unbreached entrance. Conall caught his lower lip between his teeth and tried to take his weight on his heels.

And cried out, softly, as Josh reached out with his free hand, and clasped Conall's hand tightly. "I've got you, baby." The human's dark gaze caught his, held it. "I promised you I'd make it good, didn't I?"

Hard, blunt, smooth heat pierced the tight ring of muscle at Conall's entrance; he gasped, and clamped down, and fought the clamping, sweat coming out on his brow. It *was* good. It was so much better than good. And the groans and the soft ecstatic curses that flowed from Josh as he worked his oiled, throbbing cock deeper inside told him that it was also better than good for his SoulShare.

"So full." Conall could barely form words; his brain had no interest at all in working, all it wanted to do was revel in the sensations as Josh eased one of Conall's cheeks aside to allow himself deeper. "I never knew…"

"Shh." Josh's hand tightened, where it held Conall's. "Just enjoy. God, I could watch you all day."

And then, what couldn't get better, got better, as Josh reached around with his free hand and started to stroke and pump Conall's cock. Conall's back arched involuntarily, sending his aching member up into the human's grip but nearly causing the cock in his hold to slip free. "Shit," he whispered vehemently.

Josh laughed, a delicious sound that flowed over Conall, touching him in places no hand or mouth ever could. "You *do* know how to curse." He guided Conall back down, pushing into him and making tiny tight circles with his hips, stroking, demanding pleasure with a skill the Fae suspected was born both of long practice and an intense desire to please. "Do it again, baby. Let me hear it."

The next curses that escaped Conall's lips were *as'Faein*, and had no translation. And needed none, because Josh's eyes were bright, the color high in his cheeks. "Almost there. Almost. You close?"

Conall nodded, his heart pounding. Just a slightly tighter grip—or the sensation of Josh's seed, spent in the depths of his body—

"LaFontaine, just what the *fuck* do you think you're doing?"

It all vanished.

Chapter Seven

If there was a good way to be awakened from a spectacular erotic dream, wrapped around the man who'd just starred in it, stark naked and with a hard-on about two seconds from detonation, this wasn't it. Josh groaned, yanking a sheet up around himself and Conall as he glared at Bryce Newhouse, and past him at a chagrined Terry. "You could have knocked."

"It's my fucking apartment, LaFontaine." The banking family scion—the son of a bitch should have that on his business cards, properly engraved, *Banking Family Scion*—lounged in the bedroom doorway, not a hair out of place or a sweat stain showing on his linen suit despite the heat. "And forgive me, but it's early enough in the evening I didn't think you'd be bringing your bar pickups home yet."

Sorry, Terry mouthed, as Josh reddened. *He came home early*.

Conall stirred beside him, turned toward the newcomers, one hand resting lightly on Josh's arm, pale fingers interrupting the vivid patterns. Making beauty without trying to. Josh shook his head, impressed; the younger man was unruffled, totally unfazed by the glowering asshole in the doorway.

"Should I not be here?" The redhead's accent was almost musical, and Josh couldn't understand how anyone, even an impervious dick like his ex's new lover, could continue to sneer when listening to it.

"You're fine." Josh rested a hand over Conall's, and met his gaze as reassuringly as he could before returning his attention to the man in the doorway. "I wasn't aware house rules included 'no guests'." Amazing, how Bryce unfailingly brought out the worst in him. "You want to get the fuck out and let me dress? Or is there some particular reason you're standing there staring at me?"

"Maybe it's not you I'm staring at."

Josh's hands clenched into fists, either one of which he was sure was more than enough to wipe the smirk off the bastard's face. One for Conall's sake, and one for the hurt so plain on Terry's face.

But before he could move, Terry placed a hand on Bryce's shoulder. "Let's just give him the message, okay?" Terry squared his shoulders, composed himself, and pushed past the smirking financier, his gaze darting from Josh to Conall, and back again. "Did you give your landlord our number in case of emergencies?"

"I… yeah, I did, but only if he couldn't reach me, and I've been—oh, shit." His cell phone, left in his jeans pocket when he changed, was at this moment powered off and sitting on the bathroom floor, where it had been since he and Conall got in the shower. "Something's happened?" He started to sit up, but subsided when doing so pulled the sheet off Conall.

"I guess so. He called me about an hour ago, while we were packing up costumes at the end of the parade—"

"Which meant that he called *me* while I was just getting off the plane," Bryce cut in, with the air of a man whose entire life had recently been upended. "I powered up my phone, and imagine my surprise, six calls in the last half hour from my upstairs neighbor."

"You lost me." Josh's hand covered Conall's again, it beat hell out of continuing to make a fist out of it. Sooner or later he was going to swing on the pale, immaculately groomed son of a bitch if he didn't find something else to do with his hands. Probably knock the bastard's porn-star mustache around to the back of his head. And Conall's hand tightened on his arm, almost imperceptibly. *I've got your back*, Josh's mind filled in, in the redhead's soft, sensual voice. But that had to be a leftover from the dream; no one ever said that, not to him, he was the one who had everyone else's back. And there was no reason Conall, of all people, should be doing anything of the kind.

"Tiernan Guaire has the third floor studio in this building," Terry put in softly. "He's not here much, but he turns up every now and then." He turned and shot his partner a look over his shoulder that Josh wished he could catch, then cleared his throat. "He was kind of surprised to find out I was *that* Terry."

"Did he say why he was calling? What happened?" Josh swung his legs out of bed, carefully, so as to leave the sheet in place, and rose to go get his phone; paused, blushing slightly, at the sound of Terry's cough, the sight of Bryce rolling his eyes. *Oh, hell.* At least Bryce's dumbfuckery had killed his sleeping hard-on before he put himself on display; with a mental shrug, he crossed to the bathroom.

"No, just that you're supposed to call him as soon as you get a chance."

Josh spotted his phone under the sink, bent, and snatched it up, snagging his jeans and his muscle tee while he was down there, and narrowly missing cracking his head on the sink as he stood back up. Then it was down again, to grab Conall's shirt and trousers; he winced at the blood on the shirt, knowing that the other man wasn't injured, but also knowing exactly how Bryce was going to look at him because of it.

Shit, I hate being right sometimes. He handed Conall back his clothes, then sat down on the edge of the bed, pointedly ignoring Bryce, pulling on his jeans, but not bothering to fasten them before reaching for the phone. Hitting the power button, he grimaced at all the red notifications, then called up the phone and returned the most recent call from D.C.

Tiernan picked up on the first ring. "Josh, about fucking time." At least his landlord wasn't asking what he'd been doing.

"Sorry, didn't have my phone on me. What's going on?" He started, and turned a little, as Conall's fingers laced through the fingers of his free hand; giving the other man's hand a quick squeeze, he shifted his weight to sit so he could see all three of the room's other occupants. Terry was easing himself to sit on the foot of the bed; Bryce was still staring at him, his expression so incredulous as to be ludicrous; Conall was ignoring the bundle of clothes Josh had set beside him, and was watching Josh intently, green eyes seeming almost to glow in the late afternoon light.

"There's been a break-in at Raging Art-On." The voice on the other end of the phone was brisk, businesslike, and Josh supposed that was a good thing; if his business were in ruins, the other man would at least sound a little devastated, or so he hoped. "Nothing seems to have been stolen, the police have been through the place and I've had the locks replaced, but you're the only one who's going to know for sure if anything's missing."

"Yeah, I suppose I'll have to come." Josh's voice got stuck in his throat as Conall's hand tightened around his. *I can't leave him.* He wasn't sure where the rock-solid certainty came from, but the thought of leaving Conall behind was painful. An actual, physical ache.

Which was crazy. Right? A fucking gorgeous man had fallen at his feet, literally, just a few hours ago. A few hours, that's all it had been. Sure, the encounter in the bathroom had been mind-blowing, and the remaining fragments of the dream he'd just had took that sweet BJ and cranked up the heat from there, but that was it. Insta-love wasn't real, couldn't be. Hell, he didn't even know the guy's last name.

"Josh? You there?"

Tiernan's voice was like fingers snapped under Josh's nose. "I'm here. I need to come home, right?" Green eyes, watching him. A hand in his. The memory of that mouth, searching him. Pleasuring him. And joy.

"The Acela leaves Penn Station on the hour, every hour. That's probably faster than trying to get out to the airport and get a flight." A pause. "Josh?"

Hell. "Tiernan, I, uh… I have a problem." He snarled, without even bothering to look, as a snort came from Bryce's direction; he had no interest in looking at anyone or anything other than Conall. *Not walking away and leaving you here. No effing way.* "I, uh, met someone. At the March."

Struck by a sudden thought, he muted the phone. "Conall, do you have somewhere to stay? Someone who's expecting you?"

Even as the words left his lips, he knew the redhead was going to shake his head. Which he did, damp hair tumbling into his eyes in the sexiest way imaginable.

Josh unmuted the phone and continued, "He's recovering from a head injury, and he doesn't have anywhere to go." The bloody shirt and the healed head wound were two parts of a mystery that was just going to have to stay unsolved for the time being.

"Are we taking in your strays now, LaFontaine?" Bryce sneered, oblivious to the glares he was getting from both Josh and his own partner.

"I heard that." Tiernan's voice startled Josh into relaxing what had become his white-knuckled grip on the phone. "Tell Newhouse to go let the Rottweiler on the second floor suck his dick, and tell Terry I said to show you where the spare key is for my apartment on the third floor." There was a pause, as if his landlord was conferring with someone else, out of earshot. "Kevin and I were there last weekend, so there's food in the pantry for at least a few days. But you need to get your ass home."

"Roger that." Josh's eyes closed, just for a second. And there, before his eyes, was a glorious fragment of the dream he'd been yanked out of, a crystal vial of scented oil in his hand and Conall moaning in bliss as he pierced his tight virgin ring. *My ass needs to stay here…*

"Check in with me at Purgatory before you go to the shop, I've had the codes changed on the security system. See you tonight."

Terry cleared his throat as Josh touched off the phone. "What happened? You have to go?"

"Huh? Yeah — there's been a break-in at my tattoo parlor." Terry, Josh noted, looked nearly as shocked as he himself had felt at the news. Even Bryce had the good grace to look perturbed, although to tell the truth it wasn't all that different from the normal cast of his features, so there was a chance he was wrong about that. "Tiernan's taken care of things for the time being, but I need to get back."

Conall's fingers disengaged from his, and it was as if the faint tingle of an electric current stopped running through him. *I really am losing it.* But there was no conviction to the thought, and he bit his lip as he reached out to pick up Conall's clothes and hand them to him once again. "I don't have to be gone long…"

His voice trailed off, and he turned to glare at Bryce. "Would you mind getting the fuck out of here?" And, before the financier could do more than snigger, Josh reached out to lay an apologetic hand on Terry's knee. "Give us a minute?"

"Sure." Terry unfolded from the bed. With a nod to Conall, the curly-haired dancer took a startled-looking Bryce by the arm and gave him little choice about leaving the bedroom, closing the door on the start of a low-voiced conversation.

"I should go."

The whisper brought Josh's head around like a whip cracking. Conall was staring at the bundle of clothes in his hands, his fists clenched tight in the fabric.

"Where would you go, if you left?"

Conall shrugged, and the little futile gesture and the faint lines of pain around the other man's eyes tore at Josh. He reached out, intending to rest a hand on Conall's shoulder, but somehow that hand slid up his shoulder, up the side of his neck, until his fingers were buried in thick red hair. He used that grip to tilt Conall's face up, until he could look the other man straight in those amazing green eyes.

"I don't understand this. I don't understand what I'm doing. I don't pick up men on the street"—*or off it*—"and I haven't done anything like that shower since I was a young idiot figuring out what Greenwich Village was all about." He could feel himself blushing under the intensity of that gaze; he shifted his fingers slightly, feeling the silk of Conall's hair working through them. "Nothing like this has ever happened to me. But I'm not letting you go. Not like this."

Josh leaned in and kissed Conall's forehead. "Come on, get dressed. There's a place you can stay for a few days. Until I can come back."

Conall nodded.

"*Scair-anam*," he whispered.

Soul-share?

***

Josh tilted his head back against the seat rest, letting his eyes fall closed. The East Coast would keep racing by outside the windows of the Acela whether he was keeping an eye on it or not. He'd traveled light when he came to visit Terry; his single duffel was locked away overhead. And in his group of four seats, only the aisle seat opposite him was occupied, by a guy in an expensive-looking suit who had spent the first fifteen minutes of the trip carefully averting his eyes from Josh's inked arms. Just as well, Josh wasn't feeling talkative.

"I'll come back. Probably in two or three days."

***

Conall watched him from the bed, as he checked out the apartment. He found the remote for the flat-screen television, pointed out the food in the pantry, tried to figure out the seriously badass coffee maker. The discovery of instant in the cupboard was a relief to him, at least, though from the look on Conall's face, it might as well have been sawdust. There was a tight look around the other man's eyes, one he recognized; he'd seen it before, on some clients, as he wiped away blood and ink, hour upon hour. But Conall said nothing. Until he turned to go.

"Come back, *scair-anam*."

***

Josh scrubbed at his face with the heels of his hands. Terry had promised to check on Conall, and to call him if anything came up. That hadn't made it any easier to leave, especially not with Bryce's sneering face in the background. *He can't always have been this much of a dickhead. Terry would never have left me for him if he had been. Right?*

A headache was starting to set in, and Josh sighed. Why did Conall call him his soul-share? Whatever that was.

His eyes snapped open. *I understood it.* Scair-anam. *Soul-share. How?*

Chapter Eight

Washington, D.C.

"Remind me again how you're planning on keeping our shared ass from getting shot off?"

Alone in the alley that bisected the block housing Purgatory and Raging Art-On, Janek yanked down the hood he was forced to wear even at night, and blotted sweat from what was left of his forehead. That fucker Guaire's bolt of living Stone had caught him over his right eye and drilled straight through his head, leaving a hole the diameter of a quarter and turning almost half of his head into the same freakish crystal shit. Crystal shit that glowed red whenever the monster inside it was awake. Not something you wanted to have the neighborhood staring at; hence the hoodie. In the middle of a fucking heat wave. It was just one more good reason to add to the list of good reasons he already had for taking Tiernan Guaire apart, as slowly as possible.

You do not want to antagonize me now. The female inner voice was cold enough to smoke. ***Not if you expect me to spare the attention to keep you aware. And we are not going to attempt another physical entry***.

Janek sneered, even as he scrubbed at the decades-old wire-reinforced window with the already grimy sleeve of his hoodie. "And what's looking in the window going to get you breaking in didn't?"

I'm not just looking. Janek hated it when the voice sounded more male, because when his rider felt more male, it was invariably horny, and had only Janek's body to be horny with. And second-hand hard-ons sucked balls, especially with his junk in the condition it was in. *But this way of doing it is going to be harder on you. I thought I would try to spare you that, the first time.*

Janek rolled his eyes. "Quit wasting our time by pretending you give a shit."

As you wish.

The former bouncer shuddered as an unseen force shoved his forehead against the glass. The *Marfach* had one voice that wasn't a man, and wasn't a woman. And on the rare occasions when he took some fragment of awareness with him into sleep, just a whisper from that voice was enough to give him screaming nightmares.

Hold very still. And keep your eye open.

His eye would have liked nothing better than to roll back into his head and screw itself shut, but the same force that had moved his head kept it wide open and staring. And shudders wracked his whole body as his sight, his point of view, moved through the filthy window and into the darkened hallway at the back of the tattoo parlor, with a sensation a lot like what it would probably feel like to have someone take a potato peeler to his cornea. *I did not just go through that window. I did NOT just go through that window.*

Of course not. Fool. The female laugh was dismissive. *But since I have no sight of my own, I must borrow yours.* Janek caught the impression of a frown. *It should not have been so difficult to enter. The Fae must have reinforced the wards.*

Difficult for who? Janek didn't even bother to try to keep the snarl out of his thoughts. It hadn't felt like this last time. Maybe only the parasite in his head noticed the Fae wards. And anyone else forced to come along for the ride.

You have no idea what that cost. Now, silence.

The point of view that Janek was, for the moment, drifted slowly down the hallway he remembered from their first, hasty visit. That horrible peeled-eyeball sensation was still with him, and every inch of progress felt like someone was rolling his skinned eye in ground glass. *You'd better be damned sure there's something useful up here.*

You have nothing to say on the subject, Meat. The female turned his attention to the first doorway, the one that led into the studio where piercings were done. The door stood ajar, opening onto windowless darkness; he was driven closer for a brief inspection, then passed on.

As long as it's my body you're playing with, I have something to say. He wasn't accustomed to being this awake, or this alert, for this long, and he was determined to take advantage of it. *Why are we fucking around up here?*

Janek turned his gaze—no, he had it turned for him—to the ceiling, the walls, the freshly painted baseboards, the floor, giving each in turn careful scrutiny. *The Fae's wards are enough to keep me out of his own lair, the club Purgatory. But there may be a way through from above.*

The former bouncer tried very hard not to think about being forced to crawl through an air duct. Especially if something in the air duct was going to be trying to peel him. *Why do you need to get in there at all? It's the pretty boy you want, and it's not like he lives there. Purgatory is just a fucking sex club.*

The woman's laughter was as cold as the rest of her. *A fucking sex club with an infinite power supply in its basement. A supply I need, if I am to continue this miserable existence, and yours along with it.*

The ley lines.

The great nexus, more precisely. There was the door to the tattoo studio; closed, as it had been the first time. *Do you not feel yourself weakening, as I draw on the magick stored in the Stone?*

Janek was feeling the distinct sensation of his balls shriveling and drawing up into what was left of the protective warmth of his body, all the way back out by the window. *I'm not going in there again.*

Don't be ridiculous. The male voice was back; maybe the female had been disconcerted by the sensation of shrinking testicles. *You passed through the wards already, back at the window. Man up, Meat.* The male voice was a hell of a lot quicker to pick up on human thought and speech patterns. Not that that made it any more tolerable than the female. *This is just a door.*

His point of view drifted closer, until he could almost feel the grain of the wood in the door against his nonexistent flayed eyeball. And there he fucking well stopped. Or tried to. Something shoved—

White light shot through with actinic purple exploded all around Janek, searing his nonexistent retina until it gave back livid blue-white ghosts. And it was as if shards of shattered crystal lanced through the raw and dripping remains of his flayed eyeball; he covered his eye with his hands, moaning, as he dropped to the ground.

Ground? Hands? Gingerly, he felt at his eye, with fingers gone almost entirely numb. No gore, no dripping, no brilliant light; the afterimages from hell, though, were still dancing in the darkness in front of his eye, and he cursed.

Move, Meat. Janek distinctly felt a female's stiletto heel in the small of his back. He ignored it.

You heard the lady. This time the sensation was a bare foot, pushing him to sprawl face down on the concrete.

Fuck off and die.

I will not be the one who dies here. The voice was like stone dragged over bones. Janek's bones.

The former bouncer dragged himself to his feet. Or was dragged; he had no way to tell which, numb as most of his body was. Even deader than normal, whatever the fuck normal was now for the former Janek O'Halloran. And as he staggered off into the growing darkness, his consciousness switched off again.

The *Marfach* didn't need his brain to get the meat wagon home.

Chapter Nine

Greenwich Village
New York City

Conall awoke to a persistent soft knocking. Groaning, he squinted against the harsh light barely filtered by the curtains. *Morning's not my time in this world, either, apparently.* "Just a minute."

The knocking continued a moment longer, then stopped. "Sorry." The voice was muffled, and he recognized it—Terry, the smaller male from downstairs. The one who wasn't an asshole.

The word had come into his head in English, and he chuckled softly, despite the reverberations doing so set up in his head. *Plasma screen television,* Josh had called the shining black rectangle hanging from one wall. Humans appeared to be doing quite well for themselves without magick. And at least now he had a vocabulary that wasn't full of holes, though some aspects of the vocabulary he had acquired overnight were probably of sorely limited utility, and he wasn't quite sure who or what Eric Northman was supposed to be.

He looked around for his trousers, and spotted them on the floor at the foot of the bed. Sliding out of bed, he padded around to where they lay, and bent to pick them up; stopped, clutching the footboard of the giant bed, his head pounding. He waited for the pain, the dizziness to pass, settled for waiting for them to lessen, snagged the trousers with two fingers, and sat down on the edge of the bed to put them on, feeling older and more exhausted than a Fae was ever supposed to be able to feel. Barring magickal intervention, of course.

Conall grimaced at his own black humor and got to his feet, fastening the trousers and crossing to the door. He'd watched carefully as Josh demonstrated the elaborate locks; the locks, though, were the least of what kept this place safe. There was magick warding those locks.

Fae magick.

His fingers tingled as he turned knobs and slid back deadbolts. He'd become suspicious upon hearing the name of Josh's landlord; the name of Tiernan Guaire could have been Fae, yet no one else seemed to think it odd. And then the voice, readily audible to him, even through a telephone; the male spoke with an accent that could almost have been Fae, yet with subtle differences. But a Fae who had been in the human world any length of time could lose an accent, easily, or gain another one—his night of watching the television had showed him the multiplicity of human languages, if nothing else.

And then, after Josh had left, and the door had closed, the pain had become impossible to ignore. He had stood, with his hand on the cold locks, and felt the tingle shoot up his arm. And he had been sure. Earth magick, the kind a Noble would channel. Touching the keys that Josh had hung on a hook by the door only confirmed it. A simple enough channeling, but anyone who tried to force that door would never know what had turned him to dust.

"Hey, sorry to bother you so early." Terry stood on the landing, his arms full of paper bags, and the bags filled with food. "But I figured anything Tiernan and Kevin might have left last weekend wouldn't be fresh. And I need to go open up the shop. Which left me enough time for a quick run to Gristedes."

"Please, come in." Conall stepped back, letting the curly-haired human into the apartment, and followed him to the tiny kitchen. He and Terry were nearly of a height, the human a little shorter, but not as slight. "I could put those away. I wouldn't want to make you late for work." The words came more easily than they had yesterday, after watching what Josh had told him was *satellite television* into the dark hours of the night. Of course, the headache that followed had come easily too, but was a small matter beside the gnawing pain due to the separation from his *scair-anam*. A pain both physical and emotional, and he was hard put to it to tell which was stranger to feel.

"I have time." Terry lifted loaves of bread, bags of fruit, and other less readily identifiable containers out of the bags and set them on the sideboard beside the basin; glanced at him, trying to look as if he were doing something else, and opened a small door under the sideboard, from which cold air wafted. "Are you all right? I saw you when Josh found you. You looked pretty beat up."

"That was an old injury, nothing to worry about." Conall tried to make his tone reassuring. This human was kind enough, and Josh had mentioned he was a former lover, had even smiled when he said it, so that spoke well for him; there was only one human, though, who Conall could even remotely bear being fussed over by, and it wasn't Terry.

"If you say so." Terry opened up an oddly-shaped container and started placing eggs in the cold-box. "But you don't have anywhere to go?"

Conall shrugged, hoping the gesture meant the same thing here as it did in the Realm, and that Terry would accept it as an answer to his question. "I'm traveling. Seeing the world."

"Not the friendliest part of it, apparently." Terry's gesture encompassed Conall's bloodstained shirt; after an attempt to remove the blood magically had left him muffling screams in one of the enormous bed's many pillows, the Fae had tried to work the elaborate mechanism in the shower, with some success. His shirt, however, had not been entirely cooperative with the unorthodox cleaning method. "You know, you're close enough to my size, I probably have a few things that will fit you. I'll come back after work, if that's all right with you."

Generosity. So human. Although I suspect his Bryce isn't moved by the same impulse. "Thank you. It will feel good to get into something clean." Gratitude wasn't exactly Fae, either, but he'd seen enough on the television to consider it a safe response in this situation.

Terry straightened from the cold-box, letting it swing closed. "It's my pleasure." He hesitated, raked his fingers through his hair, and flashed Conall a tentative smile. "I haven't seen Josh look that happy in

80

a long time. As happy as he was yesterday, I mean. I like it." He gathered up the bags and crossed to the door, "See you tonight."

The door clicked closed; Conall reflexively gestured and whispered the word that would lock it, then sat down hard on the bed, gasping for breath as a spasm of pain ripped through his gut. *Fuck.* Now there was a useful word. All the equivalents *as'Faein* were too elegant.

Slowly—too slowly, more slowly than last time—the pain loosened its grip on him. He sat motionless for a few moments, just breathing, testing to see if it was really over; then, stiffly, he got up, went to the door, and closed the locks the hard way. *It's a good thing touching magick doesn't have the same effect on me that trying to channel it does.*

Yes. There was the problem. Trying to *channel* magick. It was supposed to be as natural as breathing, as walking; magick was what he was made of, him more than most Fae, and it had always been an effort for him not to channel it. And that wasn't supposed to change, in the human realm.

Conall lay back on the bed, his weight on his elbows, staring at the window with its translucent shade. He knew more about what had happened to him, what was happening to him now, than he was willing to bet most of the luckless travelers that had passed through the Pattern in the course of two thousand years had known. Mages maintained histories after most Fae had long since forgotten about the tales the history became.

He should be able to use his magick here. All the histories said so. The only problem with *that* was that any attempt to channel anything beyond the abilities inherent in any Fae—rapid healing, and in his case the gift of languages, the gift of the Demesne of Air— brought an agony nearly as great as what he almost remembered of the Pattern. Even after he stopped trying, his very bones remembered what a bad idea it had been.

And the reminder lasted longer each time. Damn, he needed something to take his mind off this. He fell back on the bed, staring at the ceiling. Mirror. *Queen's tits.* An image floated unbidden into his mind, himself lying back on this bed, with Josh covering him. The way the human had in his dream. Only this time he could see, in the mirror, and the designs on Josh's tanned back were amazing. Wings, almost real enough to fly.

Conall shook his head, and the image fled; he groaned, and covered his eyes with a forearm. The pain had started the moment Josh let go of his hand. He wasn't a romantic; no Fae was, not when you and your partner *ar a lar*, of the moment, were both going to live more or less forever unless someone killed you, not when attraction was never forever, and when there was no such thing as love, except the love of blood for blood, which was a different thing entirely. No, romance was not in the Fae lexicon. Much less so in his own.

And yet, it had hurt when Josh released his hand. Down to the bone.

Scair-anam.

A Fae who passed through the Pattern had his soul torn in half. Some truths had not been preserved, and the whole truth about what happened within the Pattern was one of those truths. It was known that half of the Fae's soul went out into the human world, to be born into a human. But as to where, and when, and how, that human was to be found, the ancient texts gave not a fucking clue.

Good word.

Conall rolled onto his side, curling in around the pain as another spasm seized him, waiting for it to pass. And waiting some more, his arms crossed over his abs in an attempt to stop the tremors. Trying to breathe. Damn, this time it felt like something was dragging at his very breath, trying to keep it from his lungs. He was smothering, a little bit at a time.

The histories all said a Fae in the human world, without his SoulShare, could never die. But the histories were wrong about other things.

Can I die?

Not alone. Maybe he could. But he *would* not. He refused. Josh would come back. Somehow, being with the human would stop the pain.

How many times had he yearned for a normal life? To be free to channel, or not. To take pleasure, with another, and not risk the destruction of that other, and everything around him. To look into the eyes of a friend, or a lover, and not wonder when he would be asked to pay in power for the gift of a moment's closeness.

Wisdom wishes not, the proverb said. *For the only fate worse than to be denied a wish is to receive it.*

Chapter Ten

Washington, D.C.

Kevin grunted as something with the approximate mass of his husband hit the bed beside him hard enough to make him bounce. Cracking an eyelid, he winced at the early morning sunlight, and rolled to face Tiernan. "I didn't have to be up for half an hour yet." But the one-sided smile on his face as Tiernan's arm snaked around him made a liar of his grumbling tone.

"I could leave if you want." Long blond hair fell tantalizingly over Kevin's shoulder as Tiernan's teeth teased at his throat. "If you'd really like another half hour's sleep more than you'd like to help me unwind."

"How crazy do I look, exactly?" Kevin tunneled his fingers into Tiernan's thick blond waves and brought his head up so he could make eye contact, even as he caught at the Fae's legs with one of his own and rolled them both so Tiernan lay between his thighs. "You're up late," he added, distracted by the fingers of living crystal that stroked his cheek, toyed with his ear.

"Had a couple of new dancers to audition." Tiernan shifted his hips, grinding himself pleasurably into the cradle Kevin made for him. "From Rio, they used to run a capoeira studio."

"No wonder you need a workout." Kevin laughed softly, running his tongue along Tiernan's pierced eyebrow, toying with the gold ring. "Are you going to hire both of them?" As the owner of Purgatory, the hottest all-male sex club in Washington, D.C.—or the whole Eastern Seaboard, in Kevin's opinion and limited experience—there were aspects of club management Tiernan found less than exciting, but Kevin also knew auditioning new talent was one of Tiernan's favorite activities. As was coming home afterward and telling his husband all about it.

"Hell, yes." Tiernan caught Kevin's mouth, scorched him with a kiss. When the kiss ended, though, the Fae pulled back a little, and a slight frown creased his brow. "I also stopped by the tattoo parlor on my way out."

"Something wrong?" The word *mercurial* might have been invented to describe the Fae race, and Kevin was beginning to get used to his husband's turn-on-a-dime-and-give-back-change mood shifts. He smoothed a hand down Tiernan's back, gently cupping one ass cheek and drawing him closer.

"Nothing I can put my finger on." Tiernan slipped a finger into Kevin's mouth, with a slight lift of his pierced brow; Kevin nibbled lightly on the offered digit, and Tiernan flashed him a quick smile. "Josh came into the club as soon as he got back from New York, didn't even bother stopping at home to drop his bag. I took him upstairs, and he looked through the whole place. He doesn't think anything was taken, and nothing seemed out of place."

"You don't look convinced." Kevin raised up on his elbows to let Tiernan slip his arms around him, then tipped his head back in response to a growl and a nudge.

"Probably because I'm not." Tiernan's voice was slightly muffled in the skin of Kevin's throat, as he ran a line of gentle bites up to his ear. "I thought I felt the wards go off again, before he got back, but there was no sign that anything had been broken into. Although the magick snapped back again, until it was just surrounding the room where the tattoo equipment is. Not the room where he does the piercings, and not the waiting area in front." A tongue probed Kevin's ear, teased the lobe into Tiernan's mouth to be worried at. "I *might* have just fucked up when I reset the wards."

Kevin sucked in a breath between clenched teeth. "Someday I'm going to figure out how you manage to talk business and drive me crazy at the same time. And when I do, you're not going to be walking properly for at least a week."

"I don't think I've walked properly since I met you." Tiernan's crystal hand slid down between their bodies and encircled Kevin's swiftly-rising cock. "Which of your girlfriends was it who used to call you Elephant Dick?"

"All of them, I think, eventually." He arched up as best he could into his husband's hand. "Did you tell Josh about the second break-in?—if that's what it was."

The Fae shook his head, sending blond hair cascading down around Kevin's face, almost blocking out the early morning sunlight. "No way to back up the story. The new security system is working, and it didn't show anything." Tiernan's grip around his erection tightened, and Kevin's eyes closed with pleasure; the tip of a tongue touched his eyelids, stroked them. "My wards suck, anyway. Elemental magick's not much good for that sort of thing, you need pure magick. So I want to keep an eye on things, myself. No more weekend jaunts to New York for us for a while."

Things. Such as the possibility the evil force that had tried to kill him and enslave Tiernan might be planning another attack. There was no trace of the *Marfach* in the ley lines any more, Tiernan had been able to tell that much; the logical assumption was that all of the creature was living, or whatever it was it did, within the living Stone that Tiernan had used to kill— or try to kill—Janek O'Halloran, the former Purgatory bouncer. Obviously the attempt hadn't worked, since the man had been responsible for at least one murder after he and Tiernan had left him for dead on the floor of Purgatory's basement, with half his head either gone or turned to crystal.

Kevin fought back a shiver, and opened his eyes. The look he surprised in his husband's eyes sent another shiver chasing after the first; a fierce, hot, almost predatorial protectiveness that spoke of an unpleasant death for anyone who threatened Kevin Almstead. "*Lanan…*"

Tiernan shushed him with a finger over his lips, then followed the finger with a heated kiss. "Fuck the break-ins." Kevin could feel Tiernan's lips moving against his own, breathe in his words. "I want you." Teeth caught his lower lip, nipped sharply, followed by a long, slow lick—

And the fucking sound of a fucking alarm clock. "Shit," Kevin whispered, along with a few choice curses in the Fae language that his husband had inadvertently taught him.

Tiernan growled and rolled off him, to lie flat on his back. The Fae's crystal hand moved down to stroke his proud, curved erection; Kevin swallowed hard at the sight. "Dress slowly," Tiernan instructed, his gaze never leaving Kevin's. "I want to watch."

***

Kevin was greeted with the roar of a dysfunctional air-conditioner as he pushed open the door and walked into the front waiting area of Raging Art-On. "Josh?" The waiting room was deserted, the late afternoon light slanting through the window display of flash and body hardware to fall across the chairs grouped around a table covered with magazines, and the display case full of studs and rings and pretty much everything he could ever imagine any man wanting to stick through some part of his body. "You here?"

"Kevin? Is that you?" The voice came from down the hallway that opened off the back of the waiting area; Kevin looked around the corner, then entered the tattoo studio. Josh was seated beside the tattoo machine, and after nodding a greeting, he turned back to inspecting the gun-like attachment. His jaw was set in a hard line, and his expression was inward-turned, instead of his usual easy, open smile.

"Yeah, it's me. Am I interrupting?" Kevin eyed the heavily inked artist uncertainly. "I can come back later—"

"No, no." Josh set down the piece of equipment and turned his full attention to Kevin, with a smile that, while genuine enough, still seemed far away. "What can I do for you?"

Instead of answering immediately, Kevin motioned toward the tattoo apparatus. "Tiernan told me about the break-in. Is your equipment all right? Nothing damaged?"

The younger man shook his head. "No. I don't think they even got into this room. I'd know if anything were out of place."

Kevin believed him. Judging from the way Josh had held the gun, and the possessive way his gaze, and his hands, lingered on it, and on the racks of pigments and all the other equipment that he used to—by all accounts—make magic in this tiny space, he'd wager that anyone who fucked with Josh LaFontaine's livelihood would be in serious shit. Anyone other than the *Marfach*, anyway.

"So, did you just stop in to say hello?" Josh's good cheer seemed more forced than genuine, and Kevin frowned. "You okay?"

Josh shrugged, the bright designs on his well-muscled arms rippling. "I'm having a little trouble getting my breath today. Probably just the humidity or some shit." He grinned apologetically. "Can I do something for you?"

"Yeah, actually, you can, or at least I hope so." Kevin reached into his suit pocket and withdrew his phone; scrolling through his stored pictures, he quickly found the one he wanted. "I'm thinking about getting some ink; I want to match Tiernan's." He laughed softly as he looked at the picture, remembering his husband's reaction when he'd asked to photograph the magnificent tattoo that rode his left hip, the elaborate Celtic-*cum*-tribal design which was the claiming-mark the Pattern left on a Fae who passed through its sieve. One picture had led to another, and in the end Kevin was just damned glad his phone was password-protected.

"Let me take a look." Josh reached for the phone.

Kevin was totally unprepared for the other man's reaction. Josh was staring at the phone in his hand as if he seriously expected it to bite him. "What is it?"

For a long moment, Josh didn't answer; Kevin was just opening his mouth to ask what was going on when the other man cleared his throat. "I, uh, I've seen this design before. That's all."

Now it was Kevin's turn to stare. *That's not possible.* "Where?"

"The guy I met at the march this weekend. He has this design all over his upper back."

"Oh, Celtic knotwork." Kevin let out a breath he hadn't even realized he'd been holding. He'd seen some incredibly intricate Celtic tattoo work since he'd started coming to Purgatory—had it really only been six months ago?

"No." Josh was expanding and enlarging the image on the phone. "He had ink just like this. Same color, same quality work. I meant to ask him where he had it done. I was jealous as hell." Josh moved the picture around, enlarging it, studying it intently, and suddenly grinned. "I see your husband kept the Prince Albert. You enjoying it?"

Kevin felt himself turning red. "Very much so."

Josh laughed, and there was no way to tell if the

sound was a little tight. "Anything I can do to brighten your days. Or nights." He went back to perusing the tattoo in the picture. "I doubt I can pull off an exact copy of this, it's just too damned good. And I hate to ask you to settle for second best." He looked up at Kevin, brows a questioning arch. "Have you asked Tiernan where he got his? It would be better if you could go back to the same guy."

Kevin shook his head. "I want to surprise him." Which was true. And it wasn't as if Kevin could somehow pass through the Pattern himself; Tiernan had made clear the portal was one way only. Kevin had seen at least part of the cost of that passage in his SoulShare's nightmares, too, for weeks after they had met. Maybe if he'd been there when Tiernan had first entered the human world, if the Fae hadn't had to spend a century and a half alone, the pain would have been less. As far as Tiernan had been able to tell him, though, there was no way for a Fae to know where, or when, the other half of his soul would be born into a human.

"I get that." Josh shook his head thoughtfully. "That's going to be hard to do, though, no matter who does it. If you want that much ink, and a design that intricate, you're looking at at least two sessions. I'd want to do the outlining first, and hell, that alone might take two
sessions. Think you can keep a big-ass bandage a secret for two or three days, maybe more?"

"Not a chance." Kevin tried not to look crestfallen. Sure, the ink had been at least partly an excuse to come in here and have a look around for himself, though what he thought his untrained eyes might uncover that Tiernan's magick hadn't, he had no fucking clue. But he genuinely did want to surprise his husband with a matching design, maybe on the other hip. "I feel like an idiot, thinking I could just come in and have it done."

Josh laughed and clapped him on the arm. "Most ink virgins are pretty clueless, don't sweat it." He slid off the stool he'd been perched on, circling his shoulders as if he'd been hunched in on himself for a while. "Think about it and let me know. I'm going to have to go back to New York soon, plus I'm booked a ways out, but if Tiernan's going to be out of town for a few days, I'll try and work you in so we can get the whole thing done before he has to see the work in progress."

"Thanks. If we can do it that way, I definitely want to do it." Though it wouldn't be happening soon, not with Tiernan insisting on staying close to home. Kevin took a deep breath, squared his shoulders, and put out a hand; Josh shook it, his palm sweating. "I'll let you know."

The breath of air he took back out on the sidewalk, before plunging into the safe cool dimness of the stairwell leading down to Purgatory, would have seared Kevin's lungs if it hadn't also been as humid as the inside of a fishbowl. *Christ Almighty, if anyone down there says 'hot enough for you?' I swear I'm going to feed him his jockstrap. It being early enough in the evening that they're probably all still wearing them.*

It took his eyes most of the walk down the stairs to adjust to the comparative darkness; his ears told him he'd arrived before his eyes were entirely sure. The music wasn't yet the driving, pounding, consuming beat that would fill the dance floor later in the evening. No, this was the Monday-after-work scene, and most of the late-night dance whores and leather boys were still stuffing their ties in their pockets and having quick cocktails before heading home to change. And the dancing boys didn't even look warmed up yet; their gyrations were slow, languid, more suited to the sticky sultry air outside than the flashing lights of the dance floor.

Kevin grinned at Mac, who was in the process of sliding a beer across the bar to his bald, stocky fireplug of a partner, Lucien, then made his way down into, and through, the as-yet-empty cock pit to the door that opened into Tiernan's cubbyhole of an office. He knocked, softly, then opened the door.

Tiernan turned away from the pair of computer monitors on the top of his desk as the door opened. One monitor was cycling through live digital images of the various "hot spots" in Purgatory, all the places a conscientious owner would keep an eye on in order to be one step ahead of the law in dealing with any issues that might come up. The other monitor stayed focused on one image, a black leather chaise longue in the middle of the floor of an otherwise bare, concrete-walled and floored room. The first thing Tiernan had done after taking title—well, the second thing, after hiring Mac to tend bar and Lucien as a bouncer—was to wall off that part of the basement storeroom over the ley nexus. Only he and Kevin could get in there, now, or so they both hoped and Kevin, at least, prayed. And this was the monitor that Tiernan had been trying to stare a hole through when Kevin knocked.

"*Lanan*," Kevin murmured, bending and tipping

Tiernan's chin up into a hungry kiss, and laughing softly into the kiss as Tiernan took hold of his tie and used it to hold him firmly in place. "I have no problem with letting you use that on me, but I have some news you might want to hear before you start messing with my airway."

The Fae's grip lessened fractionally. "I'm all ears."

"No, you're not." Kevin's downward glance took in his husband's swiftly-growing arousal. "You like breath play too much to just let an opportunity like this go." He grinned, but quickly sobered. "Look, I've just been upstairs talking to Josh. And I think there's a chance his new friend is Fae."

Tiernan's first response was to let go of Kevin's tie as his hand fell to his side. "What makes you think that?"

"I, uh, showed him a picture of your ink." *Well, there goes the surprise, probably. But that doesn't really matter. Much.* "And he recognized it. Said his friend had the same markings all over his upper back."

"Shit." Tiernan sat back in his chair, head falling back, eyes half closed in thought. "I can't say I'm exactly astonished, Cuinn did say there would be more coming." Cuinn was the sandy-haired Fae who had crashed their wedding reception last month; it had been his warning to keep the nexus safe that prompted Tiernan to set up the system of wards that protected Purgatory, and to a lesser extent the building over it, from intrusion. His warning, coupled with a noticeable crawling of Tiernan's skin every time he thought about the *Marfach*, and the possibility of that creature of pure evil magick getting at the great nexus.

Although Cuinn an Dearmad hadn't seemed overly worried about the *Marfach* regaining the nexus, to hear Tiernan tell it—Kevin hadn't heard the oracular pronouncement directly, as he'd been off discovering the veteran with the prosthetic leg taking in Purgatory's pole dancers had been his father's Marine Corps buddy Mac. After all, the creature had been living in the ley lines for some unknown amount of time before Tiernan and Kevin had accidentally drawn it out and hadn't managed to destroy the world yet. No, Cuinn's main concern had been that Tiernan ensure no Fae who had yet to find and bond with his SoulShare touched it. He'd made Tiernan promise not to let that happen, on his own life.

Tiernan's thoughts were, apparently, running in tandem with those of his own SoulShare; slowly, his head came up, his gaze fixed on Kevin's. "If the male in our apartment is actually a Fae… and if he goes down to the basement and finds the minor nexus down there…"

"Fuck," Kevin breathed.

Tiernan nodded grimly. "We have to get him the hell out of there. Somehow."

Chapter Eleven

Greenwich Village,
New York City

"Baby? Are you there?"

"Yes. I'm here." *Wherever 'here' is.* Conall was surrounded by a grey fog almost too dense to swirl in the cool breeze that caressed his naked skin. And Josh's voice was too damned far away.

"Keep talking. Maybe I can follow the sound."

Conall strained to hear. And that was so strange; a Fae of the Demesne of Air never had to strain to hear anything. Anything the air could carry, he could hear and understand. "This way." He closed his eyes, and tried to get his breath. So hard. "Hurry."

"Damn." The voice was fainter. "I'm trying, baby. I just can't move."

"Baby?" Despair edged Josh's voice, and Conall wanted to take that edge away. He needed to hear Josh's voice; it eased the pain he'd been in ever since the human had gone away. *SoulShare.* Not a complete bond, not yet, but it would happen. If Josh would come back. "I thought your Terry was 'baby'."

A soft chuckle floated through the fog. "He was,

once. You're right, though. I should call you something else. But 'Conall' seems so formal."

"You sound closer now. Keep moving."

"I wasn't moving. But you sound closer, too." Again the quiet laughter, wrapping around Conall in a blanket softer than the fog. "This has to be one of the weirdest dreams I've ever had."

"Dream. Of course." Conall groaned. *Maybe Mater was right, and the only thing my brain is good for really is to keep the light from shining straight through from one ear to the other.* "Stop trying to move, then, *lanan*. Stay right where you are, and just talk to me." Dreams in the Realm had their own logic; maybe that was true here as well.

"That makes as much sense as anything." A pause, and it almost seemed to Conall that he could hear the human breathing. "So, something to call you besides 'baby'?"

Now it was Conall's turn to laugh; and, to his amazement, he actually *felt* like laughing. He could sense Josh somewhere, nearby and coming nearer, and the closeness eased the awful tightness that had settled round him like a noose the moment Josh had left his sight. "I never said I didn't like 'baby'." Actually, he *did* like it. A lot. He'd never imagined anyone calling him anything of the sort. "But *lanan* is a good word, it means 'lover'. Or maybe *viant*, that means 'desired one'." Conall felt himself going red; this was odd language for someone like him, even in a dream.

"That's a beautiful language."

The voice was almost in his ear; the temptation to reach out was great, but Conall resisted. Because there was no way Josh could be there, and the

97

disappointment of knowing that to be true was more than he could bear, even in a dream. "It's my native language."

"Does it have a word that means 'impossible'?"

If he closed his eyes, Conall could almost feel warm breath in his ear.

"Because that's what I thought, when I first saw you. Dreams don't just fall at anyone's feet like that. Certainly not mine."

Conall felt a tightness, in his throat and in his heart, a sensation foreign to any Fae. Sympathy. The changes the SoulShare bond was making were already profound, and if he were awake, he would probably be alarmed. But here and now, the wistful sadness in Josh's disembodied voice caught at him, made it hard to breathe. "*D'orant,*" he whispered. "But I'm not a dream."

"You are mine." So close, the pain was gone. "Ever since I can remember. *D'orant.*"

A shiver ran down Conall's spine. "Please, *dar'cion*. Please talk to me. It helps."

"Helps what?"

"The pain." Conall swallowed hard. "Being separated from you. It hurts."

"Christ, I wish I could touch you." A pause. "Would that help? Does it help more if I talk about touching you?"

"I—yes. I think so." Conall's heart raced, he could feel a thin film of sweat on brow and cheekbones. "Yes. It helps."

"Then I'll tell you what I was thinking, all during that long train ride back to D.C." It seemed as if the fog swirled beside him, as if a figure were sitting there, making itself comfortable. "I couldn't think of anything but you, that's for damned sure. The sight of you, going to your knees in front of me, I must have relived that a hundred times on the way home."

Josh's voice *did* help. Conall could breathe again, and the trembling that had followed him even into the dream state was gone. "Did I please you? Did I get it right?"

"Get it right? Christ, *d'orant*, it's never felt like that in my life." A soft groan, the sounds of weight shifting, as if the speaker were trying to ease himself. "I want to give you that. I need to try, at least. I need to know what you taste like, what you sound like when you let go."

Conall closed his dreaming eyes, let his hand drop. Of itself, it found his own rising shaft, weighed it, gripped it. "I want that, too. I want to give you that. But I can only have it in dreams."

"Damn." The word was half a groan. "The dreams are good—hell, the dreams are amazing, I had a dream after the shower that was almost as hot as the shower—but it's not the same as having you, it can't be." The sound of flesh on flesh, a stroking hand, carried clearly through the mist.

"I wish we could have finished the dream," Conall murmured. "I wanted to feel you inside me. I still do." No secrets from his SoulShare. "I want you that way." There was no way to know if Josh could arouse him safely—if the needs of the SoulShare bond were stronger than a lifetime of refusing the touch of others. But he would glory in touching, and in being able to bear the touch, as long as he could.

"That dream—it was real?" Josh's voice was choked. "We shared it?"

"Yes. Just like we're sharing this one." It *was* dreamwalking. It had to be.

Josh's breath hissed through clenched teeth. "I was so close, damn it. Almost in you. Would *that* have been real?"

Conall shivered. "I don't know. But I need it. Need you. What would you have done to me? What is it like?" How real *was* a shared dream? A SoulShared one? He bit his lip, gripped himself. "Tell me, *scair-anam*. What will it be like, when you take me?" *Talk to me...*

"It's going to be as fucking amazing as I can make it for you, *d'orant*." Josh's voice dropped to a low murmur, almost a purr. "Just the sight of your ass gets me hard enough to cut glass, you're so beautiful it hurts to look at you. I'll put you on your knees on the bed, bend you over, get you pillows for your head so you can turn and watch. I want to feel your eyes on me. Damn, I want them on me now."

Conall couldn't help himself; he reached out toward the source of the voice, and groaned as his hand passed through empty air. "Then what, *dar'cion*?"

"What does that mean?"

"Brilliant color." If he closed his eyes, he could see the exquisite patterns, the beauty he had thought at first all humans wore.

"You make it sound incredibly sexy." Low, soft laughter. "And next? Oil. As long as we're both dreaming. My favorite oil would fuck up a condom."

Another new word, with a history in the human world and a host of implications. "You won't need a condom with me, I can't carry disease and I can't be infected."

Another long silence, and Conall shuddered and wrapped his arms around himself as the malaise threatened to reassert its grip. "Josh, *please...*"

"I'm sorry, baby. It's a lot to take in, more dreams coming true." Soft laughter floated through the mist. "Oil it is, then. Warmed, and drizzled all over my cock—which is huge right now just thinking about this, by the way—and then down the crack of your ass." The laughter slowly gave way to a low, breathless intensity. "I'll work it into you with my fingers. Just one at first, nice and slow, but then two, and three. And what will you do then?"

Conall swallowed hard, the pain once again forgotten, his ass cheeks tightening hard around the fingers his imagination obligingly supplied. "Rock back on you. Try to make you go deeper."

"Will you moan for me?" There was a thickness to Josh's voice that hadn't been there moments earlier. "Let me hear what your pleasure sounds like."

"I... can't." Conall forced the word out reluctantly. "I can't let go like that, I've never been able to." *Even when I'm pleasuring myself. Because I've never been entirely sure I'm safe, even then.* Control. Always control.

"You will, for me." The human was whispering, now, almost in Conall's ear. "I'll keep you safe, you can let go with me. I promise. Let me give you that." Now it was Josh who groaned, a low unsteady sound, and coming as it did so close to Conall's ear, the Fae's shaft jerked, spilling clear drops down its length. "I'll reach around your body, grip your cock, stroke it. Are you hard?"

"Are you insane?" Tears had come to Conall's

eyes, as the human promised him what he'd never had, never even imagined. And hard on the heels of the tears came laughter, a sweeter laughter than any he had ever known. "How did you say it? Hard enough to cut glass?" Pure delight welled up in him, a wave of it almost as strong as the one that had come close to breaking his waking resolve in the shower. It had to be something to do with the SoulShare. And what a wonder; joy, even more arousing, more compelling than a lover's touch. "I want you. *Now*." His voice broke on the word, and for once he didn't care—

An ear-splitting buzz sounded, oddly distanced; Josh cursed explosively, at almost the same instant; and Conall sat bolt upright in bed, the sweaty and twisted sheets clutched in his hands and his eyes gone wide and panicked. The apartment was quiet, serene in early morning light; almost mockingly so, considering the groans the walls absorbed last night, the pain that reverberated around the spare white room until he had fallen into an unconsciousness that only superficially resembled sleep.

And the pain was returning. Not yet back to its full, harrowing intensity; Josh's presence, even in a dream, had been enough to drive it away. But it was coming. He could sense it, like a gryphon circling, waiting for its moment to strike. And he didn't have the strength to endure another onslaught like last night. If he could stop trying to draw on his magick, he could hold the pain at bay, at least until his SoulShare returned to shield him.

Stop trying to channel? It would be easier to stop breathing. *Which I just might do. Soon.* Conall swung his legs off the bed, rested his elbows on his knees, and clasped his hands behind his head, curled in on himself, waiting, trying to brace himself against an attack that would come from within. Yes, the preserved lore held that a Fae in exile could not die, as long as the SoulShare bond was unconsummated. And as mind-shattering as his experience of Josh's pleasure in the shower had been, he knew that there had to be more than that to the consummation of the bond. But he also knew what the pain of being closed off, unable to channel magick, was doing to him, and he was unable to imagine surviving much more of it.

Sweat prickled his forehead, his cheeks, his chest. He shivered, as much in anticipation of the pain as of the pain itself.

The soles of his feet tingled.

What the hell? It was a soothing feeling, almost a coolness. Sweetness.

Magick.

There was magick, somewhere below him. Some kind of magick, impossibly, here in the human realm. Could it keep him alive until Josh came back?

Conall lurched to his feet and staggered toward the door; then stopped, turned. If something happened, if he didn't find what he needed, or found it too late, he had to leave word for Josh. He'd seen a book, on the night table—yes, there. A battered, leather-bound sketchbook, tied up with a drawstring and an elaborate metal fastening that might be Fae craftsmanship. The property of the Fae who had enchanted the locks, no doubt. A charcoal stick was entangled in the laces, and fell out as Conall undid the lacing with a trembling hand, smudging the white bed linens before he could pick it up.

103

The book fell open in his hand to a sketch. A dark-haired male looked off the page at him, broader of face than Josh and with a shadow of stubble shrouding a strong jaw. His dark eyes glinted wickedly, his smile was full of promises, and light gleamed off a ring on the fourth finger of the hand on which his chin rested.

Conall turned the pages quickly, looking for a blank page on which to write. More pictures of the same male greeted him, some in what looked like formal attire, others in jeans, a great many in nothing at all, and several of *those* would have given Conall pause had he been in less of a hurry.

At last, a blank page. Conall gripped the charcoal tightly, trying to steady his hand. And groaned, as he realized his dilemma. The gift of Air, the gift of languages, extended only to understanding, and to speaking. Not to writing.

He growled softly. If a Fae lived here, then that Fae could translate.

'Siad na aslin agann ronnte fíor, Iós, m'lanan. Tá tú a's mé ra lath amáin anam. Fan anso g'dí mé. Bei mé a'tacht aras cugat.

The dreams we have shared are true, lover. You and I are two halves of one soul. Wait here for me. I will come back to you.

Conall let the book fall to the bed, knowing that now he was truly in a race, against the pain that would make it impossible for him to trace the magick to its source. He hurried from the room, his steps uneven, the door slamming behind him as he all but fell onto the landing.

The cool tingling was like music, and he followed

it down, as blind as any courtier mazed by a bard. Two flights down he went, and found himself outside the stairwell door of the apartment to which Josh had brought him. But the music, the relief washing over him came from somewhere below.

And now the magick was warring with returned, redoubled pain. His body was a battleground, magick pulling at him and his own body's rejection of it tearing at him. He had to find a way down, immerse himself in the source. Leave his traitor body no choice but to take it in.

He stumbled to the back of the entry hall, and there, behind the stairs, was a heavy wooden door. The knob turned easily, and he let himself into the darkness beyond.

No. Not darkness. There was no light, but he could see. Power streamed up the stairs with all the energy of a spring torrent, more than enough energy to light the way down. Conall almost felt sorry for the Noble who lived upstairs; there was a trace of elemental magick here, the sort that male would use, no doubt enough for him to sense, but it was all but lost in the rush of strangely sterile, unloving magick from somewhere below Conall's feet.

The source of the power was plain to see, once he reached the bottom of the stairs. In the floor of a cellar, its walls all but invisible behind piles of papers and rows of shelves and machines the functions of which a Fae could only guess at, two lines glowed, one touched with blue, the other with silver-white. The power he had felt, coming down the stairs, rolled off the place where these lines joined like spray off the base of a waterfall. Conall averted his gaze from where the two

105

lines crossed, one hand going up instinctively to shade his eyes.

Had his pain been any less, or the prospect of rescue any nearer, he might have stood there in awe, forgetful of time and place, rapt in contemplation of a force of magick even greater than his own. A few of the ancient stories from the time of the Sundering hinted that some kind of magick had been left behind in the human world, and said only living magick, the kind that made up the flora and the fauna and the Fae, had been separable from the parent world. They were stories no longer, and hints no longer; he was staring at the truth of the matter.

Conall had no more time to stare. He walked out into the center of the dank, musty room, feeling the magickal force swirling around him, like the fog of his dream. But Josh was nowhere in this fog, though his eyes kept trying to create his image there; if there was any relief from his pain here, it was before his eyes, where the two lines crossed and the light danced.

Slowly, Conall knelt. Be damned if he was going to fall. He was stronger than his pain.

Movement caught his eye, and he startled. But it was only an old mirror, meant to hang but leaning now against some shelves, and his own reflection coming back to him. Shirtless and barefoot and in a pair of Terry's jeans; a pale, drawn face looked back at him, eyes almost glowing, feverish. *Behold the greatest power in two worlds, rider of storm, master of hurricane. How the mighty mage has fallen.*

He grimaced at himself, and reached out a hand; it was lost to view even before his fingertips brushed the floor, vanished in the light that was not light.

Fingertips brushed dank cement. Nothing.

And then—everything.

A force surged up through the floor, strained to enter his body. Overwhelmed, panicked, he tried to fight it off, or to control its entry. But there was no controlling this. It seized him, it coursed through him, it met the walls of his flesh and thundered back into his truncated soul, flaring for an instant as bright as the sun, as cold as the moon.

When the glare faded, the streams of light were gone, as if they had never been.

And so was Conall Dary.

Chapter Twelve

Washington, D.C.

Janek O'Halloran was not going to claw out his remaining eye. This was not for want of trying, but because his fingers refused to obey his increasingly urgent demands. He stumbled along the pitch-dark concrete tunnel, fighting his rider's control to keep one hand outstretched to touch the wall.

Move your hand. This was the voice he loathed, the one that spoke in whips and blood. The male had tried demanding, the female cajoling, and now he was left with the obscenity.

"Like hell." He tried to squeeze his eye closed, and groaned as it was forced open against his will. "Damn it, I can't see in that kind of light." He tried not to sound like he was pleading, but they both knew that he was. They *all* knew. Whatever the fuck.

You do not need to see. I will see for you. The sound of the monster trying to be reasonable was more than enough to turn his stomach, but the fucker wouldn't even stop to let him retch. ***The hand. Move it. Now.***

"Fuck off and die."

108

Janek snarled as the hand that had been keeping him oriented grabbed the wrist of the hand that covered his face and forced it away. Briefly, his eye stared out into the darkness, and what he saw felt like a spoon digging into his eye socket. A few dozen yards down the subway maintenance tunnel the *Marfach* had guided him into, a line cut across the ceiling. A line that was made of light, except that it was no light that human eyes had ever seen, or at least not the eyes of any human that wanted a shot at staying sane. Fortunately, he no longer had to give a fuck about that. The light was shed by one of the four ley lines that ran underneath the city and met under the sex club owned by the soon-to-be-dead asshole Tiernan Guaire.

And the light crawled. It wavered. It warped the rocks and the air until Janek rammed his head into the concrete to make it stop. Human eyes were never meant to see by this shit, although his remaining eye was only human if you were prepared to stretch a definition.

There was a light switch under his hand. Thank *God.* Before the *Marfach* could take control away from him, he dragged his hand over the switch, and sagged against the wall in relief as his surroundings stopped moving. Maybe some people would call what he'd been seeing beautiful. Odds were that any such people still had both of their eyes, and more functioning brain cells than he had.

Fool. He could almost feel the monster's spittle. Which, considering that it was inside what was left of his head, was almost as much fun as not being allowed to puke while trying to see by that bad-acid-trip light. *Do you think no one watches these tunnels?*

"Do you think I give a shit?" Janek dragged a forearm across his forehead to wipe away the cold sweat, trying to ignore the sensation of stone against flesh when his arm passed over the place where his right eye and most of that side of his head had been before Guaire gave him a lobotomy and a permanent passenger.

As long as you don't mind a little extra work. The male voice carried more than a hint of a snigger. *If anyone finds us, you're in charge of taking care of it.*

Without waiting for an answer, the *Marfach* turned him around and resumed force-marching him down the corridor. The monster was obviously still looking for the light source his eye wasn't equipped to handle, but the nausea was manageable now that there was also some light he could actually see by.

As far as Janek could tell, the narrow concrete corridor down which he presently shambled was about half a block from the building that housed Purgatory and the sleazy establishments that shared its ground floor. Trying to get in that way had been one piss-poor idea, and the club itself was apparently protected by magickal shit even the *Marfach* couldn't break through. Even with his presently limited onboard memory capacity, the former Purgatory bouncer was never going to forget the time his rider had tried to make him simply walk down the spiral stairs and into the club. Just remembering it felt like that fucker Guaire had figured out how to take the rest of his head, from the inside. And he never wanted to hear the *Marfach* scream like that again. Ever.

So here he was—here they were—wandering

around the maze of maintenance tunnels under and around the Washington, D.C. subway system, with the *Marfach* hoping for a less defended underbelly, and Janek hoping for a chance to rip the head off the male who had turned him into a motherfucking zombie. Once the *Marfach* had finished with whatever it was it needed Guaire for. *Just leave him alive enough to feel what I do to him, you son of a bitch.*

Incoming. The male voice was laughing, a sound only a little more pleasant than a scream would have been. ***Work off some of that bloodlust, Meat.***

A few seconds later, Janek could hear the approaching footsteps himself.

"Hey, buddy, this is a restricted area—"

The hoodie Janek wore concealed the hole in the back of his head, but even the extra-large eyepatch he'd improvised in the early days of his new existence couldn't completely hide the entry wound. And when he flipped up the patch as he turned around, and the gray-haired security guard got a good look at the throbbing red crystal-lined hole that was most of the right side of Janek's head, whatever the guy had been about to say turned into an almost comical gurgle.

During those first weeks after he'd surprised the hell out of himself by waking up on the gore-covered floor of Purgatory's basement storeroom, Janek had gotten a charge out of playing up the whole horror-movie zombie routine when he killed someone; groaning and lurching and making sure the dumb sons of bitches got a good look at the whole lot of empty in his face before they died. But the game got old fast, and it had nearly gotten the rest of his head blown off once. He wasn't sure he could die, in his current condition, but being shot still hurt like a motherfucker. And the Metro security guard was wearing a gun, and was going for it, albeit clumsily. So no, no *Brainnnnssss* routine today.

"G-get away from me!"

Janek laughed harshly as he charged forward. The guard couldn't get a grip on his gun, his hand was shaking so badly; all Janek had to do was step around him, wrap one arm around his scrawny neck, grip his jaw with the other hand, and twist. The vaguely wet crack of the guy's neck breaking was almost an anticlimax; he would have preferred to use his knife, but fresh blood all over his clothes would have been a pain in the ass to try to conceal once the *Marfach* let him out of this fucking tunnel.

He stepped back to let the corpse fall to the concrete floor, and growled as his rider forced him to his knees beside the body. "What the hell do you want now?"

He will have identification. The female's cool precision grated on him. *You might need it.*

Janek grimaced, but started rifling the sorry bastard's pockets. Taking the guard's gun was, of course, out of the question; the *Marfach* wasn't going to risk giving him such an easy ticket out of slavery. It could stop him from using a knife on himself—and had, twice—but there was at least a chance that Janek could be quick enough with a gun to catch the monster off guard. Or at least, that's what he guessed. Not that he wanted to take that way out, most days. But the *Marfach*, he was learning, never left anything to chance.

He flipped the guard's driver's license over in his hand, ignoring the smell of urine that was slowly permeating the narrow corridor as the guy's bladder let go, a thin stream puddling near shiny black uniform shoes. The picture on the license wasn't going to do him any good, not unless whoever was looking at it was dumb enough to think the fucking tunnel through Janek's head was a bald spot. And the age was all wrong, of course. The poor bastard had been maybe a year shy of retirement. *Too bad, so sad.* Still, he pocketed the license, and the accompanying work I.D., now that could be useful—

Why the hell am I waking up on a concrete floor with my face in a puddle of piss?

For the space of a couple of really loud heartbeats, the only sound that came out of the *Marfach* was a groan. "Hey, asshole." Janek spat; not that he could really taste what he was lying in, but a guy had to have some standards about what he'd allow into his mouth. "What just happened?"

You can be silent. Or you can be made to claw out the rest of your pathetic forebrain with your fingernails. Choose.

The monster sounded in deadly earnest, and Janek opted for silence.

On the outside, anyway. *Motherfucker. Like it would kill you to tell me.* Slowly, he started to push himself up onto his elbows, testing as he went to be sure that everything still more or less worked.

Unless... He froze. *Unless it really* doesn't *know?*

And it was while he stared blankly down the corridor that the third thought hit him. *It should have smacked me down for that.* He was so used to being internally bitch-slapped, there were times he'd just pause, and wait for it, and then go on with whatever

113

he'd been doing. And his eye *ought* to be staring backward at what was left of his brain right now. But his rider sure as hell seemed oblivious; it was grunting, and from the way the inside of his head was trying to crawl, it was doing its best to shake its head. Which, since it didn't have one of its own and had to borrow his, creeped him the fuck out.

It can't hear me. He tried to keep the thought small; something told him he had to hide it, get it out of the way. He'd never been known for being particularly imaginative, and cleverness was *way* beyond whatever he was at this point, but he managed to come up with the image of a box. The cardboard kind homeless dickheads tried to sleep in, until dickheads like him came along and kicked them in. He took that little thought, and he hid it in there. It was quiet in there. Nice.

His body started to lurch to its feet, and Janek groaned. Leaving the thought in its hiding place, he came out to await orders.

And those orders weren't long in coming. He staggered against the wall, caught himself, and started back the way he'd come, tripping over his own feet in his haste. "Where the hell are we going?"

Union Station. His hand was forced into the pocket of his hoodie, and fumbled to be sure his stolen credit cards were in there. ***You're getting us on a train to New York, Meat.***

"In broad daylight. What a joy that's going to be." Janek forced himself to verbalize, not sure how well he could keep the secret place a secret when his rider was concentrating on communicating with him. "And what happens when we get there?"

114

The male voice actually hesitated, and now Janek was reasonably sure the world was at least starting to end. Whatever had just happened, it had scrambled the monster's brains. *There's another Fae there. I want him.*

Janek felt suddenly cold. Which was no mean feat, considering he'd gotten curious once and taken his own temperature, and found it to be exactly 67.5 degrees Fahrenheit. "What's wrong with the one you almost have?"

Shut the fuck up. Janek felt as if he were being shoved by a hand between his shoulder blades.

When the voice came again, it was the woman's, wheedling. *There is nothing wrong with the Noble Fae. But this other may be less well guarded. And I can find a use for another one easily enough.*

The bitch is lying through her teeth. Its teeth. My teeth. Whatever.

Janek held his breath, once the thought was out, but his rider didn't seem to pick up on it.

It's lying. Lying was one thing Janek O'Halloran was an expert in. *Any fucking Fae will do, for whatever it wants. It just hasn't known about any others until now.*

He barely suppressed a growl.

Is it really going to give me Guaire?

Chapter Thirteen

Washington, D.C.

Cuinn had started hauling his shirt off over his head even before the apartment door slammed shut behind him. *Central air, my taut tanned ass.* If he were back in the Realm, he could probably spare the magick to drop the temperature twenty degrees or so. In a little bubble around him, would that be so bad? Of course, in the Realm they'd never heard of such a thing as a fucking heat wave. Maybe it was time to go back for a real vacation, instead of one busman's holiday after another.

Tossing the sweat-soaked T-shirt on the leather sofa, he headed straight for the bedroom. Or, more to the point, for the master bath. A cold shower would cure what ailed him. For a little while. When the humans' Hell needed heat, surely it sent out to Washington, D.C. At least this summer. If he didn't have to keep an eye on the great nexus, he would be on the first plane, train, automobile or dogsled headed north, and to hell with Fae claustrophobia.

He was unbuttoning his jeans when his gaze happened to fall on the book laying open on his bedside table. The page that had been blank when he left an hour previously now held an elaborate piece of silver-blue knotwork. *THOU ART SUMMONED*, it said, not in an alphabet, nor yet in pictograms or code, but in the sharpness of its curves and the subtlety of its weaving. *D'aos'Faein*, a language spoken by no Fae now living, existing only in its written form.

"Oh, fuck me backwards." Cuinn flung himself onto the bed, grabbing the book in one hand and the stylus beside it in the other; growling, he propped himself on his elbows and looked down at the design that was to all appearances inked onto the page. Touching stylus to paper, he widened out the curves, added flourishes, expanded one set of whorls and arches. *YOUR HUMBLE SERVANT AWAITS ENLIGHTENMENT*, the new design said.

He waited a moment, then turned the page, and grinned broadly. Curled in elegant scrolls from one edge of the page to the other, *BLOW IT OUT YOUR ASS* looked back at him. *THIS IS SERIOUS.*

Sounds like Aine. He grinned, his stylus flying over the blank page, leaving streams of knotwork behind. Of all the Loremasters, Aine was probably the closest to understanding what he was dealing with, here among the humans. And she'd certainly come the farthest in picking up human speech patterns. He remembered her, back in the days before the Sundering, bright copper-red hair, sparkling grey-blue eyes like the sea in storm, and even a smattering of freckles. Leather and feathers and lace, oh my. *SO EDUCATE ME, O MY MASTERS*, he shaped.

An image began to form on the blank right side of the page, quickly, as if sketched. An unmistakable piece of knotwork, for all he'd only seen it once before, purely abstract but suggesting two halves of a whole, chained together. The *d'aos'Faein* shaping for *SoulShares*.

Cuinn's gut twisted, just a little, but he ignored it. After all, the first pair of SoulShares had already found each other, and bonded, and apart from the fucking *Marfach* nearly running fucking amok, nothing all *that* bad had happened. Surely this pairing would be no different.

He started crafting a reply even before the design had completely filled itself out. *WHICH FAE IS IT?* He and his fellow Loremasters had done the best they could, two thousand years ago, but there was simply no accounting for all the variables involved in creating a world of living magick, then sealing it off from the world that had given it birth, and *then* trying to arrange for passage back and forth. Every safeguard for the Realm meant another bit of control over the portal lost; when a Fae went through the Pattern, there was no telling where—or, more to the point, when—the half of his soul so carefully detached in the process would be reborn in the human world.

And of all the scores of Fae who had come through in the millennia since the Sundering, only one, so far, had found his SoulShare. Tiernan Guaire, Noble of the Demesne of Earth. But where there was one, there would be more; the Loremasters were most definite with him on that point. To the extent the process could be guided, it was being guided; with all the grace and finesse of a blind toreador in a body cast, to be sure, but guided nonetheless.

He could read the answer even before the sketch was completed. *CONALL DARY. THE SUMMONER.* The shape that spelled out name and function was the same, and both were now etched in that Fae's flesh in silver-blue ink, just as those of each of the Loremasters were etched in silver magick in the floor of a cold stone cell in the Realm. Each Loremaster but one.

Cuinn's stylus flew. *CAN'T BE. HE ONLY CAME THROUGH TWO DAYS AGO.* He knew—he'd been there. The worst part about being the only Loremaster left walking the sundered worlds was being the only Loremaster in a position to make sure the cack-handed guidance the rest of them were able to give was delivered. The Lady Liadan certainly hadn't been capable of getting the mage to the portal herself, and would never have thought to bring truesilver with her to do the deed. Plus, Cuinn had discovered over the course of two thousand years that when he was involved with a transition, the time distortion that could otherwise accompany a Fae's transit between the worlds was eliminated. So that got tacked on to his job description, on top of everything else.

Frankly, Cuinn had not been, and was not, eager to play babysitter to this particular Fae. Conall Dary was known to the Loremasters; he was easily the most powerful mage since they themselves had last inhabited the Realm, and in terms of raw power he just might outdo any one of them, Cuinn included. Fortunately, the male had had the sense not to use his talent at shaping living magick indiscriminately, because the sorry son of a bitch was probably capable of siphoning off half the magickal power remaining in the Realm if he put his mind and his magick to it. Of course, that lack of practice meant he had all the control and training of an unhousebroken Rottweiler, but one couldn't have everything.

119

Rory Ni Coileain

*THEN HIS HALF-SOUL PRECEDED HIM.
OBVIOUSLY.* This shape surrounded the SoulShare
motif, in a dry, pedantic shaping very different from
Aine's.

Obviously. Cuinn's eyes rolled. And once they
stopped rolling, he noticed something else unusual.
When the Loremasters had given him the shaping of the
first SoulShares, Tiernan's and Kevin's, the halves of the
figure had very obviously been chained together. This
pairing also bore the chains, but they only wrapped
around one side of the image and hung free beside the
other. He used the stylus to modify the image, lightly
tracing where the missing chain should have been.
*COULD YOU POSSIBLY BE LESS CRYPTIC? JUST
THIS ONCE?*

THE BOND WAS NOT COMPLETED. Cuinn had
to turn the page again to get this one. Fuck, he was going
to talk his fellow mages into learning how to use an iPad
if it was the last thing he did this side of oblivion.

Shit. Cuinn raked the fingers of his free hand
through his hair. *ANOTHER FLAW?* One imperfect
pairing might be of no concern, though the defect in
Tiernan and Kevin's bond could have ended the
Loremasters' plans before it had properly begun. But
two? That could be the start of a pattern. Or a Pattern,
pardon the expression.

*AS FAR AS WE CAN TELL, THEY SIMPLY
HAVE YET TO COMPLETE THE COUPLING.*

Cuinn shook his head at the careful precision of
the shaping. *Damn, you all have been disembodied too
long, if that's all the enthusiasm you can muster at the
thought of sex that's probably hot enough to register
on a seismograph.*

BUT WE ARE CURIOUS. YOU REFER TO 'ANOTHER' FLAW?

Oh, balls. He hadn't wanted to try to explain his theory to the other Loremasters until he was more sure of it, or of himself, but now that they had hold of the idea, they weren't going to let go of it any time soon. They had precious little else to occupy their time, other than conversing with him, or about him. Well, that and flaying the souls of maybe a half-dozen Fae a century, and then turning the survivors over to him to nursemaid. If it could be called nursemaiding when all he could do was stand there and watch as they learned to cope with life in the human world. Or didn't. Some of the didn'ts were epic.

THE BONDING OF TIERNAN GUAIRE AND HIS HUMAN DIDN'T GIVE THE HUMAN ENOUGH STRENGTH TO SHIELD THEM BOTH. WHICH IT SHOULD HAVE DONE. Absently, he chewed on the end of the stylus. *GUAIRE HAD TO INTERVENE, TO REINFORCE THE BOND. I THINK THE BOND WAS WEAKENED BECAUSE GUAIRE'S SUNDERING WAS IMPERFECT.* He took a deep breath. Which was idiotic, considering he didn't need to breathe to shape. *AND IT WAS IMPERFECT BECAUSE OF THE FLAW IN THE PATTERN.*

The page before him was blank for so long that Cuinn stared wondering if his magickal connection with his fellow Loremasters had been broken. *BY 'FLAW', YOU REFER TO YOUR ABSENCE FROM THE PATTERN.* The shape was slow to form, and halting, as if the shaper were uncertain, or reluctant. The names, the powers, the very essences of all of the Loremasters had been required to separate the realms, and wall off the *Marfach* from what it had come so close to destroying.

All the Loremasters but one. *I DO.*

This blankness lasted even longer. *YOUR NAME CANNOT BE PART OF THE PATTERN. YOU MUST BE FREE TO PASS BACK AND FORTH BETWEEN THE REALMS, AND THAT WOULD BE IMPOSSIBLE IF YOU WERE BOUND TO THE PATTERN.*

He sighed. *I KNOW. BUT JUST BECAUSE THERE'S NO CHOICE DOESN'T MEAN THERE ARE NO CONSEQUENCES.* Tiernan and Kevin had overcome the flaw in their Sharing. But what if another pair weren't so lucky?

A charge shot up Cuinn's spine, a sensation like barbed wire being pulled through his spinal column from his ass to the base of his skull. And then things got scary. He froze, twisted into a position like a fish out of water, just long enough for every muscle to spasm hard enough to bruise and his vision to flare from actinic white to pure blackness. At last he collapsed, faceplanting on the open book.

Dizzy, he raised his head. And when it stopped hurting to try to focus, he saw Aine's spiky shaping, just under his nose. *WHAT THE MOTHERFORNICATING HELL WAS THAT?!?*

Oh, sweet fuck. The edges of the pages of the book were charred.

Somehow, he was still holding the stylus, and he scrabbled at the page until an image started forming. *GIVE ME A DAMN MINUTE.*

Cuinn fell back onto the bed, his eyes closing. He didn't have to reach out, not really; his magickal sense was still seared with after-images. And there was no need to stare straight into the sun to know approximately where it was. His awareness traveled north, as if drawn by the biggest fucking magnet a mad human scientist could devise.

He was wincing in anticipation long before his inner eye was within range of New York City. His fellow Loremasters hadn't seen fit to warn him about Tiernan Guaire's *pied-a-ligne* in Greenwich Village, assuming they'd known about it before he did, but once the first pair of SoulShares had come onto his radar, and he'd started doing his own watching, he'd discovered the third-floor walk-up soon enough. And whatever it was that had just reamed him out, it had come from that same place, sending a surge of pure raw proto-magickal energy down the ley lines that would have knocked him flat on his ass if he'd been standing. *Son of a bitch.*

FOLLOW IT. The shaping was still identifiably Aine's, but softer, quietly urgent. *FIND IT. SPEND MAGICK WISELY, BUT DO WHAT YOU MUST.*

Cuinn nodded. He was ordinarily very parsimonious about his use of magick in the human world, because anything he spent, he would have to replenish upon returning to the Realm. The humans thought they had a problem with their fossil fuels? The very stuff of which the Realm was made was being depleted, with every use of living magick, one channeling at a time. And he was going to have to draw even more magick out of the fiber of the place the next time he was there to replenish what he was going to spend in these next few minutes. But there was no help for it.

Grabbing his shirt from where he'd thrown it and

shrugging it hastily back over his head, he Faded, slowly vanishing from his apartment in D.C.

When he reappeared, just as slowly, he was standing on the landing outside the door of Guaire's apartment. The nexus, obviously, would have to be several floors below him, but he was damned if he was going to risk touching it accidentally, even for an instant. His warning to the Noble, at the wedding reception he'd crashed last month, had been in deadly earnest. An unShared Fae who touched a nexus invited disaster. The human half of a SoulShare, so the Loremasters' theory went, grounded the Fae, allowing him to channel that unthinkable energy without burning himself out. An ungrounded Fae would invite all the energy in a nexus to use him as a conduit. There was no telling what would happen after that, other than it wouldn't end well for the luckless Fae.

Oh, fuck. What if that was what had already happened? Almost-a-Loremaster Conall Dary was wandering around the human world, after all, and here was a ley nexus unguarded. Whispering a stream of Fae curses, Cuinn took off down the stairs at a dead run, pounding down three flights, yanking open the basement door, and all but flying down the last stairs. And at the bottom, he found...

Nothing. Not a damned thing. He could barely sense the power of the nexus; the ley lines were there, but so faint that he could only find them because he already knew they *had* to be there. It was as if they were a mile underground, or sealed away behind something harder than diamond.

There was a flicker of movement in a far corner, and Cuinn spun, every magickal and mundane sense on full alert. The smothered nexus didn't even give off enough magickal light to see by; early morning sunlight slanting in through a grimy window high in the wall showed him a basement used as a storeroom by tenants apparently spanning a number of years, or even decades. And where he'd seen movement, or thought he had, an old, cracked mirror leaned against an even older metal shelving unit piled high with musty, water-warped books. For a moment, he almost thought he could make out a shimmering in the air, like heat hovering over a road in the middle of a baking hot summer day. Then dust tickled his nose, and by the time he was done with a string of violent sneezes, whatever he thought he'd seen was history.

Son of a bitch. Cuinn shook his head, glaring around the claustrophobic storeroom, daring it to give up its secrets. It wasn't taking dares, though, and soon he snarled and headed up the stairs, taking them two and three at a time, to Guaire's apartment. Anything magickal there would still be resonating with whatever it was that had just happened in the basement; with any luck at all, he might be able to get a sense of what he was dealing with.

The locks to the apartment glowed, almost imperceptibly, with magickal light; not living magick, nor yet the proto-magick that pulsed in the ley lines. No, this was a faint trace of elemental magick, the kind of which Royal Fae were made, and given to the Nobles to play with at the time of the Sundering. Which they no doubt thought by now they'd been wielding since the dawn of time. And it was never meant to be used as a ward, the way it had apparently once been used here, though Earth magick was better suited to that purpose than any of the other elements; Cuinn rested a hand on the top lock, and his magickal sense rang with the sound of struck crystal, an Earth ward's indelible imprint.

But only for an instant; then it was as if the memory of a nova flared up right in front of his eyes, temporarily blinding him. *Fuck, yes, someone touched the nexus.* The ward that had been on the lock was still quivering with the echoes of whatever had collapsed it, and small wonder; alone, an Earth ward would simply frustrate any attempt to penetrate without permission or the counterchanneling, but add pure magick, and arc welder's glasses would be a prudent precaution.

Just to be safe, Cuinn pulled the remaining trace of magick from the locks before opening the door. *I'll ward them again before I go.* He grunted, bemused, as the door swung open. *Not locked?*

Inside the tiny apartment, everything was pristine. Everything, that is, except the bed, which needed only blood to look like a battlefield. The sheets were twisted, sweat-soaked, spilled half onto the floor, the pillows likewise. *A Fae in transition dreams? Guaire shouldn't still be having those, he's been on this side of the Pattern for a century and a half, and besides, his SoulShare bond was consummated months ago.*

Cuinn's gaze fell on an open book, nearly lost in the chaos of the bed. It was a sketchbook; the left-hand page was a breathtaking charcoaled nude of a male Cuinn recognized as Kevin Almstead, Tiernan Guaire's human SoulShare. *I need to start cultivating a few of these human gods, because a Fae needs something to swear to when he sees a cock like that...*

The other side, though, was just as remarkable in its way. Writing, in the curling yet spare Fae script.

'*Siad na aslin agann ronnte fíor, Iós, m'lanan. Tá tú a's mé ra lath amáin anam. Fan anso g'dí mé. Bei mé a'tacht aras cugat.*

The dreams we have shared are true, Josh, my lover. You and I are two halves of one soul. Wait here for me. I will come back to you.

A chill ran down Cuinn an Dearmad's spine, despite the heat and the sweat on his brow. *Fuck me oblivious. It* is *Conall Dary. Was.* He reached for the book, his hand unsteady. *Where the hell is he?*

Before he could touch the page, the image began changing. The curves and whorls of a shaping took form on the page in front of him, covering over and erasing the elegant script, and replacing it with a single stark declaration.

IT IS COMING.

Chapter Fourteen

Josh tilted back in his chair, balancing his sketchpad on his thigh and reaching without looking for the cup of coffee on the small wooden table beside the padded one on which his clients usually sat. His phone was propped up on the larger table, displaying the photo Kevin Almstead had sent him, the tattoo the lawyer wanted copied onto his own hip. The one his husband bore. The one that was for all intents and purposes identical to the one across Conall Dary's shoulders.

Josh took a sip of the hot black coffee, and grimaced as he looked at the design he was working out on the sketchpad. He was willing to swear he was copying the photo exactly; as many years as he'd been at this, he knew how to do a preliminary sketch, for God's sake. But each time he compared his work to the picture, there was something wrong. Something out of place.

He set the cup back down and reached again for the pad. This set of designs shared a page with an elegant twining of jungle creepers around a black panther, an inquisitive squirrel that had ended up being purple, Rainbow Brite on a rampantly erect pony—proof positive, as if any were needed, he did not come up with all his own designs—and an early black-and-white rendition of what had eventually become Terry's Firebird. The attempt at Tiernan's ink he was about to snarl at looked more tribal than Celtic, spiky rather than smooth, but he could have sworn that was what he'd seen on the phone at the time. Never mind that a lovely piece of Celtic knotwork was presently sitting smugly on the screen.

This is starting to piss me off just a little. Josh had to laugh at himself. He'd grown accustomed to being able to make the magic happen at will; his customers had called it that so often, he was almost ready to believe it himself. Magic. Making art of ink and flesh had been his calling ever since he could remember; he was never happier than he was when he was sitting in this chair, wielding the tattoo gun, bringing something to life.

Never happier until a few days ago, anyway. Maybe the magic wasn't working now because his mind kept going back to Terry and Bryce's apartment, and watching his own hands fisted in red hair as his aching erection went deep in a willing throat. Or back to a bed, where he lay curled around a dreaming lover who thrashed in his sleep, until they both found ease, and then found something more.

Conall. Maybe he was losing his mind. He couldn't remember a guy ever haunting him like this. Those eyes, no shade of green he'd ever seen. That mouth—hell, just thinking of it, and what it could do, was enough to make him need to rearrange himself. The beautiful ink, across his shoulders; Josh hadn't been able to keep his fingertips from it, and then his mouth, as Conall slept, before he'd joined him in sleep and in dream. Those hands. How anyone who claimed to be a virgin knew how to touch him like that was beyond him.

But it was more than just the fact the other man was every wet dream Josh ever had. So much more. The look in Conall's eyes, when he'd seemed to literally appear on the ground at Josh's feet, battered and bewildered, drew him in from that very first instant; as if Conall Dary were a drowning man, and Josh LaFontaine a lifeline. And the way the slight redhead held on to him, as he'd made his way through the crowd on the sidewalk; maybe Conall looked weak, gentle, but there was a strength to him that made Josh shiver, remembering it.

And yet Conall had trusted him. Utterly. Maybe *that* was what was so compelling about him; all that power, that force of will simmering just under the surface, and yet the other man had given himself into Josh's hands. Christ, if he replayed the memory of Conall going to his knees in the shower one more time, he was going to need to go home and change clothes and it wasn't even eight in the morning yet. The thought was making him even shorter of breath than he already was. Fuck this humidity anyway.

He glared at the sketchpad again, as much to get his mind off remembered sights and sounds and scents as anything else. Yeah, that was working *so* well.

I need to get back to New York. To hell with his waiting list—though he'd work Kevin in as soon as he could, once he got back, assuming he could ever come up with a design he liked. Josh groped for his coffee cup, his mind already a few hundred miles away. Despite Tiernan's suggestion he was still needed here, there wasn't anything more he could do to assist in the investigation of the break-in. Assuming there *was* an investigation. Given the volume of illicit activity downstairs at Purgatory, and until a few months ago in the massage parlor next door, police presence on this block wasn't exactly anything most of the tenants welcomed—

Josh's hand jerked violently, spilling coffee all over his lap, the sketchbook, and the floor. Not that he noticed; he was doubled over, smacking his forehead into the wooden frame of the padded table so hard a bright light flashed in front of his eyes. He couldn't breathe, couldn't see. But he could hear. His name. Shouted, raw and aching, with the last breath to leave Conall Dary's lungs. How he knew that, he had no idea. But he knew.

Slowly, he became aware of another sound. It was his phone, chirping at him with the ringtone he used for business. He groped for the phone, activated it solely by touch. "Raging Art-On." His lips felt numb, stiff. Which was probably a good thing; numb kept away panic. So far.

"Josh?"

It was Tiernan Guaire, and from the ragged edge to his voice, Josh guessed that his landlord was almost as shaken as he was himself. Which made no fucking sense whatsoever. "Yeah," he croaked.

"Where are you?"

What the fuck? "In the shop."

"Perfect." There was a pause, a low urgent exchange between Tiernan and someone else, barely audible to Josh over the phone. "Meet me in my office. You know where it is, right? Back behind the cock pit."

"Right." Josh tried to sit up, wrapped a forearm around his gut. *Shit.* "When?"

"I'll be there by the time you get downstairs."

***

By the time Josh made it down the stairs, fumbled the elegant silver key out of his pocket, and let himself into the cool darkness that was Purgatory in the early morning, he felt at least a little less dizzy, though there was still a sensation like an iron band around his chest, keeping him from getting a decent breath. The darkness within was total, save for the scant light coming in through the door he still held open, and brighter light spilling out from the door to Tiernan's office, on the far side of the maze of leather sofas and loveseats that was legend in the D.C. gay clubbing community. *How the hell did he get down there so fast? I didn't see him come down the stairs.*

"Close the door, Josh." Tiernan's voice was muffled by the mostly-closed and heavily-soundproofed door. "Kevin has his own key, he'll be along in a few minutes."

Josh let the heavy door swing shut, then cursed softly. "Tiernan, I can't see a damned thing. Where are the lights?"

"Here, let me."

Josh wasn't sure what he was expecting— probably the throwing of a switch from within the club owner's sanctum—but it most definitely wasn't the flickering glow that materialized somewhere beside his knees, lighting the floor immediately around his feet. "What the *hell*?" He rubbed his eyes with the heels of his hands, glared at the spot. Nope. Still there.

"Hurry, will you?" The voice sounded strained. "I can't do this for shit, normally, light's not my thing."

I suppose it was overly optimistic to start expecting

things to make sense at this point. Josh took a step forward, and the light moved along with him; he let the glow herd him down through the cock pit and up the steps on the far side, where it merged with the light streaming out from where the door stood ajar. He pushed the heavy door open, enough to allow him to enter.

Alice down the rabbit hole had nothing on the stairs down to Purgatory. Tiernan Guaire sat in a generously padded black leather chair behind a spare, elegant teak desk, two computer monitors behind him. He wore nothing but a rumpled expression and an apparently hastily-donned white silk robe, which he hadn't even bothered to belt and was holding closed in front of him. Holding with a hand made of pure, clear crystal.

"Pardon my state of undress." One of the blond's eyebrows quirked up, the one with the gold ring in it, and it caught the light as he nodded toward one of the chairs opposite the desk. "And have a seat. You have a lot to learn, and not much time to do it in."

Slowly, Josh sat, his gaze never leaving the man on the other side of the desk. "Tell me why none of this is surprising me. Much."

Tiernan laughed; leaning forward in his chair, he let go the robe and propped his elbows on the desk, lacing his fingers together, glass with flesh. "You tell me something, human. You know what *scair-anam* means?"

"Soul-share." It was out before Josh could think, or even wonder why the hell his landlord was calling him 'human'. "Why?" Although, with that hand, maybe he didn't need to be wondering. Now that he thought about it, every time he'd seen Tiernan Guaire before today, the man had been wearing gloves. Even in the middle of a truly infernal D.C. heat wave.

"Because it's what you are. You share a soul with a male like me. Your new boyfriend isn't human, he's a Fae. He lost half his soul coming to this world, and you got it. And I'm not sure, but I think he just managed to attract the attention of an entity that makes your human Satan look like Hello Kitty."

"Wait. *Wait*." Josh sat back in his chair, pressed the heels of his hands against his closed eyelids, and took a deep breath, fighting the slowly-tightening phantom band around his chest. The panic he'd managed to fight off upstairs now threatened to overwhelm him; he dropped his hands and sat forward again, hands braced on his thighs. "Conall's in danger? And how the hell do you even know about him?"

"Second question first, it's easier. I know about him because my husband told me how you recognized my ink. He'll be along in a few minutes, by the way—Kevin can explain a lot better than I can about what it's like to be the human half of a SoulShare."

Josh gave a slight, disbelieving laugh. "SoulShare. As in, I share a soul with a guy who fell at my feet during a parade?" The laughter was more for show than anything; a sane man would be cutting Tiernan dead right now, maybe making a surreptitious 911 call, but he was feeling about as far from sane right now as he'd ever felt. It all made sense. The instant connection he'd felt with Conall, the shared dreams, the need to be closer to him than skin.

All he had to do was believe something totally impossible. The man of his dreams was from another world, and wasn't human.

Tiernan shrugged. "That pretty much sums it up, yes. I came over about a hundred and fifty years ago. The coming over isn't a pleasant process, by the way. Your boy is probably pretty fucked up."

Josh growled softly. "Conall's not my 'boy,' and if you know everything about this, then tell me what I can do for him."

"Right this minute? Haul ass back to New York and find out what the hell he just did, though I'm afraid I know. I'm assuming you felt it?"

"I felt *some*thing." Josh was unsure whether the tremor that shook him at the thought was a memory or an aftershock. "What could cause something like that? Is he injured again?" *Christ, is that why I can't breathe? Because he can't?* His heart raced, and sweat came out on his forehead despite the air-conditioned chill.

"Calm down. If you haven't completed the SoulShare bond, he can't die. Probably. And if you have, if he were dead, you'd know it. I'm pretty sure." The fingers of Tiernan's glass hand drummed softly on the desk. "The important thing is what he might have attracted. Because if he *can* die, the *Marfach* would be just the monster to make it happen."

The look in the blond's eyes at that moment, as much as the freakish follow spot, or the first sight of the glass hand, convinced Josh the man on the other side of the desk was telling the truth when he said he wasn't human. "You cold son of a bitch—"

"Take it easy, Josh." Kevin's voice came from the doorway, just a little short of breath. "Fae don't get along with each other all that well, from what I can tell, but Tiernan doesn't wish your *lanan* any harm."

He crossed to the chair beside Josh's, stopping on the way to share a brief but heated kiss with his husband before offering Josh a hand. "Sorry you're having to find out this way."

"I think I already know a lot of it." Josh was reasonably sure Tiernan's intentions were good, but he still found it easier to talk to Kevin for the time being. "Conall and I have shared a few dreams; I don't remember them clearly, but what I do remember fits with what your husband's been telling me."

"Shared dreams?" Kevin looked askance at Tiernan. "Have you been holding out on me? Can you all do that?"

The blond snorted. "If I could have you sleeping and waking, I'd die exhausted and happy. And Cuinn would probably have an infarct."

"He may anyway." All lightheartedness left the lawyer's face, replaced by a grim determination. "If you're right about what's happened."

For a brief moment, Josh felt like waving his hands in the air, jumping up and down, anything to get the attention of the two men in front of him. "Just for the hell of it, will someone pretend I don't know what's going on and tell me what's happened to my *scair-anam*?"

That was enough to get them both staring at him. "Damn, it feels strange to hear that word coming from anyone but you," Tiernan murmured at last, the words directed at Kevin though his gaze remained on Josh.

"Cuinn did say there would be more. And yes, I know that Cuinn pisses you off simply by breathing, but it's time to deal with the idea." Kevin turned slightly in his chair, to face Josh squarely. "We think your Conall tapped into a magical power source he wasn't equipped to handle safely. It might have injured him—probably did, if Tiernan's past experience with a similar source is any indication. And there's a creature out there, pure evil, and the mortal enemy of the Fae, that probably noticed. And best guess is that it's heading for your *scair-anam*, since he's so thoughtfully broadcast his location to anyone sensitive to either him or the ley energy."

It sounded insane. It probably *was* insane. But it also made a terrible, beautiful kind of sense. And Conall was in danger. Josh could sense that all the way down to the bones thrumming in tortured sympathy with whatever had happened to his lover. His Fae lover. "So what can I do?"

Kevin opened his mouth to reply—and whatever it was he was planning to say, he didn't look happy about it—but was cut off by Tiernan. "Maybe more than you realize. Depends on what form your magick takes."

"My what?" Josh and Kevin traded blank looks, before looking back at Tiernan, who was sitting back in his padded chair with a decidedly cat-eating-canary expression. "I haven't tried magic since I got the hots for David Copperfield when I was in seventh grade."

Tiernan snorted. "Not that kind of magic. I should have realized what was going on after the break-in." The blond leaned forward again, elbows on the desk. "The *Marfach*—the creature—was behind the break-in at Raging Art-On. It couldn't get into the room where you keep your tattoo equipment, though, and when I was checking things out, I sensed magick in the equipment."

Kevin cleared his throat. "News to me, *lanan*."

Tiernan flushed. "Slipped my mind. I thought it was just spillage from the nexus in the basement. It honestly didn't occur to me at the time that Josh, here, might be using magick himself."

"I'm not," Josh blurted. "There's nothing at all magickal about me."

But even as he spoke, things started falling into place. No, he'd never cast a spell in his life. But his art, now... How many times had his clients suggested the same thing? He glanced down at his arms, his thighs where they emerged from his cutoff shorts, his gaze running over the designs he had put there himself. The brilliant colors, the unique designs; under his wife-beater, a hawk of his own design spread its wings in flight across his chest. Conall had touched it with something close to reverence, and had whispered a word he couldn't quite understand.

Tiernan and Kevin, too, were eyeing his ink. "I don't think you're *using* magick." Tiernan's voice was softer now than it had been. "Humans can't, as far as I know. But it finds you, somehow. And I think Conall's going to need that. Whatever has happened to him, whatever he's done to himself, he needs you."

Kevin's sudden movement startled Josh, as he reached across the desk to clasp Tiernan's hand tightly. It was as if Josh wasn't even there; the other two men had eyes only for each other, lost in one hell of a shared memory from the look of it. Josh felt a sudden, deep pang; once he'd thought he and Terry had that.

Now?

Iós...

As if they heard it too, Kevin and Tiernan turned back to him. Their hands were still clasped, and Josh caught a glimpse of scars around the blond's wrist. Scars like chains.

"Josh, what the hell just happened to you?" Kevin said, staring at Josh's left arm.

"I don't..." Josh followed the direction of the lawyer's gaze. The gold dragon around his left forearm—the first design he'd inked on himself after he bought Raging Art-On—had moved. Where the dragon's head had previously rested on Josh's wrist, its tail now curled around it, a glittering bracelet.

"If I had to guess, I'd say you just inherited some more of your *scair-anam's* magick." From Tiernan's expression, this was not good news.

"Get your ass on a plane, Josh." Kevin's hand tightened on his husband's. "Find your *scair-anam* and get him the hell back here."

"Before the *Marfach* finds him," Tiernan added grimly.

Chapter Fifteen

Greenwich Village
New York City

Conall stared fixedly at a cut glass knob on an old chest of drawers on the far side of the cellar from his accidental prison, one that caught a hint of the sunlight trailing in through the grimy window somewhere back behind him. Struggling for calm, trying to focus. It was bad enough to have awakened to find himself trapped; then add the shock of the abrupt appearance of a Fae mage he'd thought dead for two thousand years, a name and a face out of myth. A name and a face, he'd quickly discovered, that couldn't see him, or hear him, or sense him in any way. He'd shouted, screamed—as Cuinn an Dearmad had turned to go, he'd actually tried to channel magick, one last desperate attempt to get the other Fae's attention.

Which had been a useful lesson, really. He now strongly suspected, stories or no stories, an unSoulShared Fae could actually die. Or at the very least, wish he had a god to pray to for such a desired outcome.

Slowly, he turned his attention from his makeshift

focus to the spot on the floor that had flared so brilliantly in magickal light as he staggered down the stairs. Now, there was nothing visible at all, though he thought he could still feel a faint vibration through the floor. Though how he was able to feel anything at all, in his present condition, was a mystery to him.

His present condition. He would have snorted, if he'd been corporeal. Or even three-dimensional.

All adult Fae could Fade. It was the easiest way to get anywhere; at least, anywhere you'd ever been before and knew well enough to go back to. Fading was the first thing a Fae learned to do when he or she first came into the birthright of power; one slowly disappeared from where one was, and reappeared where one wished to be.

But there was another kind of Fading, one rarely attempted, and then only in extremis, as a way to avoid grave physical danger. It was possible to lessen one's physicality; to become insubstantial, invisible to anyone looking on, even with the magickal sense, and barely there even to one's self.

To call it dangerous was an understatement. It was the kind of thing drunken post-adolescents in the first flush of their powers dared one another to do, and an inability to reconstitute oneself after this sort of Fading was thought to be one of the few things that could kill a nearly immortal Fae. It was, of course, difficult to be certain, since no one could ever find the Faded ones to come to the truth of the matter.

Conall was trying very hard not to think about that right now.

He'd never Faded involuntarily before—hadn't known it was possible to be forced to Fade, at least not without another Fae doing the forcing. He'd already known his ability to channel magick was gone, completely blocked. Yet in the moment he touched the nexus, the surge of power had forced the barrier, and his body had channeled magick—all the magick that had flowed out from the buried power source in response to the touch of a mage. And the magick had seized him, and shaken him, and savaged him. Had flung him aside, in the end, Faded and broken. What had they called that device, in that old movie he'd watched during that endless night of pain and television? An electric chair. A good comparison, if one could plug such a device into an infinite power source.

That wasn't all, though. No, one-of-a-kind calamities were waiting in line to dance a figure with him in this wretched minuet. When one attempted this sort of Fading, one was wise to cover any mirrors in view. Or at least, to close one's eyes.

A mirror could trap a Faded Fae. A mirror had.

Son of a pox-ridden chancre-licking whore. And whatever gods these humans followed, please bless public access television and its vocabulary-expanding wonders. *I can't die. All the tales, all the lore, they all agree. Once a Fae passes through the Pattern, there's no dying without SoulSharing first.*

But what guarantee is there those tales are true? He wasn't sure why he doubted. Other than the fact that he couldn't move, couldn't breathe, and was still in every bit of the pain he'd been in when he made his way downstairs. In a way, it was more frightening to imagine *not* being able to die, being forced to live this way for a full Fae lifespan. Or maybe forever. Of all the ends he'd ever imagined for himself, becoming one of the 'magick mirrors' of Fae legend had never once appeared on his list.

He wanted to breathe, needed to breathe; he no longer had a body needing air, but his mind was accustomed to breathing and was becoming frantic at his inability to do so. He fought it as long as he could, but it eventually became more painful to suppress the urge than to give in to it, and he tried to gasp in a great breath.

Screaming was bad. Very bad.

Damn. I was so close.

The magick had seemed tantalizingly accessible at first, as he made his way down the stairs, swirling around him as if he waded a creek in flood. Yet it was separate from him, as if some unbreakable glass came between, dooming him to sense, but never touch, the power that he had once channeled with such ease.

He'd fallen to his knees beside the brilliant eye of the nexus, as if something grasped him and pulled him there. He'd reached out, his hand unsteady. But then his hand clenched into a fist, as another vision came between him and the swirling brightness.

Josh.

For an instant, he'd thought the vision real, real enough to drive back the pain, to stir a spark of the joy the human's presence woke in him. But it had only been his desperate imagination, of course, and the beautiful dark eyes and patterned skin dissolved back into the shifting light before he could speak.

Could his SoulShare have returned him to himself, given him back his magick? Maybe. But there had been no time left, no time to wait, or so he had believed, and he'd reached out and opened himself and invited the magick in.

Conall came back to awareness at a sound, nearby. Beady black eyes looked back at him. Well, no, not back at him, into the mirror. *Eiscréid*. Or, to be less elegant and more to the point, *shit*. He'd hated rats ever since his cousins had dropped one in the bathing-pool with him when he was seven.

Nothing said he had to keep watching the rat, of course. Unfortunately, closing what passed for his eyes simply invited memory back in.

The memory of touching the nexus felt like being turned inside out, and then flayed. Conall wasn't sure what was more painful, the physical effect of the raw form of pure magick or the thought that magick itself had turned on him so brutally.

Unconsciousness had been swift, and the return of awareness slow. And now memory was back full circle, showing him once again the movement on the stairs. The other Fae, magick simmering around him like the air around a forge, a rage of power barely banked. Even his own aura, back in the Realm, had been nothing like this. *A Loremaster*, he remembered thinking. And then came recognition. *Cuinn an Dearmad. He has to be. But that's impossible. He's dead. They're all dead.*

Conall groaned again, remembering the moment of utter despair when the other mage had turned to go, oblivious to his shouts. If he was invisible even to one so gifted, surely not a soul would ever know where he had fallen.

Not a soul, except his own.

Iós...

Invisible tears were hot on Conall's cheeks, and his nonexistent body was wracked with pain as he tried to gasp in another breath. *Iós, lanan, scair-anam.*

This time, when he turned within himself, it was the dream he saw, the one he'd shared with Josh. The scent of the oil filled him, without the need to breathe; he felt the human's hands on him, the warmth of his kisses, the heart-quickening insistence of a slick hard shaft at his entrance.

I will not die. Not before I know the truth behind that dream.

Chapter Sixteen

Josh lost patience with the Greenwich Village traffic somewhere around Perry Street. He hadn't been long on patience to start, and going through security at National Airport in D.C. with the TSA people making smart-assed comments about his piercings had consumed most of his limited store. He'd been restless through the flight, sweating, unable to get his breath, and pretty sure the flight attendants thought he was strung out, as he checked his ink every couple of minutes to make sure it hadn't started moving again. Then the wait for a cab, and the fight with traffic into the city; he had a sick feeling the Acela would have been faster.

And now Seventh Avenue was slowed to a crawl. Growling, Josh waited for the third full stop at the same light, pulled some of the cash Tiernan had forced on him out of his pocket, shoved it at the startled driver, got out of the cab, and started to run.

He was still enough of a New Yorker that ignoring oncoming traffic was second nature; he sprinted across Seventh, easily dodging the traffic that had started to inch forward again, and bent left on Waverly, trying to ignore the burning in his lungs.

There's nothing wrong with me, damn it. But knowing it was Conall's breathlessness threatening to cripple him was no help at all.

By the time he arrived on the block of the little three-story brownstone, black spots were dancing around the edges of his vision. There was one very bad moment when he was sure he'd left his keys, to the building and to Tiernan's apartment, on the table beside his bed; he leaned against the streetlight on the corner for support, gulping in air as he dug through his pockets.

As his fingers closed around the tourist-trinket key ring, the frosted-glass door of the brownstone opened and Bryce Newhouse exited, dressed for the gym and moving like a man on a schedule. His gaze raked over the corner where Josh stood, then passed on without pause, and he headed off in the opposite direction. Which was fine as far as Josh was concerned, as he was in no mood to wait around and exchange unpleasantries. Not even waiting until the insufferable prick was out of sight, he ran the rest of the way to the door and let himself into the blessedly cool interior.

The door swung closed behind him, barely noticed. Three long strides took him to the stairs. With any luck, Conall was only two flights away, and he was only moments from reuniting with... well. A stranger, of barely three days' acquaintance. But also the other half of his own soul. Three days ago he would have laughed at the thought. Now, his caretaking instinct was in overdrive; all he wanted to do was make certain Conall was well and whole.

Before he could start up the stairs, though,

something caught his eye. The basement door, opposite the stairs, standing open and giving onto darkness.

It doesn't matter. Someone else will take care of it. Conall's upstairs.

But he crossed to the door all the same, and, a hand on the knob, he peered down into the dimness. Not a sound came up from below, and once again he turned to go, but instead found himself bending to look farther down the stairs.

He wasn't sure what he'd expected, but the room below him was just a basement storeroom, with the vague shapes of shelves against the walls, boxes and furniture and other miscellany filling most of the space except for a spot in the center. Off to one side, a cracked mirror leaned against some metal shelving, giving back a gleam of light from a dust-covered window. Nothing remarkable. Certainly nothing worth tarrying for, not with Conall waiting upstairs. *Please, God, let him be waiting upstairs.*

Yet something in him wept, as he closed the door. To lock it from this side required the use of a key he didn't have, so he left it as it was, and with a soft groan, he turned and bolted up the stairs.

The door to the apartment where he'd left Conall was unlocked. Heart pounding, he opened it, just enough to slip inside. And once again he was met by the unexpected—not Conall, *Christ, he's not here*— but a sandy-haired man in board shorts and a t-shirt, sitting cross-legged on the bed, which looked as if it had been ransacked and then hastily made up, pondering a sketchbook open in his lap.

He looked up from the book, a lock of hair falling

in eyes of a disconcerting pale spring green. "About fucking time you got here. Name's Cuinn." He gestured, and the door slammed shut behind Josh. "Sweet ink, by the way."

Oh, shit. "You're another Fae."

"Your powers of observation are matched only by your obvious intelligence. And stunning good looks."

"What the hell did you do with Conall?" Josh took a step toward the bed, reaching for the neck of the other man's shirt—and found himself frozen in mid-stride, lip just starting to curl in a snarl, as Cuinn lowered a hand Josh hadn't seen him raise.

"Ordinarily I'd have more fun with this, but we don't have time." Cuinn sighed, leaning back on his braced arms and shaking his head. "I haven't done anything with your *scair-anam*, in fact I'd give my left nut to know what happened to him. And if you'll promise to cut the bullshit, I'll let go of you so we can figure this out. Deal?"

Josh's head was released just enough to let him nod. Which he did, and staggered, off balance, as the rest of him found itself able to move again. Steadying himself, he stared at the Fae, unsure what to say. The other man looked nothing like Conall—long sandy hair framing his face in waves, instead of Conall's haphazard red-gold thatch, and a face intense and sensual, with none of Conall's delicacy. Yet there was something exactly the same. Something about the eyes.

"Sit down, will you? You keep looking at me like that, you'll be trying to buy me flowers next, and even I won't stoop to poaching another male's *scair-anam*."

"Narcissistic much?" Josh lowered himself to the bed, there being nowhere else to sit, and continued to watch the Fae's eyes. There was an almost gemlike quality to them, as there was to Conall's. And Tiernan's, too, come to think of it.

Cuinn shrugged. "I'm a Fae. Comes with the territory." He sat forward, abruptly all focus, all intensity. "Time's short. Why would Dary have gone after the nexus before you two finished Sharing? And without you there?"

"I might be able to answer that better if I knew what the hell you were talking about."

Cuinn noticed the sketchbook on his lap, grimaced, and tossed it aside. "Fuck. Guaire didn't tell you *anything*?"

"Nothing about a nexus. Although Kevin said something about ley energy—does it have to do with that?"

"You might say. There are two lines crossing under this building, one strong, one not so much. Or there were, until your boyfriend got at them." Cuinn grimaced. "I'm pretty sure he managed to short out a whole fucking nexus."

A chill ran through Josh at Cuinn's words. Not so much the words, as the way the other man said them. "What would that have done to him?" He looked around the tiny apartment. *Conall, where are you, God damn it?*

"No one Fae could possibly channel that much magickal energy. Not even a Loremaster." Cuinn smirked. "That would be me, since I'm the last one." The smirk quickly faded, though, giving way to a pensive expression. "And I can tell you in dead earnest, I would not touch even a minor nexus unshielded."

"Why are you so sure he was unshielded?" None

of this was making any sense at all, but it was getting easier to talk as if it did. As long as it seemed the conversation was getting him closer to figuring out where Conall was, anyway.

Cuinn's eyebrows arched. "Because you're his shield, *buchal alann*. That's a human SoulShare's job, to protect his Fae. Well, part of it."

"What the hell does that mean, '*buchal alann*'?" Josh's hands clenched into fists; with an effort, he made them relax. "And I would have been there if I'd had the slightest fucking clue that was where I was supposed to be!"

The Fae was regarding him with a cool curiosity. "It means 'beautiful boy.' Which you are. And you weren't meant to know. The SoulShares have to find their own ways."

"Find their own ways, my ass. You knew Conall was in danger, and you didn't do anything." Josh could feel the red of anger creeping up the back of his neck; he glared at Cuinn, a muscle in his jaw jumping as he fought not to snarl.

Cuinn, for his part, simply looked bored. "Don't make me spend magick again, there's a good boy. If I could intervene on behalf of any of the Fae, believe me, I would. I've watched more train wrecks than you could possibly imagine, these last two thousand years. But my hands are tied."

For a moment, Josh almost believed him; the disconcerting green gaze was shadowed, waves of hair fell around Cuinn's face as his head bowed. But then those eyes glinted up at him again, with something that could have been amusement, or mockery, and the moment passed.

"So why haven't you two finished the bond?"

Josh's mouth opened, closed. *How do you know we haven't?* warred with *what the fuck business is it of yours?* and *what do you mean, finished?* And in the end, none of them won. "Tell me what I need to do and I'll do it. Whatever I need to do to keep him safe."

"Whatever?" Cuinn laughed harshly. "What if I told you that the only way you stand the proverbial snowball's chance in your human hell of keeping him safe is to get as far away from him as you possibly can?"

"I'd say fuck you, I'll find another way." The answer came without hesitation, without rancor. A fact, simply stated.

"I wish it were that simple." Cuinn got to his feet, apparently driven by an excess of nervous energy; he all but bounced on the balls of his feet as he crossed to the window and leaned on the sill to look out. Unfortunately, that particular window gave onto nothing but the brick face of the taller building next door, and the view didn't hold the Fae's attention for long; he turned back to Josh, hands clasped behind his back. "You have to complete your bond, I know that much. But I don't know when that's supposed to happen, and for the moment, this is probably the least safe place on two planes of existence for you. And, coincidentally, for me."

Josh looked around, alarmed, but saw nothing that hadn't been there a minute ago. Only a spare white room, an enormous bed, and an agitated Fae. Kevin and Tiernan's words still resonated within him, though; he'd thought of very little else, on the plane. "The *Marfach*?"

Oddly enough, Cuinn almost looked relieved. "At least his Grace told you something helpful." Soon, though, relief gave way to tension; the Fae paced, slowly, his bare feet almost silent on the wooden floor. "Yes, the *Marfach*. An evil it cost the lives of most of the Fae of my generation to contain. It's loose, and it wants your boyfriend. And if it gets him…"

Cuinn's voice trailed off, and the slow inexorable tread stopped. His back was to Josh, and it seemed he started to speak, then stopped, and tried again, though Josh could barely hear him over the hammering of his heart in his own ears at the thought of losing Conall. "Then everything the Loremasters did is going to be undone. And both our worlds could fall."

"This *Marfach* is really that evil?"

Cuinn turned and nodded grimly. "And Conall is that powerful. If the *Marfach* takes him over, I know I couldn't stop him."

The set of Cuinn's jaw told Josh exactly how grim a prognosis the Fae had just given him. "You're assuming the *Marfach* can find him."

"I'm not going to wager two worlds that it can't," came the quiet reply.

I am losing my goddamned mind, was Josh's perfectly reasonable thought. *I'm sitting here with one of the hottest men I've ever seen in my life, except that he isn't really a man, straight-facedly chatting about protecting my boyfriend, who isn't really a man either, from a monster that wrecks worlds for shits and giggles?*

"So why are you talking about getting *me* out of here?" Sanity was highly overrated, at least when the subject was his *scair-anam*. "Conall's the one in danger. We should be finding him and getting *him* to safety."

"Twinklebritches isn't here, in case you hadn't noticed." Cuinn shook his head, crossed to the window and leaned on the sill, forehead resting against the glass as if he thought he might see the missing Fae in the bricks of the wall opposite. "You, though, I have right here and can do something about."

"I'm not going anywhere until I know what's happened to Conall."

Cuinn turned, at this, and Josh worked not to flinch away from the intensity of his gaze. "You don't have a fucking clue what we're dealing with here. You are in no way equipped to deal with the *Marfach*, and trust me, the only option you have that's going to keep you breathing long enough to get back together with your boyfriend and help him do what he has to do is get the hell out of here. Now. Because it's coming. And if it can't find your boyfriend, it'll be perfectly happy to take you and settle in to wait for him."

The Fae started for the door, apparently assuming Josh would follow. Josh didn't. His jaw set, and the patterns on his arms twitched as the muscles under them jumped and bunched. "You might as well save your breath, hot pants. I'm staying right here*." Until I can take Conall with me, get him back to Purgatory.*

Cuinn's teeth clenched; his hand twitched, as if he fought not to raise it, not to gesture and probably paralyze Josh all over again. "Fuck, I don't dare, I can't afford the magick it would take to drag your ass out of here." He sighed.

When Cuinn's startling pale-green gaze met Josh's again, it was almost reasonable. Almost. "Listen. I'm not trying to get you to betray your SoulShare. As freak-ass as that is for a Fae to say, because generally we don't give a downstream piss about turning on our own kind. SoulShares are an exception, and you and Twinklebritches—" He paused at a glare from Josh. "You and Conall are an even bigger exception than the norm."

"Go on." Josh arched a brow. "Why?"

"Because a half-souled Fae on this side of the Pattern is invulnerable. Physically. Completely. Until he finds his SoulShare. It's one of the protections built into the Pattern. Once you two both get your wicks dipped, he'll be vulnerable again to the physical shit, but the tradeoff is that he'll have you as his protection against all things magickal and be safe to tap into the great nexus without fucking killing it. Which is why we have to hook the two of you up. Once it's safe. *Only* when it's safe."

Josh felt his face turning crimson as Cuinn spoke. "How do you know we haven't both... *what* did you call it?"

"Dipping your wicks. Knocking boots. Whatever the hell you want to call it. I use 'fucking' for so many other things, it's kind of lost its original meaning. And as for how I know, I have my sources." Cuinn made a chopping motion with one hand, physically cutting off that line of conversation. "What I *don't* know is what happens if you get *your* ass killed before you two finish what you started. And believe me, the *Marfach* might not recognize your ass before you finish *scair'ain'e*, but it's perfectly capable of killing it. Or much worse."

Those words were still hanging in the air when the sound of a crash made its slightly muffled way through the apartment door. "*Shit*," both men cursed at once; Josh, being closer to the door, got there first and eased it open, barely enough to let him see out.

No reason for things to start making sense now. He watched, catching glimpses through turns in the stairs, as a vaguely familiar figure let itself in through the broken front window and crossed to the basement door, opened it. "What the fuck? He's supposed to be dead."

He heard Cuinn's breath catch—felt it, the Fae was leaning that close. "Who?"

"I forget his name, he used to be the bouncer at Purgatory. But I heard he was killed in a break-in or something."

Cuinn grabbed Josh's arm and hauled him back, away from the door. "We are fucking out of time. It'll be here any minute."

"It?"

Eyes like clear green gems blazed with an inner light almost too beautiful to look at. "There's only one place I can take you without Fading you. Hang on tight, human. And if you like to pray, pray I have the magick left to pull this off with a passenger."

Josh opened his mouth to protest—closed it in shock as the room in which he stood tore, parted like a heavy curtain, and the light of another world shone through the rent. Water splashed somewhere within earshot; he caught a glimpse of a small waterfall, and sunlight shining through the spray. A bird sang on the other side, its melody almost a language, teasing at his ears.

Cuinn yanked on Josh's arm. Twisting to grip the Fae's elbow, he stumbled forward, his shoes sinking into soft grass.

The curtain fell, and the room was empty.

156

Chapter Seventeen

Janek picked slivers of glass out of his hand as he descended the stairs. *You could at least have let me pull my sleeve down over my hand.* He knew better than to speak aloud, having been warned before he shattered the glass pane set into the door of the brownstone. 'Warned' as in almost brought to his knees.

You felt nothing. The male voice sounded distracted, and Janek's passenger kept forcing his gaze down the stairs, into the storage space below the staircase. *You feel nothing unless I allow it.*

Nothing but pissed off. Janek was careful to keep the thought confined in the small box that marked the part of his mind he could call his own. Getting onto the train from D.C. without attracting unwanted attention had been more than enough of a pain in the ass. But enduring the use of what was left of his human flesh to try to sense the location of the other Fae the *Marfach* was so hot for was much, much worse.

His shitkickers had barely touched the floor when he was rocked with a snarl of rage so vicious he staggered and nearly fell. He was being forced to stare at the only empty spot in the whole dismal basement, a spot in the middle of the floor, and he was dully surprised that he could do it without needing to throw up. *There's nothing there.* He made his inner voice as cheery as he could.

There has to be something. Yeah, this was bad news, if the obscenity was out. The sound of that voice reminded Janek of the time he'd t-boned a Lincoln on his bike and broken his leg; the monstrosity's voice reminded him uncannily of the sound of bone grating on bone.

You weren't seriously expecting to find another Fae lying there in the middle of the floor, were you? Not that he had a clue what the *Marfach* did expect. There had to be more to this wild goose chase than just another goddamned Fae, but his passenger had kept its thoughts to itself all the way up the coast.

Janek was actually surprised he'd remained aware for the whole trip; usually, when the *Marfach* was preoccupied, it meant lights-out for him. Come to think of it, though, he'd been left alone quite a bit, since he'd waked up next to the stiff.

Shut up, Meat. There have to be ley lines here. I need your eye.

Suddenly, he was on his hands and knees on the floor, staring at the grey cement, with no idea of how he'd gotten there, the male's snarl still echoing in his ears. A wave of dizziness swept over him, but it wasn't nearly as bad as it had been down in the tunnels under Purgatory. His eye wasn't even trying to roll back in his head. Much. Forced to stare at the floor, he could just barely see the wavering that was all his human eye could make out in the presence of magick.

The *Marfach* let out a scream of pure fury within him and slammed his all too human fist against the concrete, over and over until the skin was split and the bones cracked. "That's not doing any good, damn you!" he finally shouted aloud, not caring if the creature punished him again. He didn't feel the pain now, but he sure as hell would later.

The creature wasn't done raging, though. Not by a long shot. The *Marfach* drove his body around and around the basement, using his feet to kick in boxes, his arms to overturn furniture. *Like a fucking baby with the tit taken away.* He cursed again, as his already-wrecked hand punched through the side of a chest of drawers.

After a few minutes, though, the monster's tantrum started to feel good. Rage was one of the few emotions Janek had left, after all; soon his snarl echoed through the basement right along with the one that echoed in his head, and the place was a ruin.

In the midst of his rampage, something moved. Janek cursed, and turned, and stumbled back at sight of a monster. It was a grotesque creature, six and a half feet tall, lurching like a drunk, with a badly shaved head, dull black and red ink, a ragged eyepatch, bleeding hands, and a glowing red cavity where half its head should be.

The female voice laughed, chilly, mocking, her anger drained away. *Have you frightened yourself, Meat?*

Janek roared, an act which contorted the face that glared back at him from the mirror even more. Not even stopping to think, he raised his shitkicker and shattered the motherfucker, snarling in satisfaction at the sound of falling glass, grinding the thick soles of his boots into the shards that fell from the frame.

Seven years of bad luck. The male voice, too, was laughing.

Don't laugh at me, asshole. Slowly, Janek forced himself to calm. On the outside. Deep in the small private place in his mind, he was thoroughly enjoying the act of rimming all three manifestations of his tormentor with a broken beer bottle. Well, two. No fucking way was he touching the obscenity.

Now that the *Marfach* was done with its shit-fit, Janek's gaze was forced back toward the stairs. His stomach lurched as he saw what he'd managed to miss on the way down, traces of magickal energy on the stairs. A trail, of sorts, one that came down to the middle of the chaos he'd just created in the middle of the floor, and stopped there. *A Fae has been here.* The female's voice was suddenly so cold, smoke seemed to come off it and hang in the air. ***Possibly more than one. If you could only see better, Meat, I might even be able to tell who it was.***

Pardon me for being kind of human.

Janek was urged back up the stairs, stumbling a couple of times thanks to the numbness in his feet. *What the hell are you doing now?*

Perhaps someone here has seen whoever it was. A hint of the mocking laughter returned to the female's voice, as Janek nearly faced on the stairs.

Watch where I'm going, asshole. Janek emerged into the dimly lit hallway and looked around. *And you obviously haven't spent much time in New York. Nobody sees nothin' here.*

Humans are easily persuaded. The voice was cool, confident, and utterly dismissive.

"What the *hell* is this?" The voice came from

160

outside, through the empty air where the glass pane in the front door should have been.

Janek wheeled—as best he could, given his shitty balance—to see a toned but pasty man, shining dark brown hair immaculate, mustache like a 70's porn star, carrying a gym bag as if to pronounce to the world that he could work hard and still look fuckable as all hell, glaring in through the mostly missing square of glass.

"Maintenance." Janek yanked up his hood, glad of the nondescript dark grey hoodie; it mostly hid what was left of his face, and it had been mistaken for a uniform before. It would do for that purpose now, at least until this new prey item came inside.

"Thank *God*." The dickhead reached in through the broken pane to let himself in, closed what was left of the door behind himself. "Considering what we pay in common area fees—*urk*."

His complaint ended in a very satisfying strangled sound, as Janek grabbed him around the throat and pinned him to the wall. He needed no instructions for this part of what was going to happen; this was the part of his job in which he took real pleasure. Slowly tightening his grip, he reached up with his free hand and pulled away the patch over the cavity that was half his face. The poor little pissant tried to scream at the sight, but the best he was able to do was a pathetic squeak. Which made Janek smile. Which made the pissant try to scream more.

Ask him about the Fae, the woman's voice wheedled.

His temporary good mood fled, Janek grimaced. *How the hell am I supposed to do that? He wouldn't know a Fae if one bit him in the ass.*

Use your imagination. The male voice dripped contempt. As it usually did, when it wasn't dripping something more disgusting. ***They're blond more often than not, try that.***

"The blond man. Where is he?" *When they make a movie out of my life, I want a different scriptwriter.* Another thought to tuck into the box.

"Which one?"

What the hell? Tighter still. "How many are there?"

"Two. Kind of. I guess." The breath whistled oddly through the guy's throat, and Janek unclenched a little. "Guy named Tiernan Guaire has the upstairs apartment—"

This time it was more a wheeze, as the hand around the throat tightened and a knee came up into the dickhead's gut. "You did *not* just say that."

You are not allowed to kill him yet. The woman spoke sharply enough to cut. ***Guaire might be one of the ones we seek, but there is at least one other. I am sure of it.***

"Who are the others?" Janek spoke through clenched teeth, and all of his thoughts went straight into the box. *I don't give a shit about anyone else, give me Guaire. I want to make him bleed.*

But, fuck it, the asswipe grew a set. Pale and gray, he shook his head. Tightening the grip didn't help, leaning in with the knee made him squeal interestingly but didn't get any more information.

Idiot. The male voice practically spat the word. ***If you want a job done right…***

Janek's hand was forced to his belt. To the sheath of the knife he wore there for special occasions like this trip, the knife he'd stolen from Kevin Almstead. And should have used to kill him, except his boy-toy got in the way.

I thought you said you didn't want him killed.

Shut up.

Janek drew the knife, and looked down to where the dickhead's abdomen was heaving as he fought to breathe. He watched, fascinated, as the knife in his hand stabbed deep, in a very careful, deliberate way. Tightened his other hand again to stop the screams. The narrow blade didn't make much of a wound, but a satisfying spill of blood welled up and poured out nonetheless. And Janek's hand didn't entirely stop the screams. Which was all right too.

Then the blade moved toward Janek's face.

Can we talk?

Shut up.

The gleaming, blood-streaked blade went straight for the hole in Janek's ruined face. It was useless to try to fight it, but that didn't stop him from trying. *I am fucking not making a sound.* He couldn't see what the blade was doing, but he sure as hell felt the cutting and the burning when it scraped at the living Stone that made up so much of his head. The knife fell to the floor unheeded, and when his hand came back into his field of vision, it was carefully holding a tiny chip of crystal in numb fingers. It gleamed even in the dim light, and probably would be beautiful if he wasn't in too goddamned much pain to notice.

Then things got really interesting. Janek watched his hand take the little piece of Stone and push it into the wound the knife had made, his finger disappearing into the prick's gut to the second knuckle. And as he withdrew his finger, the wound healed, leaving a small, gnarled scar like a knot.

Much better. The female was back, self-satisfied as hell, practically preening. *You can release him now, Meat.*

Janek snarled and let go. To his astonishment, the asswipe merely stood there, rubbing his throat and looking perturbed.

Ask him again about the others, the female voice prodded.

Janek gritted his teeth. "Other blond men?"

"Only one, that I know of." The other man coughed. "Twink named Conall. Conall Dary, I think. Though he's more a redhead. We wouldn't take him in, so Guaire's letting him stay up there."

The name meant nothing to Janek, but he could feel the monster within him come instantly to rapt attention. *"Get out of here until you're summoned."* Now it was Janek's turn to rub his throat, as his rider took direct control of his vocal cords, growling the order at the bloodied man before making Janek bend to pick up the knife. *"I will have a use for you. Later."*

After fixing the hapless man with one more one-eyed glare, Janek turned, or was turned, and ascended the stairs at as close to a run as he could manage. He tried not to look at the stairs as he climbed, because the treads were shifting under his feet with hints of magickal energy and he was fucking sick of trying to hand himself his stomach.

Janek passed the second-floor landing without a glance, his gaze already locked onto the last door. He could almost feel the *Marfach* quivering with anticipation inside his head, fixated on new prey. A slow boil started, deep down in the box, taking advantage of the thing's focus elsewhere.

It doesn't give a shit about Guaire. Whatever it wants, it can get from any Fae. And what does that mean for me?

No time to think about that. He'd arrived at the top of the stairs, at a plain wooden door that was at least holding still.

Not even warded? The woman's disdain was palpable. ***Too easy.*** He reached out and opened the door.

Jesus fucking Christ. Janek's human eye insisted on seeing nothing but an empty room, an apartment not much bigger than his own, with a badly rumpled bed taking up most of the space. The creature looking through that eye, though, saw things overlaid with a constantly shifting glow, except for a dead spot near the edge of the bed. Janek kept trying to look at the dead spot. The *Marfach* kept not letting him, forcing him to examine the glow despite his wrenching stomach, getting more and more jiggy in his head as the glow started to resolve into two different patterns.

Two. The female voice sounded more excited than Janek could ever remember hearing her. ***Two besides Guaire. And both so very much stronger.***

Janek shut down his thoughts so fast it was a wonder the bitch didn't get her fingers caught when the steel shutter slammed down. *It's playing me. It has been all along.*

He watched as his bleeding hand ran over the sheets, the headboard of the bed, wondering if the *Marfach* could feel the magick there, because he sure as hell couldn't. He wasn't paying much attention, though; what was left of his mind was working frantically. *It was pissed when it didn't find ley lines. It expected to. But it's creaming its panties over these new Fae. It wants them.*

Which means I don't want it to have them. Fuck, the thing was using his vocal cords to giggle with glee. *I want Guaire. Maybe these two are good enough for the monster. But they're not good enough for me.*

He sat down hard on the edge of the bed. His hand reached for a book that someone had discarded in the middle of it, a book that made his eye ache even when he didn't look at it full on. Oh, hell no. No clues. And anything with that much magick in it was one motherfucking huge clue. With an effort that would have left him sweating if he could still sweat, he pulled his hand back, and turned his head toward that dead gray spot. *What could have caused that?*

He could feel the *Marfach*'s attention go from the dead spot to the book, and back again, and held his breath. Whatever it was that happened while he'd been down in the tunnel, if it had rattled the *Marfach* enough to give him even a little bit of influence over it, it was the best thing to happen to him. Under his new, lower standards for 'good,' anyway.

All of the magick has been sucked from it. He could almost feel immaculately polished female fingernails drumming on a tabletop, somewhere in his head. *A mage in the Realm does this, when he channels. Dary could have done this.*

How do you know? He needed to keep it talking, keep it distracted. Time for a little bit of his late unlamented Uncle Art's blarney. *You've never met him.* In a parody of casualness, Janek struggled to cross one leg over the opposite knee, and dug an irritating sliver of mirror out of the sole of his boot, flicked it away with a bloodied finger. *I mean, if you had, you would have offed him. Assuming you can.*

I've seen him. Until I left the ley lines, I could see everything that happened in the Realm. The male's laugh was harsh. **The fools, imprisoning their only predator where it could watch its prey's every move.**

Yeah, and I can't help but notice what good use you made of the opportunity.

Pain gripped his gut, and he doubled over. **You're forgetting your place, Meat.**

My 'place' is to get you into Purgatory. Though it was a safe bet the creature wasn't being straight with him about its reason for wanting to get in there, either. He gritted his teeth, waiting for the pain to pass. *So you can pay me off.*

Ah, yes, your revenge. Janek shuddered at the grating sound, and wished like hell he could close his eye to the image of itself the monstrosity was branding into his brain. **We are such a tidy symbiosis, you and I. And Guaire might make a better beginning than either of these two, at that. A means to an end, now.**

Janek froze, the better to hide his inmost thoughts. *It's not going to let me have him. But as long as it still wants him, it'll get me closer. And once I'm within range, we'll see if it can play its games before the motherfucking Fae bleeds out.*

But he will have felt the same thing I felt. The voice morphed in mid-sentence this time, from monster to woman. And the next words from it confirmed Janek's long-standing suspicion that the

167

female was the real brains of the unholy trinity in his head. *He will have felt this lesser nexus go dark. And he will be taking steps to safeguard the great nexus. We must move quickly.*

Despite himself, Janek groaned at the thought of another ride on the Acela. Hiding his thoughts from the *Marfach* for that long, with nothing to distract either of them but their own thoughts, was going to be next to impossible.

Bored? Janek could feel the male smirking. *You're going to wish you were bored, Meat. I'm in a hurry now. And I don't feel like having company while I plot. Time to get you home and tuck you in bed.*

Janek was too confused by the *Marfach*'s words to pay much attention to the obscene snigger in its inner voice. *You're in a hurry?* His natural belligerence muscled its way to the fore. *What do you want me to do, hold the engineer hostage so he'll drive the train faster?*

The *Marfach* snorted. *As enjoyable as that might be, no. I've been considering this for a while, and I think I can Fade you once or twice without killing you.* It paused, thinking. *Once, at least.*

What the hell is Fading?

Something only magickal beings can do, Meat. The female purred, and Janek distinctly felt a fingernail run down his spine. *Don't worry, I'll be very careful. I still need my ride, after all.*

But Janek didn't fade out. Everything around him did. Going colorless, and then transparent.

And then all the breath was sucked from his lungs.

Maybe this was a bad idea…

168

Chapter Eighteen

Conall wished like hell he could rub his eyes. What a stupid, petty thing to be irritated about. Yet irritated he was. He was seeing everything through a haze of blood, the blood of the deformed man-monster who had shattered his prison.

'Deformed' was just a guess, of course. Even now, he would shudder, if he had a body, remembering the sight that had borne down on him in that cursed cellar. If the aura around Cuinn an Dearmad had seethed with power, the aura around the head of the black-and-red-tattooed freak who stomped the mirror had been a maelstrom of it. There had been living magick there, and elemental magick; but most of all, a force malevolent beyond all comprehension, twisting and horribly distorting both forms of magickal energy. He had only been able to bear the sight for a moment; but a moment had been all he'd had, before his mirrored prison shattered under the hulking male's boot.

The breaking of the glass hadn't freed him. Not that he'd thought it would—there hadn't been time to think, only to react. As pieces fell away from the mirror, he'd drawn himself in, shifting from one fragment to the next, until, by luck or design or both, he found himself in the sliver of mirror that wedged into the behemoth's boot-sole, and carried up the stairs.

To be deposited right back where he had started from. The irony was far from lost on him as he stared up at the ceiling, essentially his only option at the moment. Staring at the edge of the bed, and past it at the mirror on the ceiling. He could see the sketchbook, in the mirror, the one he'd penned the brief lines to Josh in. It was upside down, now. No way to tell if his message had ever been read.

Josh.

Tears were a thing of the mind, more than the eyes, and Conall's insubstantial vision blurred with them. He'd had only a glimpse, when his *scair-anam* appeared at the top of the stairs. More than he had ever hoped to have again, but not enough.

Whatever he'd thought the SoulShare bond would be like, it was certainly nothing like the reality of it, or at least the partial reality he knew. Not that he'd ever given the matter much thought, but he'd probably given it more than most. Mages were about the only Fae who ever indulged any kind of interest in history, probably because they were throwbacks themselves, echoes of a forgotten time when all Fae shaped magick at will and Loremasters walked among them.

An exile's soul is torn in two, one old scroll read. *One half to be reborn, beyond the Pattern, and regained only by love*. He'd laughed, reading it. If there was one true thing about knowing one was going to live a thousand years or more, it was that no ties other than blood could possibly endure that long. The

Fae raised pleasure to an art, and vendetta to a science, and between the two there was no room for anything like love.

And yet here I am. Since the moment he opened his eyes, amidst all the noise and confusion and pain, he'd been bound, in the only prison a Fae could bear. Bound despite fear, despite mistrust. Had a smile, gentle hands, a kiss undone all that? The mightiest mage since the Sundering, made captive by dark, intelligent eyes, intimate touches, a marvelously inked body.

Body. Had he really done... *that*? Yes, he had, and his cold sharp prison was nearly forgotten, as he remembered falling to his knees, desperately fighting the destructive force of his own arousal so he could safely give pleasure to a male he barely knew.

How had he known what to do? He'd read, of course, and there had been dreams, dreams to make him tremble when he recalled them in the light of day. But this had been different. Real. And it had been the most natural thing in the world, his tongue sweeping over Josh's heavy sac before tracing his length, teasing at his sweet spot before taking him deep, his arms curling around strong thighs as if he'd braced himself this way a thousand times. Pleasuring a lover with a skill he'd never had the chance to show, and a hunger he'd never dared to let himself feel.

Surely it hadn't been love. He could be certain of that much, at least, if only because he'd known what it was, and Fae knew nothing of love. Himself least of all, with no knowledge even of friendship. As wonderful as it had been, and as much as he ached now for more of it, it hadn't been love.

But the sensation that gripped him, shook him, scattering everything resembling thought to the five winds, when Josh released? Joy, a joy so intense even the memory of it made him desperate for a voice to cry out with it.

Josh…

Delight in the male his arms were wrapped around, in the taste of him, in the sound of his voice, in the way his knees threatened to buckle under him and he'd laughed softly as Conall held him upright. In that moment, he'd wanted to make it all happen again, to make Josh feel that way again. Even if he, himself, could never share it.

That could be love.

But he'd lost it. No trapped Fae had ever come out of a mirror, in any tale he knew—that was why they were *cautionary* tales, if they had happy endings every idiot post-adolescent in the Realm would be placing bets and then vanishing into the nearest bit of silvered glass. He could imagine no way out of his tiny prison, no direction in which he could move that might free him. Any attempt simply reminded him he was caged. Which was a very bad thing to remind a Fae of. So far, the thoughts of Josh kept the panic at bay, but how much longer could that continue?

Of course, there was no hope of channeling magick to set himself free. Even the thought threatened to bring on mind-shattering pain; that hadn't changed when he became incorporeal.

A glint caught what passed for his eye, here, a flitting dazzle of light. A phantom? Reflected sunlight? How could anything be moving, in this tiny space? No matter—it was movement. Which meant it might show him a way out, because none of his efforts had led to any movement at all.

He focused on the light, and it moved away from him. It moved. Hope stirred within him, and he followed. Beautiful, dancing, the light kept just out of his incorporeal reach. What had begun as a rainbow scattering became a spark, a tiny flame, teasing him, warming him. He pursued, intent, mesmerized. Time ceased to be important; all that mattered was following the light.

Until he started noticing more flickers, darting at the edges of his vision. He stopped, looked around himself. And a low cry of terror rose in the throat he didn't have, as he watched a thousand reflections of the light dance around the walls and floor and ceiling of a mirror maze. An unbroken mirror could never harbor such a thing. But the laws of magick allowed his shattered prison to hold within it an infinite labyrinth, crafted from sunlight and the magick of which he was made.

And the light he had followed? The betraying sunlight, at first, no doubt. But then a phantom, a figment of his own imagination, born of his desperation to be free.

So beautiful. And forever beyond his reach. Perhaps it was love.

The light, and all its kindred, went out, plunging this deeper prison into darkness.

He would not scream. He would not weep. He would not. For who would hear him?

Josh…

Chapter Nineteen

The Realm

"You know, most guys who hold my hand this long at least buy me dinner."

Cuinn snorted. "You don't want me letting go, believe me. And to be on the safe side, I wouldn't recommend eating anything while you're here. You never know."

Josh didn't answer; he looked as though he was still fighting nausea and was frantic besides. Not a happy combination, Cuinn guessed. The human raked his free hand through his hair, and the dragon tattooed around his wrist flexed its wings and glared balefully at the Fae.

The son of a bitch channels when he inks. He's human, and he channels. He'd nearly lost it the first time he saw one of Josh's designs animate; he was getting used to it now, though. *If he got Conall's ability to channel magick when Conall went through the Pattern... shit.* The most powerful mage since the Sundering unable to channel, and his ability gone rogue in a human?

"Explain to me again why you have to physically

hold on to me?" Josh was looking at the creature too—
he'd taken the revelation that his ink was magickal a lot
better than Cuinn had thought he would, for some
reason, but had said he'd be relieved to get home and
have it lie down again, just the same. "I know you told
me, but at the time I had vertigo that would have killed
a large farm animal and I wasn't paying much
attention."

Cuinn snickered. "I could tell. You were an
interesting shade of green. And I'm your only way
home." He leaned back on his elbows in the soft grass,
feeling the magick of the place slowly permeating his
body. Too slowly. It was going to take him a long time
to recharge, after everything he'd been up to in the
human world of late, and especially after opening up
that rift without being properly prepared. *Panic makes
a pretty fair substitute for arousal, in a pinch,
apparently.* He didn't dare consciously siphon magick
out of his surroundings, because that ran the risk of
killing nearly everything he could see from where he
lay. Not permanently, but close enough. And he
needed to be sure he could get the human home. His
fellow Loremasters had made it very clear to him some
time ago a SoulShared Conall Dary was an essential
part of their plan. Which plan he wasn't allowed to
know. "I'm the only sentient being who can pass back
and forth between the Realm and your world."

Josh pushed up and looked around as well; Cuinn
was pleased to see him looking better than he had on
arrival. The combination of adrenalin and
disorientation when he'd first been pulled through the
rift had caused the human to spend his first few
conscious minutes trying very hard not to puke all over

him. "So why does that mean we need to play handsy?" Another pointed glance at their joined hands.

"Time does strange things, where the worlds touch." Cuinn tipped his head back, closed his eyes, and concentrated on drawing in power. Slowly. "When I pass through, I don't disturb the flow. The flaw in the Pattern that lets me go back and forth is shaped to me. And anything I happen to be touching." He smirked, without opening his eyes. "Would have been interesting if my clothes went to another time every time I passed through. But nobody asked me for my input on that subject."

"I wonder why."

"I heard that." Cuinn opened his eyes again, solely so he could roll them properly. "Play nicely, human. If I were to lose contact with you right now, even for a moment, I'd have to open a new passage to send you back, instead of just letting go of you when the time was right, and there's no telling when you'd return to your world. Today, last week, a hundred years from now." He shrugged. "Those stories you hear, about humans wandering off after fairies, and reappearing a hundred years later with their brains scrambled? I started most of them. You don't want to run into me when I'm bored and drunk."

Josh's eyes narrowed. "Is that a Fae thing? Dicking around with humans?"

Cuinn laughed. "You bet your ass it is. Don't you read your own legends? It's not just me. We haven't been gone *that* long. You still have stories."

The human turned away from him, staring off along the winding path that led to the pool beside which the two of them lounged, one hand trailing back behind him so Cuinn could continue to hold his wrist. Hints of ink peeked out from around the neck and sleeves of Josh's sleeveless T. From what the Fae could see, he guessed that Josh's broad, well-muscled back was covered with wings. These tattoos didn't move, though. Which made sense, because Josh probably hadn't done his own back. It was only the ink he'd done himself that sparked to life at the touch of the Realm's magick.

"Are you all like that?" Josh didn't turn to look at Cuinn as he spoke, and his voice was tight.

"Not really, some of us are worse."

The muscles tightened, tensed.

Oh, fuckitall. Sympathy was not something that came naturally to Cuinn. Or any Fae. But something told Cuinn he needed to dredge some up ASAP. "We save our worst for each other. And SoulShares are different. Or they should be."

"Should be?"

No relaxation at all. Damn, that was a lovely back. *Down, Cuinn.* "The Loremasters didn't have a chance to test anything we did in the Sundering. We took the best ideas we had, and we made them happen. But we didn't know how they would all play out. We couldn't. So, yes, 'should be.' But no guarantees."

Now Josh turned. "How is it *supposed* to work? The SoulSharing?"

Cuinn considered. He wasn't supposed to tell the SoulShares a damned thing. His job was to observe, and report back to the other Loremasters on the progress of their grand design. And if the SoulShares knew they were being watched, if they knew *why* they were being watched, it would most likely all have been for nothing. And he, Cuinn an Dearmad, would never be called on to play his other role. Whatever the fuck that was.

But the need-to-know rule was for the Fae, not for humans. This particular human would more than likely forget everything he'd seen or heard here, as soon as he crossed back to the reality he knew. And two thousand years was entirely too fucking long to be carrying some secrets around.

"Your boyfriend was supposed to lose half his soul, crossing over to your world. And find it again, eventually, after getting to know the human world. He should have been able to do everything a Fae in the Realm could do, after crossing over, except die. But there's a flaw in the Pattern. The first part of the gig went the way it was supposed to, but Twinklebritches landed right at your…"

Cuinn's voice trailed off. *Fuck. That cannot have been a coincidence.* If Conall had landed, literally, at his SoulShare's feet, it was because he had been thrown there. Which meant his fellow Loremasters had been *able* to throw him there. Which, in turn, meant they'd been able to control a variable they'd never been able to control before.

And tighter control in one place meant letting go somewhere else. It was like trying to hold sand in your fist; the tighter you gripped, the more got away from you. Cuinn kept his face impassive, with an effort. If the Loremasters of the Pattern were going to fuck with any Fae, Conall Dary was a mind-blowingly bad choice. *What did they lose control of?*

That question, at least, answered itself, as the dragon on Josh's arm blinked its eyes of faceted ebony and hissed at him. *The human can channel. Which, by logical deduction, means the Fae can't.* And what could the Loremasters have wanted Conall in the human world for, if not to use his magick in some way? *Shit. We have to get this fixed.*

But there was the little matter of the mother-humping *Marfach* in the way.

"So something went wrong." There was an edge to Josh's tone. "Something that put Conall in danger?"

"Who the fuck knows?" Cuinn lay back on the grass, one forearm over his eyes, trying to focus. *Have to get my powers back. Have to get the human home. And not drop him in the Marfach's lap. That's it, I'm asking for a raise.*

Muscles tensed rock-hard under Cuinn's hand. "I'm lost. I admit it." Josh's voice was even, quiet; underneath the calm, though, there was a strength that even a Fae had to respect, however reluctantly. "I don't understand half of what's happened to me since Conall arrived. There have been times I've been sure I've lost my mind. But I know I have to find him, and I have to keep him safe. I have to do that like I have to keep breathing. And right at the moment, what's keeping me from doing that is you."

Cuinn moved his arm, and cracked an eyelid. "You aren't threatening me, are you, human? Seriously?"

Josh had turned, and was propped on an elbow, looking down at the Fae, his jaw set in a grim line. "I'm not that stupid. But I want you to send me home. Now."

"Not yet." Cuinn groaned and pushed himself up to a sitting position, still holding Josh's arm, and then to his feet, hauling the human up after him. "No matter how careful I am when I send you back, there's going to be a certain amount of time slippage, just because time doesn't necessarily pass at the same rate here as it does there. And if I drop you on top of the *Marfach*, you have no clue how dead you're going to be." *Dead buying me time to get the fucking rift closed again before the* Marfach*'s fucking golem forces his way through it.*

Going through with the human himself wasn't an option, either. Even assuming his race's ancient enemy wasn't lurking on the other side waiting to hand him his own ass, which it most assuredly *would* do if it came down to *mano a mano*, if he went through before he'd replenished the store of magick he carried within himself, he'd be trapped there. No way for *him* to tap into the ley lines.

"You don't understand." The human's voice was rough, strained. "I'm losing my sense of him. Every minute I'm here, it's getting weaker. I thought it was because I felt like hammered cat shit, but that's not it, because I feel better now, and I'm still losing him."

Cuinn's head jerked up. "You can sense him? Here*?" Even with the SoulShare incomplete. Fuck me oblivious.*

"I have since we... since he..."

Under other circumstances, Cuinn would have had a field day with Josh's obvious discomfort. Now, though, it was one more thing standing between him and what he needed to know to keep this situation from turning into a fail that could take two worlds down with it. "Can you communicate with him?"

"You mean, contact both ways? Only in dreams." The blush that had started moments earlier deepened.

"All this connection tells me is that he's alive. And in pain."

Probably because he can't channel. Son of a bitch. "That's better than nothing." Cuinn's hand slid up Josh's arm, to his gloriously inked bicep—inked, fortunately, with abstract designs that weren't sizing him up to determine what might taste good. Damn, the male was gorgeous. For a human. "And if the two of you dreamwalk, you just might have a chance of finding him. The only chance."

"Sleep is about the last thing I'm going to be capable of when I'm back."

Cuinn waved a hand casually; as Josh's gaze flickered to it, he gestured, and the human froze, unblinking. *I hate to spend the magick, but we don't have time to fuck around.* The arousal that fueled the working of magick was easily come by, he was halfway there already and all he had to do was look this particular male up and down a time or two. Then directly into his eyes, drawing in magick with his breath, and sending it into the mind that lived behind those eyes, into the Fae soul that the human shared with Conall.

Bei tú coladh. Bei tú asling. Gobaidh tú do scair-anam.

You shall sleep. You shall dream. You shall find your soul-share.

The last bit was, of course, pure wishful thinking on his part, since there was no way of knowing what had happened to Conall. The surge of magick he'd felt had been strong enough to burn out a ley nexus. There was no telling what it had done to the Fae that had triggered it.

Another gesture, and he released Josh, who glared at him. "What the hell was that?"

"You're going to forget almost everything you saw and heard here." Cuinn shrugged. "I wanted to make sure you didn't forget the important part."

"You could have asked." Josh rubbed the back of his neck with his free hand. "Damn."

"If there had been any point, I would have."

"More dicking around." Josh's eyes went unfocused; his breath caught sharply. His lips moved silently. *"Conall."* A tear slipped down one of the human's cheeks.

Cuinn cursed softly, almost reverently. *Their bond. Even incomplete, it works between the worlds. Damn.* "He's calling you?"

Josh shook his head, eyes still closed. "No. Yes. He needs me." His eyes opened, and more tears fell free, unheeded. "You have to send me back. Now. He's lost."

Chapter Twenty

Conall, damn it!

The connection was still there. The thinnest thread imaginable, but it was still there. Cruel, only letting Josh feel his lover's terror. *At least if he's afraid, it means he's still alive. Somewhere.*

Josh opened eyes he hadn't realized he'd closed. He'd been doing a lot of the eyes-closed thing, since coming to the Realm. Not that his surroundings weren't beautiful. They were. Too beautiful. So beautiful it bent his brain. *No wonder they say wanderers who get lost here go mad.* Human eyes, a human mind couldn't encompass what was around him. Why he was still sane, he hadn't a clue. No clue except that thread, the one leading back to a love he'd never hoped to find and now might have lost.

The ugliness he saw when he opened his eyes was startling, after all that beauty. Cuinn cursed, kicking at the grass around the two of them, which had gone from brown and withered to limp and matted, and was starting to mold.

"Shit, this is going to be close." Cuinn's gaze was measuring, as he studied the blasted circle, and it was obvious he didn't like the result he was getting. "I'm going to have to tap into the Realm's stored magick directly to open a rift to get you back, I'm not replenished enough yet to do it all myself."

"I don't care how you do it, just do it." Josh was looking at Cuinn, but he wasn't really seeing him. He was seeing thick red-blond hair, fair skin, sensual lips, vivid green eyes. Lips that shaped his name, again and again, and eyes that stared unseeing into darkness. "Right fucking *now*."

"Easy." Cuinn's eyes narrowed, and the grip around Josh's arm tightened. "You can't comprehend the forces at work here."

"I haven't comprehended a goddamned thing since Sunday afternoon at the Pride march." With an effort, Josh kept his voice low and even. "That's not going to stop me from getting Conall back. I'm not going to let it."

Cuinn whistled softly, tunelessly, under his breath. "Is that the SoulShare bond talking?"

"Fuck if I know. All I know is that I love him. I don't care why." *I never believed in love at first sight. But some things are real whether you believe in them or not.* Josh looked pointedly at the hand that still encircled his arm. "I just need to find him. Now."

The Fae grimaced, and closed his eyes. It seemed to Josh he could feel a humming, through his arm. He felt the dragon's wings stir on his forearm, and the brush of the feathers of the hawk on his chest. *I always knew I made magic when I inked, I just never knew what kind.*

A gap opened in the air in front of him, and widened just enough to let him see darkness through it. "Go." Cuinn's voice was barely above a whisper, as if he couldn't even spare the energy to speak. "The longer it's open, the worse the time-slip. And if the *Marfach*'s still there, then at least one of your gods help you."

The hand on Josh's arm urged him forward, but he needed no urging. The gap wasn't wide enough; well, he would make it wide enough. He put his head and shoulders through the rift, bent his knees and braced himself and pushed.

He fell, awkwardly, in the middle of the bed, in Tiernan's apartment. It was quiet—no rampaging monster, thank God—and dark, with only the light from the streetlight on the corner coming in at an oblique angle to light the small, austere space. *Shit. How long...?*

A faint sound behind and above him made him turn; the chime of a tiny bell, or crystal lightly struck. Where he had just come from, there was a momentary swirl in the air, not-quite-light disappearing as though down a drain. Then, nothing at all. As if he hadn't just been standing on solid ground, feeling sunlight, hearing the splash of a waterfall.

He shook his head, swinging his legs over the side of the bed, scrubbing his face with the heels of his hands. No time. He had to find out how long he'd been gone. And he had to find Conall. He surged to his feet—

—and a force equal to his own shoved him back on his ass on the bed. *What the hell?*

You will sleep, Cuinn's voice whispered inside his ear. *You will dream.*

I'm not being left much choice. But that's a good idea. Josh pulled himself back to the middle of the

185

bed, but his feet were still hanging off the edge of the bed when his eyes closed as if the lids were weighted.

***

Fog. He remembered this fog, from the last dream he'd shared with Conall. When he was in D.C., and Conall was here. Did this mean Conall was hundreds of miles away this time, too? *Fuck.* His hands balled into fists. *I'm not giving up.* "Conall?"

He strained to listen, trying not to move, not even to breathe. Nothing that would make noise. "Josh?"

So faint, fainter even than Cuinn's whisper, yet perfectly clear. "I'm here, *d'orant.* I've been to the Realm, but now I'm back. I'm right here." Josh took a deep breath. *You're blithering, you moron. Get a grip.* "I'm in Tiernan's apartment. Where are you?" *Tell me where I need to go, what I need to do, to get you back.*

"I'm lost."

Was he only imagining that the voice was stronger? A little? "Do you know where?"

"So close you could touch me. But I can't get out."

Josh looked around, turning all the way around several times. "All I see is fog, *d'orant.*"

"And all I see is dark. I'm in a maze. But your voice draws me."

"Just like last time." He nodded. "Do you need me to keep talking?"

"Please." The voice still sounded lost, but there was a touch of dry humor to it just the same. "I want you to tell me—" Conall's voice broke off abruptly.

"What?" Even in a dream, Josh's heart raced. "Tell you what?"

"I was going to ask you to tell me what happened to you after you looked down into the basement." Conall cleared his throat, or at least made a noise like it. "But what I really want you to tell me is what we're going to do, once I get my body back." Yes, that was a sigh. "I need hope, *dar'cion*."

"Get your body back?" Josh thought about it, shrugged, set it aside. One more strangeness, in a day filled with so many of them, his mind should have buckled under the strain of them all.

But it hadn't, because of Conall. He wasn't used to having his strength come from someone else; he'd always been the strength of others, and his own as well, when it was needed. He would never ask anyone to shoulder anything he wouldn't carry himself; and if he could carry it, why ask someone else?

He couldn't carry this, though. Everything he'd thought was real had fallen apart when Conall had fallen at his feet. And he needed his Fae lover, the lover he'd never actually taken but needed in order to find his way in what his world had become. "Whatever you need, *d'orant*."

"I thought I'd never hear you call me that again."

"You're going to hear it over and over." Yeah, he felt a little shy, a little stiff; he'd never been particularly into phone sex, and that was what this felt like. But he'd get over it. He'd make it good for Conall. "Listen, lover, let me do this for you. You want to top, the first time?"

"You decide. For now." Josh could actually hear Conall's smile. "You're much more of an expert than I am."

Josh's heart was pounding. "I'll top you. I've

187

been wanting to since I first saw you. Did I ever tell you you're every wet dream I've ever had?"

"You might have. But I don't mind hearing it again." Conall laughed softly. And damned if he didn't sound at least a little closer than he had.

"You are." Even in a dream, he was sweating. "I'm putting you up against a wall. You're naked, I'm in jeans." Josh swallowed. "Your body… God, you're beautiful. Just the sight of you has me hard enough to drill concrete. And with your head bowed, just a little, and your hands spread on the wall to take your weight, you're just screaming *fuck me, lover.*" Josh groaned, softly, adjusting himself.

"Will you?" The hoarse voice was definitely closer. "F-fuck me? The way you want?"

"Hell, yes." Adjusting himself wasn't doing it; he unzipped, freed his length from his jeans, and cradled it in his hand, the potent weight of it hot against his palm. "Until you're screaming my name and pounding the wall."

"I like that thought. Keep going."

"First, I need to get you ready. Make you beg for it. For me, in you." Slowly he stroked himself, his throat working with the pleasure of it. All he had to do was close his eyes, and it was no longer his hand touching him. He could see Conall, feel the Fae's hands glide up the backs of his thighs and grip his ass. Feel hot breath on his cock, and then a long, slow, hot swipe of the tongue that made his hips jerk.

And made his eyes open. *Damn.* But he kept stroking, tugging at the loose skin as it slowly tightened. "I wish you could see this, baby," he murmured. Then, more loudly, "I'm reaching around you, letting my cock rest in the crack of your ass while I take yours in my hand. Gripping you tight." A sudden thought made his breath catch. "Has anyone else ever done even this much for you? Touched you this way?"

"I never dared allow it." A soft, breathless laugh. "Fae are the next thing to asexual until their powers awaken. And when mine did... well, I knew I would never be able to let anyone else arouse me. My magick is—was—too strong. And someone else touching me would only have magnified it."

"Fuck the 'was,' *d'orant*. I'm getting you back. And you're getting your magick back."

"Body first, magick later." More of the soft laughter that seemed to go straight to Josh's groin and caress him like hot velvet. "Keep talking, *dar'cion*."

Josh cleared his throat. Glancing down, he saw the first clear drops beading the head of his cock; palming them, he coated the length of it and continued to play his hand up and down. "I'm touching myself. Like I want to touch you. I'm gripping you hard, around the base. Are you..." Even in the dream, he could feel himself coloring. *Idiot*. "I've only seen you soft. Are you big when you're hard? Small? Not that I care one way or the other," he added hastily. "I just want this to be as real as I can make it."

"I don't exactly have a lot of points of comparison." It sounded as if Conall was trying to muffle his laughter, now. "And I suspect that a direct comparison to the one I do have would be as ill-mannered in the human world as it would be in the Realm."

"So you're bigger than I am."

"I think so."

Josh had never wanted anything so badly as he wanted to kiss that laugh. *Right fucking now.* "Are you any closer to getting out?"

"Yes. I think. It's easier to move. Keep talking. Or…" There came the distinct sound of a throat being cleared. "Make other sounds."

"Jesus, I think I'm going to explode," Josh murmured, his hand tightening around his shaft. "Whatever you need, *d'orant.*"

He worked himself in earnest, now, groaning with each firm stroke of his hand. Still trying to speak, between the involuntary pleasure-sounds. "I can still see you. Waiting for me. Open. Looking back over your shoulder."

"Watching you." The whisper was almost inaudible, filled with longing. "I need to get out of here… I need to see you."

"As much as I need to feel your eyes on me?" Josh's tip was weeping copiously; when the clear trickle stopped, he'd know the fuse was lit and explosion was imminent. "No one's ever looked at me the way you do."

"That can't be. You're so beautiful you hurt my eyes." Conall's whisper cut off abruptly. "I'm out of the maze. I'm out. But I'm still trapped."

"Trapped? Where?"

"Shh. I can see you. Your feet, hanging over the edge of the bed. I can hear you. You snore like thunder."

Josh laughed despite himself. And somehow, the laughing didn't even take the edge off his arousal. If anything, he wanted Conall even more. The laughter made him think of the joy that had nearly buckled his knees in the shower. And thinking of the shower brought him to rigid attention, his cock curved so hard it hurt, a sweet throbbing ache. "Conall." He could barely get the word out.

"*Dar'cion. Lanan.*" A low murmur, all promises. "Let me give to you, this time. And I think… no. *Dóchais laurha, dóchais briste.*"

Somehow, Josh understood. *Hope spoken is hope broken.*

"I'm selfish, this time." Conall's voice was like warm honey, pouring over him. "I want to see you. Kiss you. I'll use my hands, wrap them around your cock…"

Josh's eyes drifted closed, as the soft voice went on, flowing into him, touching him from the inside. He could imagine Conall better this way anyway. His own hand had to substitute for Conall's, but that was all right. For now. Harder, faster. Moans hung in the air, throbbing with the insistent pulse in his shaft; the foggy, swirling air was heavy with his scent, and the memory of Conall's.

"Are you close, *dar'cion*?" Conall's voice was tight, unsteady. "Will my mouth help? On my knees in front of you, your hands in my hair—"

Josh's head fell back and he shouted his pleasure, thick white ropes coating his hand where he gripped his pulsing shaft. Bright white lights were flashing around the edges of his vision, and his knees were going to give out on him any second. *Have to hold on to the dream—please, God, don't let me wake up, don't let me lose Conall!*

Another cry joined his. "*Ta'sair!*" *I'm free!*

Conall was so much closer now, and even panting and dizzy as he was, Josh turned and looked, and turned and looked again. "Where are you?"

"I was trapped in a piece of mirror that got tracked upstairs by the creature that broke it. And now I'm next to the bed. But don't wake up—I don't have a body. Yet. This is the only way we can talk, for now."

Josh leaned forward, braced his hands on his thighs, and tried to get his breath back and collect his thoughts. Of the two, the breath was a hell of a lot easier. "Was that why none of us could find you?—were you here, all along, only without a body?"

"Yes. I saw you, at the top of the stairs." The pain in Conall's voice cut Josh. "And I saw another Fae."

"Cuinn."

"I thought so. Yes. And one other." Conall's voice slowed, caught. "A male. Evil."

Josh wasn't sure if he somehow heard Conall shudder, or if he actually felt it himself. Whichever it was, he shared it. "The *Marfach*."

A long silence followed. "How do you know that name? — are you sure?"

"I'm sure. Cuinn told me."

"*Bod lofa dubh.*"

"You going to tell me what that means?"

"No. I want you to think I'm reasonably civilized."

Josh shook his head, straightened. He couldn't keep himself from looking around again, even though he knew that nothing physical was anywhere near. "You sound so calm, baby."

"Calm?" A short, breathless laugh. "I thought I was going to be trapped in that damned mirror for the rest of eternity. And I'm still trapped, I lost my body when I touched the ley nexus and I can't channel magick to try to get it back. Calm isn't happening, *dar'cion*. Believe me."

"You can't?" What was it Cuinn had said? "Maybe that's why I can. Channel magick, I mean." So hard to think. Conall might not have a body, but that didn't mean Josh didn't know he was there. Right beside him in the fog, and apparently right beside him in the apartment.

"You can *what*?"

"Cuinn says I channel, at least when I'm inking. Some of my tats came alive, a little, when he took me to the Realm to get me away from the *Marfach*. He said the only way it could happen was if I'd been channeling when I inked them." Josh's eyes kept trying to form Conall's image out of the swirling fog; each time, he closed his eyes to banish the illusion. *No. I want the real thing.*

"*Damn*."

Conall's vehemence startled Josh. "What's wrong?"

"If I'd only waited for you to come back, instead of going downstairs and trying to tap into the ley energy myself, I might not have overloaded the nexus. We could have tried to use its energy somehow, with you doing the channeling, to get my magick back."

"Wait." Josh held up a hand and closed his eyes. Something was teasing at his memory. "When I talked to Tiernan and Kevin, before I flew up here, one of them said something about ley energy. And a nexus." He opened his eyes again, staring into the mist. "Under Purgatory. The club that's in the basement of the building where I have my studio."

193

"*Another* nexus?"

"Yes." The excitement in Conall's voice made Josh's heart race.

"Then I have a plan, *dar'cion*."

Chapter Twenty-One

Greenwich Village
New York City

And I thought it hurt when he wasn't here.

Conall followed behind Josh as closely as he could, as the human descended the stairs to the ground-floor apartment. Keeping up was difficult, even though Josh evidently remembered the plan the two of them worked out while the human was still dreaming; take it slow, because a Fae in a physically Faded state moved only a little faster than an eddy of smoke in a gentle breeze. That would soon change, if the plan worked, but for now it was a pain in two asses, one corporeal, one not.

Josh raised a hand and knocked on the door that opened out into the hallway; the door opened to the length of a security chain, and Conall smothered a groan at the sight of Bryce Newhouse's face in the gap.

Josh didn't bother to muffle his own groan, at least not much. "Is Terry home?"

"I thought you were in D.C."

Josh just stared, until Bryce backed down. "Terry has rehearsal tonight. I'll tell him you came by."

"Thanks, but I need to come in. I would rather have talked to Terry."

Bryce's expression darkened, and Conall felt an irrational urge to laugh. He didn't know Terry well, but he suspected the male's small size concealed a very large heart, a trait uncommon among the Fae but one that had been a treasure to discover under the circumstances. Bryce, on the other hand... well. *Other hand? I could have three hands, and I wouldn't want him on any of them.*

"What do you need?" Slowly, the other human stepped back, closed the door enough to slip the chain free, then opened it again.

"Conall left something here. A chain." Josh walked past Bryce, into the apartment.

Conall moved to follow. And froze, stricken, staring at Bryce. It was impossible, but there was magick about this human, too, a small dark knot of swirling, gut-wrenching evil centered on his midsection, but tainting everything about him. Conall had seen that pattern before, in the face of the monster who had smashed the mirror. The *Marfach*.

"Your twink?" Bryce smirked, but under the casual expression there was something else. Almost a hunger.

Conall drifted past the human, careful not to touch, just as the door swung closed. *If the* Marfach *itself couldn't see me when it was forced to use a human eye, there's no way this human can possibly see me. But that doesn't mean I want to touch him.*

Josh apparently decided not to dignify Bryce's dig with a response. "A silver chain, maybe a couple of feet long. Is it here?" He walked down the short, narrow entry hall and into the living room, probably headed for the bedroom at the back of the apartment.

Conall followed, leaving Bryce behind by the door, and hoping the human stayed there. Even if the truesilver of which his chains were forged had gone completely inert, he would still be able to see residual traces of its magick. He hoped. How he would get Josh's attention, if he saw it and his human didn't, was something he hadn't quite worked out yet.

"I haven't seen it." Damn, Bryce was following them. "But if he wanted it so badly, surely he would have dragged his delicate ass down the stairs at some point."

Bryce shut up in mid-syllable as Josh wheeled around, fists bunched and mayhem in his gaze, looking straight through Conall toward the unfortunate financier. "You can shut the fuck up, or you can let me shut you the fuck up. Your choice."

Conall turned just in time to see Bryce backing up, hands raised, palms out, until he bumped into the wall of the hall outside the bedroom, knocking a picture askew. "Calm down, LaFontaine. I didn't realize you were so sensitive."

"Don't push me." Josh's voice was low, controlled. "The *only* thing you have going for you right now is the fact that Terry would be upset if I taught you manners."

What the fuck is he doing? Bryce was watching Josh intently, his hand wandering down to cover the dark knot in his abdomen, almost caressing it, as Josh searched the bedroom. *There's a connection to the* Marfach *there, somehow.*

"So when is your boyfriend going to be moving

out?" Bryce's tone was casual, but the expression on his face made a liar of his voice.

Damn. Don't answer him, dar'cion—

"I don't see where that's any of your business."

Conall would have let out a great sigh of relief, had he needed to breathe. Josh was carefully ignoring Bryce, searching with a quick efficiency that made Conall wonder if he'd done this sort of thing before.

"I happen to live here."

"And so does my landlord, who is letting Conall use the third floor apartment for as long as he needs it. Which is the end of the inquiry as far as you're concerned. Unless you need me to repeat the whole 'shut the fuck up' lesson."

Conall felt a sudden, unaccustomed warmth suffusing him. *He's doing this for me. To protect me. A Fae would have sold me out long before now.* He wanted to put his arms around the human, find some way to thank him. But there was no closing the distance between them, not yet.

Crossing from the bed to the chest of drawers, a shiver ran through Josh; he stumbled, and grimaced, cursing under his breath. Conall cursed right along with him. *A human's body isn't meant to channel. He can't keep this up much longer.* Undoubtedly, being taken to the Realm had made things worse in the long run. Part of him understood Cuinn had been doing the best he could at the time—probably the only thing he could have done under the circumstances. And it might have helped Josh bear the strain a little longer. But he could see the changes in the human, the confusion, the tremors, as the energy that was so utterly blocked from Conall surged through their incomplete bond and sought release. And part of him wanted to pin the cocky Fae bastard to the wall and show him exactly how he felt about conduct that endangered Josh. *We have to finish the Sharing. Soon.*

Conall saw it an instant before Josh did; the betraying glimmer of magick drew his eyes before Josh could see the links beside his foot, from underneath the chest of drawers where his truesilver bonds had been thrown when Josh cut them off him.

Josh bent and caught up the chain, wrapping it casually around his hand and forearm. "This is it." He glanced at Bryce, a small smile quirking up one corner of his mouth. "I'll get out of your hair now. Such as it is."

The other human turned a very interesting shade of dark red. "Tell your pretty boy he needs to get his own key made and give me back our spare." The words were gritted through clenched teeth, and Conall saw a vein pulsing at Bryce's temple as he drifted past after Josh.

"I'll let him know." Josh sounded just the right shade of bored by the topic. Not that that particular key was likely to be capable of being copied—judging from the ward he'd felt on the lock, a key would also have to be keyed to whatever channeling Tiernan had done.

They were back at the door to the claustrophobic entry hall again. Conall had a feeling he was going to be even more spooked by enclosed spaces than the Fae norm for a very long time to come.

Bryce opened the door and held it wide for Josh. "Don't let this hit you in your ass on the way out, LaFontaine."

199

Josh shook his head, but continued at his slow, deliberate pace, to give Conall time to get out as well. Conall had made sure he could pass through solid objects before the two of them came downstairs—the next phase of their plan depended on him being able to do so—but it wasn't a pleasant or quick process, and Conall shuddered at the thought of being shut up in that apartment with Bryce, and whatever Bryce was carrying around with him.

"I'm wagering that would be more action than *your* ass has seen in a while."

Conall, laughing, barely managed to dart through the door before Bryce made good on his threat, or promise, or whatever the hell it had been, and slammed it behind Josh. As soon as they heard the lock shoot home, Josh made for the back of the entry hall, in the sheltered place under the stairs. The Fae followed, all levity fled; if he had a heart, it would be hammering.

Josh set his back to the wall, and held his right arm out in front of him, unwrapping the truesilver chain from around it. The chain glimmered magickally in the half-light from the fixture three stories up, as it dangled from Josh's left hand. As did the dragon tattooed around Josh's left forearm. *Shit. It's getting worse.*

"Conall, baby, I hope you're here." Josh's murmur was barely audible; the human glanced around, grimacing faintly as his gaze swept over and past Conall without a pause.

His lover held his arm out further, and took a deep breath. "Just like we planned it. I'll give you a slow count of twenty, then I'll start. One…"

Don't think about it. Just do it. "Two…"

Conall drifted closer. Closer. He reached out a hand. "Three."

Slowly, the hand disappeared. Into Josh. "Four."

Conall shut out all awareness of the count. He needed to focus. Passing through a solid object had been difficult, and unpleasant, when the solid object was the surface of the bed. But when the solid object was his *Ianan*'s body? *Damn… it feels good.*

But it was slow, torturously slow. *Never going to make it by twenty. Time to try something else.* He withdrew his hand, moved to stand in front of Josh, and carefully backed into him. Letting his lover close around him like a cloak.

"Uh, *d'orant*?" Josh laughed softly, and how strange it was, it almost felt as if Conall were laughing himself. "Screw counting. Is this supposed to be making me horny? Because if it is, it's working."

Now Conall *was* laughing himself, as he worked his way in and held out his arm to mimic Josh's, letting his arm disappear into Josh's decorated flesh. *It's supposed to be the sex that calls the magick, not the magick that calls the sex.*

"Conall?" Josh barely choked off an exclamation, turning a nervous gaze to the door into Bryce and Terry's apartment. "Conall, is that you?" The whisper was harsh, urgent.

I seriously doubt it could be anyone else. For all the light tone of the thought, Conall held his figurative breath, waiting for Josh to answer.

"Sweet bleeding Christ."

The hand Josh held out in front of him was shaking, and Conall could almost feel the magick coursing through him, plucking at his nerve endings, chafing them raw. The magick that should be charging Conall's own body. *Something went wrong when I came through. It must have.* He felt a faint shiver ripple through Josh's body, and groaned. *Dar'cion...*

"Hey. Don't feel bad. It's easier when you're here." Conall felt Josh smile. "Ready to try the chain?"

Do it. We need to get out of here.

Josh nodded, and quickly wrapped the chain back around his wrist and forearm.

Now it was Conall's turn to shiver. Was he only imagining he felt different? Because he expected to? Needed to? If the truesilver was doing its job, if it was binding magick, then bound he would be, and he and his lover off to the nexus in Washington. And if not...

Would it be better to be the *scair-anam* who couldn't die? Or the one who would?

"Hang on to your skivvies. Or mine." Josh pushed away from the wall and took a few quick strides toward the front door.

Conall moved with him.

There are not words for how strange this feels. He was dizzy with relief. And with vertigo, especially when Josh turned and walked back to where he'd been standing, then plowed a hand through his hair. *Now I know how a puppet feels.*

"Sorry."

Conall shook his head. Or tried to. *You have nothing to be sorry for. Just hold still for a minute and let me get used to this.*

"A minute. But we need to get out of here before Terry comes home."

Shit. I forgot. Conall closed his eyes—at least he

could still manage that much, he wasn't dependent on his *scair-anam* in order to blink—and tried to settle himself. He'd expected to feel closed in, trapped. He'd expected to panic, frankly. But he wasn't even close to panicking. He could feel Josh's strength, not quite as if it were his own, and knew himself sheltered.

He had a strength of his own, too, even in his present state, strength he could share. Or hoped he could. The strength to bear the magick. Even if he couldn't channel it, this power was as familiar to him as breathing; it had flowed through him since he came into his birthright. *Let me bear this for you*, m'lanan.

He felt Josh's breath catch hard. *What? What is it?*

Josh's whisper, when it came, was rough; Conall could almost feel the way it caught in his throat. "No one's ever said that to me."

And I've never said it to anyone. Anyone who came close only wanted to take—no one ever waited for him to offer. *Damn.* He wanted to hold, and be held, and in this state he could do neither. *How long is the train ride, again?* Josh had explained airport security, and how unlikely it was that they would make it through without him having to remove the chain and risk losing Conall.

"A little over three hours."

Too damned long.

"Agreed." Quickly, quietly, Josh went to the door, and let himself out into the sultry New York night. "But I'll have you all to myself, for three whole hours. And maybe that will be enough time for you to explain what you are. What I am."

What we are, scair-anam.

Chapter Twenty-Two

Between New York City and Washington, D.C.

"Are you going to be all right, *d'orant*?"

I'll be fine. Especially if you keep looking out that window.

"I can do that. I'm sorry, I didn't realize how hard this was going to be for you."

Neither did I. These train cars are no more enclosed than that hallway outside Terry and Bryce's apartment. I don't know why I panicked like that.

"Maybe it was the thought of getting into something that's going to move? You did mention that you're used to Fading."

Or riding horses. And thanks so much for the reminder—oh, shit, here we go.

"Shh... it's all right, *d'orant*. Would it help if I close my eyes?"

Not really. In fact, please don't.

"I'm sorry. This is going to take some getting used to."

You're telling me. Why is that male in the seat opposite looking at us that way?

"Well, it might be because I'm talking to myself,

as far as he can tell. Or it could be the ink. That's a pretty expensive suit he's wearing, and people in that income bracket tend to frown on what they consider excessive decoration."

I don't think you have to speak out loud. I'm fairly sure I can hear your thoughts.

"If it's all the same to you, I think I'll at least keep moving my lips. I keep trying to make your voice in my head sound like my voice does in my head, and I need some way to tell us apart."

You're taking this remarkably well, dar'cion."

"Only on the outside. On the inside, I assure you, I'm freaking out."

No, you're not. I'm on the inside. I can tell.

"Busted. All right. I'll admit, though, I wouldn't mind understanding what's going on. Cuinn didn't tell me any more than he thought he absolutely had to. Or if he did, I don't remember it. I don't think I remember most of what happened over there."

Not surprising. The human mind can't process magickal energy properly, and it's everywhere in the Realm. Here, you only have to worry about that energy when you're actually channeling it. Which, thanks to me, is more or less all the time, now.

"Are Fae constantly doing… this?"

You might want to keep that arm out of sight, dar'cion. I'm not sure anyone who doesn't have a magickal sense can see what that dragon's doing, but best not to take chances. And no, we don't channel all the time. There's a certain amount of magick a Fae can't help—being able to Fade, the lesser gifts of the Demesnes, that sort of thing. Anything more than that, we have to use, deliberately.

"Like casting a spell?"

I think so. If I'm understanding you correctly. But not exactly. Fae are—I suppose you could say we're made of magick, that's close enough to the truth. Most of the time, channeling just draws on our own innate magick, uses it, spends it. Most Fae can't channel all that much, actually.

"What about you?"

I'm the strongest mage born since my world parted from yours, Ianan. *In the Realm, I channeled so much magick I drained it out of the land and the creatures around me.*

"You're so quiet, all of a sudden."

That talent is why I've always stayed apart from other Fae. Why I've never had a lover. And it's what's hurting you now. Going through the Pattern blocked my ability to channel my magick, and the ability had to go somewhere. So now you're stuck with it, in a body that can't handle it.

"Christ, *d'orant*. I wish I could hold you. Right now."

Your pain is my fault, and you want to comfort me? I may never understand humans.

"This isn't your fault. And you're helping. Having you inside me this way, the magick's easier to bear."

And that's another thing. Even a Fae accustomed to magick would probably be having trouble with sharing a body.

"As long as it's you I'm sharing with, I have no problem at all."

Why do your cheeks feel hot?

"I think I'm blushing. And you laughing isn't helping."

I'll try to control myself.

"No, don't. I like your laughter."

I don't think anyone's ever said that to me before.

"From what you've said, there probably hasn't been much chance for anyone to. You… haven't really been close to anyone, have you?"

Sexually, you mean? No. I can't take the chance. Couldn't.

"Not just sexually. You don't have to be someone's lover to enjoy making them laugh."

I… no. Fae don't love, not the way humans define the word. And we tend not to trust one another, even at the best of times. Factor in the kind of magickal power I wielded—practically everyone I knew wanted to use me, one way or another—and friendship isn't an idea that… what's wrong, dar'cion?

"You don't love?"

Oh, shit. Those are tears. I made you cry.

"Conall, please —."

'Please' nothing. Listen to me, lanan. *Fae are… well, we're fundamentally different from humans. I think you'd probably say we're wired differently. We live a thousand years, sometimes longer. We're never sick, we heal from almost any injury that isn't mortal. And no love can last as long as a Fae's life. We love our blood kin, but even that is more like an alliance than what you humans would call love.*

"I understand."

No, you don't. Because SoulShares are different. No Fae in the Realm knows what this is like, what you and I have. No Fae would even know how to imagine it. Not just this sharing a body. The emotions… they're entirely new to me. What I felt, when the pain of transition let go of me, when I opened my eyes and the first thing I saw was you looking down at me…

"Are *you* crying, now, *d'orant*?"

I'm not sure. I might be.

"Damn. I wish I could hold you."

You are holding me.

"I just made it worse, didn't I? Fuck… is this a bad time to say I love you?"

I don't know.

"I love you."

Dar'cion, all the understanding I have of your language, I get from you. The gift of the Demesne of Air gives me your understanding of your words. And…

"And?"

And I hope someday to have a heart large enough to hold what I see in that word. You deserve that. And more.

Are you all right, lanan? *Lover?*

"Damn. Tell me this plan of yours. What I need to do to help you get your body back. And then your magick. I need you whole."

On further reflection, I don't think I can let you help me with that.

"Like hell you can't."

You might want to lower your voice. I'm not in any position to go teach High Lord Expensive Suit across the way how bad an idea it is to call my lover a paranoid schizophrenic freak.

"I love you even more now. But you can't tell me not to help you."

Íos, I'm not telling you. It's a simple fact. You forget, I can feel what you feel. And I know now what I felt when I first entered you. The magick in you—the

208

magick you're channeling because I can't—is taking the place of whatever is supposed to power the human mind, the human body. The way alcohol takes the place of water in the bloodstream.

"How the hell do you know about that?"

CSI. Sunday night was a long night and some station was running a marathon. Don't change the subject. You were in pain when I first merged with you, and that was when you were channeling a low level of the ley energy. Low because I did something to the nexus under Terry's apartment when I touched it.

"I'm not in pain right now."

Because I can help you with it, being within you, and given that there isn't much ambient magick around. But I'm not sure this plan of mine is going to work. If we were to go back to the great nexus you say is under the club Purgatory, and I left your body, and then you tried to channel the kind of magickal energy it would take to re-form my body...

"We don't have to go all the way to the nexus. And there's one way I've always been able to channel safely."

If I ever have anything to say about it, the Fae are going to have a new saying. 'Stubborn as a human.'

"Don't tell me you're not interested."

Oh, I'm interested. But it's still too dangerous. And if you think my being interested means I'm not going to try to talk you out of it, m'dar'cion, you're living in a dream world.

"I've been doing that since a Fae fell at my feet. Why should I stop now?"

Chapter Twenty-Three

Washington, D.C.

Janek pushed himself up, palms against the cold concrete. Froze, as he belatedly remembered what happened every time he'd tried to do that since he'd finally become solid. The pain shooting down every nerve, like he'd been threaded through with rusty razor wire and someone was ripping it out. And then falling back to the floor, smashing his head a couple of times against the concrete.

This time, though, his arms held him. Slowly, he opened his eye. There was light. A little. Enough to show him his own blood on the ground. *Fuck this shit. Never again.*

For once, I have to say I agree with you, Meat. The male sounded almost jovial. **You need your strength back for what we're going to do next. I'm going to be far too busy to motivate you properly.**

Janek snarled. And caught himself just before falling again. His eye slowly adjusted to the dim light, which turned out to be coming from a telltale next to a lockbox on the wall of the maintenance tunnel he'd been in this morning—was it just this morning?—

when a perfectly good killing was interrupted by whatever had happened in Washington.

"What time is it?" His voice was nothing but a croak, but pissing off his passenger was habit by now. He'd also discovered vocalizing some thoughts made it easier to hide others away. Which was a good thing, since he was having more and more thoughts that needed to be concealed. Such as *if you ever try that again, motherfucker, you will be in a world of hurt. Now that I know that fancy knife works on you.* Didn't matter if he died doing it, being dead would be a fucking walk in the park compared to the hell he'd just lived through.

Do you see a clock down here? There was a sneer in the voice, the kind he'd loved to wipe off faces with fists, back when he'd had the freedom to decide who he beat the shit out of.

"I don't see fucking anything down here." He gritted his teeth against another wave of pain along his flayed nerves. Not as bad as the last few, maybe it was finally going to end. "I just want to know how long I was hanging there like a side of beef in that… place." Not really a place, more like a nothingness, but he wasn't feeling philosophical or poetic at the moment.

A side of beef would Fade far more easily. He could almost hear the female laughing. *It would be slightly less intelligent, and thus need slightly less care. But to answer your question, I believe it has been several hours. Each time I tried to bring you all the way through, there was time slippage; I will have no way of knowing exactly how long it was until you get us out of this tunnel.*

The *Marfach* urged Janek to his feet; it was a

211

slow process, and he needed the support of the wall, his bloodied and battered hands slipping on the slick painted concrete. Once he was up, though, movement was comparatively easy, just a matter of falling forward and not quite faceplanting. Over and over.

Janek tried the latch of the first door they came to, hoping it would give onto stairs back up to the street. Being underground was starting to creep him the fuck out. His battered, bloody, swollen hands would have none of it, though, and he lurched on. Finally, he found a street access with no door, an open stairwell, but this meant he faced narrow corkscrew stairs to street level. A long way to street level, on stairs meant for people with much smaller feet than his iron-soled monstrosities. By the time he finally emerged at the top of the stairs, he was pretty sure his nose was broken. Again. Fucking steel railings. Fucking lack of feeling in his feet. Fucking more or less everything, come to think of it.

It was dark, and well into the night, judging from the lack of traffic. Janek drew up the hood of his hoodie, just the same. No sense taking chances. "Where the hell are we?" He stuck his head out of the recessed doorway, looked right, looked left.

Shit. He'd been disoriented ever since his passenger had compelled him to go down into the tunnels, sometime in the middle of last night. Now he'd come up near the end of a block, and just past the middle of the block, a familiar dark red neon sign flickered. Purgatory. And even if his brain was mostly dead, he didn't need it to remember what it felt like to try to walk through the wards around that place. His body remembered entirely too well.

And fuck if the *Marfach* wasn't trying to force him that way again. He lurched out of the doorway and several steps down the sidewalk before he could stop himself. "Are you fucking insane?" he hissed, glaring at the passers-by who gawped at him. *Look at the crazy homeless dude* was written all over their faces, not that he gave a damn.

Just a few steps more, pet. The bitch was wheedling now, she never called him 'pet' except when she needed him to cooperate and knew he wasn't going to want to. ***You don't have to go inside, I promise.***

When you start promising, that's when I know the shit's gotten hip deep and I need waders. He kept that thought very carefully to himself, and let himself be herded along the sidewalk. Not that he had a choice. Three steps. Four.

Suddenly, the monster in his head was laughing. All three of it, a sound that echoed and bounced off the inside of his skull until Janek was ready to put his head through a wall just to make it stop. And headbutting the brick front of the building he was standing in front of at least got its attention.

Stop that, you moron. The monstrosity seized up his muscles so hard his body started to twist. ***You just passed through Purgatory's outer ward.***

"I didn't feel anything." Janek could barely gasp, the fucker had hold of his lungs, too.

Exactly my point. Just about any sound was preferable to the obscenity's laughter, Janek decided. Although at least it let go of him while it laughed. ***The energy surge I felt earlier, when the lesser nexus was triggered, must have burned out the wards.***

Janek leaned against the wall, trying to get his breath back. Gradually, what the monster said started to penetrate. And when it was all the way in, the thought was like touching a match to gasoline. *I can get at Guaire.*

Precisely. But not in your present condition.

Fuck my condition. Janek turned and started to stagger toward the sex club once again, and roared as he was yanked up short.

Don't tell me you've forgotten what the Noble can do when you piss him off. The Stone in his head throbbed in time with the male's words. **And even without magick, he's a damned good knife fighter. Lethal, in fact. And you, Meat, are likely to find even the stairs down to the club too much of an opponent for you right now.**

Janek's broken nose throbbed, as if driving the male's point home. Which it probably was. "Shut up," he growled, but his heart wasn't in it.

Go back to the doorway. It's hidden enough. Sleep. The male chuckled as Janek started to comply, turning around and stumbling back toward the door. **You sleep, I'll plan. Just for a few hours. Once the club empties out, I'll wake you. And I'll make sure you have enough wits about you to take care of Guaire.**

"Permanently." Janek gained the shelter of the doorway and collapsed in a heap, with barely enough time to pull the hood forward to shroud his ruined face before his limbs went inert.

And as his brain went switch-off, the last thing he heard was the female's dark laughter, and a velvet-soft whisper.

You go on thinking that. Just a little longer.

214

Chapter Twenty-Four

"This is going to be close, *d'orant*."

By now—after better than three hours on the train, and the world's longest cab ride from the train station—Josh had mastered the art of 'speaking' by barely moving his lips. He probably could have gotten by with thinking, at this point, but two voices in his head was one too many. He was having enough trouble telling one set of thoughts from the other as it was.

A tight mental nod was all the response he got for the moment, and a sense that his lover was turning to look out the window of the taxi, as midnight Washington slid past. Both were understandable, given the kind of panic Conall was barely keeping under control. The Fae, it turned out, had a racial horror of enclosed spaces that moved, and a terror of imprisonment running almost as deep, and both of Conall's fears had been honed to a keen edge by the experience of being trapped first in a mirror and then in a sliver of it. Getting onto the Acela had been torment, and getting into the taxi even worse.

Talk to me, dar'cion. *It helped on the train.*

"It helped me, too." Focusing on what was going

on within him helped take his attention off what was going on around him. The distortion of his senses wrought by Conall's magick had stopped being subtle right about the time Cuinn dragged his ass to the Realm, and coming back to a more normal version of reality hadn't helped. In fact, it was much worse. Everything was twisted out of joint; sight was nearly hearing, and touch as close to taste as made no difference. And sounds were a torment, like a belt sander taken to his skin.

You can close your eyes, if you need to. I don't need yours to see through. The one sound he could bear poured over him in a cool wave, easing the pain that wasn't pain, letting him breathe. *I don't want you suffering because of me. Because of my magick.*

Damn. "*D'orant*, when this is over I'm going to take you to bed and just hold you for a week. Until you understand you aren't hurting me."

I will let you hold me until I'm convinced I have a body again. Slightly breathless laughter whispered in Josh's inner ear. *And then you will let me hold you. Until you understand that you can let go, that you don't have to carry it all any more.*

One hot tear trickled down Josh's cheek, and his skin tasted the salt of it.

"This the place?"

The cab driver's voice rasped across his skin as the taxi eased to a halt outside the building that was the home of both Purgatory and Raging Art-On. The tattoo parlor was closed, of course, but the club was doing a brisk business. Steeling himself, Josh pulled his wallet out of his pocket, fished out what he hoped was enough money, handed it over the back of the seat with one hand and fumbled for the door handle with the other. "Thanks."

The sense of relief as he got out of the taxi was like nothing he'd ever felt before, and even knowing most of it wasn't his own didn't make it any less overwhelming. Only the presence of the foot traffic in and out of Purgatory kept him from falling to his knees in gratitude, maybe doing some pavement-kissing.

Well, that and a sense of haste only slightly less urgent than a cattle prod. He fumbled the keys off the hook at his belt and unlocked the deadbolt, then keyed in the combination on the touchpad, wincing as the tiny crystalline tones tried to pierce his eardrums.

Are you sure you can do this, Ianan? *There might be another way. Just let me think, now that I can.*

Josh shook his head. Letting himself into the small client lounge in the front, he locked the door behind himself and made straight for the tattoo studio. "No time. Every minute you're disembodied makes it less likely you'll ever get back, you said so yourself. And me…" He paused, his hand on the doorknob of his studio. "I'm not sure how much longer I can stand this."

There. It was out. It was so hard to say that. But it was true. And he felt a little better for it. He'd always found it easier to banish fear when he looked at it head-on, anyway. Hell, yes, he was afraid. Afraid of not being enough. Afraid of failing the lover who needed him.

No fear for yourself?

Josh's cheeks heated as he realized he'd been overheard. "No point to that, baby. If I fail you, there's nothing here for me."

There was no answer, only the sense of an embrace, and the knob cool under his hand.

Didn't you say Tiernan put a ward on this door? I don't see anything.

"I thought he did. But he's been in and out of here a few times since the break-in, I'm not sure what he's done."

Turning the knob, Josh walked into his studio. He switched on the lights, wincing at the brightness, crossing to the cabinet where he kept his ink. He wouldn't need many colors, not for the design he had in mind.

I hope you don't mind me looking over your shoulder. After a manner of speaking.

The touch of dry humor in Conall's voice was a lifeline, and Josh held on to it as tightly as he could as he collected the inks he needed. Black, a couple of grays, and a touch of white, that would do it. Enough blister packs of needles to get him through the job in one shot, and he was set.

Set. Staring at his machine, the inks, the chair, the soft cloths, as if he'd never seen their like before. *I really am going to make magick, this time.* Or die trying. For Conall.

Josh. Lover.

The quiet voice murmured in his ear, soft as a kiss, implacable as gravity. "Conall. *D'orant.*" He knew what the Fae was going to say. It didn't take telepathy, they'd had this conversation a dozen times on the train. "Please don't try to stop me. I have your magick, and you need it. You can't channel it, it'll kill you to try. And it *probably* won't kill me to channel it."

218

You're not as funny as you think you are, dar'cion.

"Just a fact." Feeling a little self-conscious, Josh stroked his own arm, gently, over the dragon tattoo on his forearm; Conall was in there somewhere, so maybe he felt it. "I've channeled all along, on some level. Tiernan suspected it, just from touching the machine. Then Cuinn took me to the Realm, and there wasn't any doubt any more. I can do this."

But what if I lose you? Conall's voice was subdued. *I'm still learning how to need. I don't want to lose the one I need before I get it right.*

Josh blinked back tears, sat down in the chair next to the padded table, and started unwinding the truesilver chain from around his wrist. "You won't." The chain quickly fell free; turning, he let it slide through his hand, to lie in an untidy coil on the table. "Get clear, lover, neither one of us knows how this is going to work and I'd hate to trap you accidentally."

I could think of worse things than being inside you forever. The Fae's tone was wistful. *But I know, we have to do this. For both of us.*

Was he only imagining, the caress of a hand over his own? The sudden sensation of emptiness that followed? "If you're still here, tell me."

The silence that followed, both inner and outer, was an ache. *Knowing he's here somewhere, invisible, untouchable… hell. I have to get to this.*

Quickly, he set up his pneumatic machine with black ink. He wanted to take shortcuts—he wanted this done—but there was no telling which omission might shatter the magick. So, outlining first.

Carefully, he stepped on the foot pedal. The buzz was loud in the small space, but not unpleasant, the way most other sounds were. *Well, if this is my magick, I suppose that makes sense.*

Normally he'd stretch a client's skin with one hand and ink with the other. No way to do that under the circumstances, though, so he made do, trapping his arm between his body and the table and flexing his wrist hard. The sensation as the needles started to nip at his skin made his breath catch in his throat. Not pain, and not exactly pleasure. Just… right. It wasn't even a touch, not really. A taste, like salt, like sweat, like tears. Like Conall.

The design took shape swiftly, the matte black outline of a chain around Josh's wrist, close kin to the one lying on the table. Even with pauses to blot away the blood that welled up, the basic pattern seemed almost to form itself.

Josh thought he saw movement, out of the corner of his eye, and glanced toward the table. For an instant, it seemed the air danced, like the air over concrete on a baking summer day. But the inking required all of his attention, and he frowned and bent to work again.

Why a chain? Leaning against the seat back, on the Acela, watching the coast speed past, and then his reflection in the glass, he'd become accustomed to the sensation of Conall within him. It was so easy to say you wanted to be closer to your lover than your own skin — well, easy for him to say, though not many of his lovers had shared the sentiment — but now he knew what it was actually like. And he wanted to remember it.

He paused to switch inks. One of the grays, though no tattoo ink could ever capture the bluish cast of truesilver. *Metal charged with living magick*, Conall had called it, as Josh had stared at it, fascinated, on the train. *Metal that knows the purpose for which it was forged.* In this particular instance, chains capable of binding a mage.

Is there such a thing as truegold?

Much rarer. Metal with a purpose of its own. And not always one that it shares with its wearer.

He stepped on the pedal again and started the careful filling process. Almost immediately, he was seized with a wave of dizziness that nearly made him drop the machine. *Shit.* Closing his eyes, he took a deep breath, and then another one; when the worst of it was past, he opened his eyes.

The thin strip of gray he'd managed to ink gleamed bluish-silver under the studio lights. And the dragon on his other forearm was blinking at him.

Fuck. I'm channeling. Josh's heart was hammering so loudly it was odd that the walls weren't giving back echoes. *This is it. Not going to be able to do this for long, not and stay sane.* It was the mind that channeled magick, and human minds weren't equipped for it.

But he had to do it, because this was the only way Conall was coming back. He bit his lip, tightened his grip on the machine, and started in again. Trying to do more of… well, whatever it was he was doing. Imagining a flow of energy coming up from the source underneath Purgatory, entering him, being channeled through the tattoo machine and emerging to ink his flesh and give substance, life, to his Fae lover. Fighting to stay focused, to keep his skin taut, to keep the needles biting into flesh, to keep the color coming. To ignore the inky tendrils of smoke curling from his dragon's nostrils.

A little of this had been happening all along, of

course, ever since he set up shop over the ley nexus. But it had all been art, nothing more. Until a Fae fell at his feet and stole his heart.

There were no other words for what happened. Well, there were a few. Mostly involving other body parts the Fae had laid instant claim to. The heart, though, was the most important one.

Let me bear this for you, m'lanan. Memory whispered Conall's words in his ear, words no one else had ever said to him, in a lifetime of being the strength of others. The Fae had never used the word 'love'—had said Fae *couldn't* love. But those few words, from one who had spent his whole life escaping those who would use him as their tool, spoke exactly the same truth.

Maybe he would go insane, channeling the magick Conall needed. But a reality without Conall in it would be bleaker than the most blasted landscape of madness Josh could imagine.

"Are you there, baby?" His hand threatened to tremble, the one holding the machine; he gripped it more tightly, and kept going. Four links complete, six more to go. No need to fill in more colors, different shades of gray, the magick was doing it all.

"Josh."

The whisper was so faint, he nearly missed it over the whirring of the tattoo machine. His head whipped around, toward the source. At first he was sure his eyes were deceiving him, his rogue senses creating what he needed to see. No more than an outline and the faintest wash of color, red-blond hair, green eyes.

Eyes that turned to him, wild, pleading. "Hurry. I'm… slipping."

Josh's jaw set in a grim line. His grip tightened on

the pneumatic machine; tearing his gaze from Conall's barely visible one, he set to work once again. Gradually, he found himself slumping in the chair; he braced his foot against the leg of the chair, arresting his slide. The dizziness got worse, the more intensely he focused; sweat poured into his eyes, burning, blurring his vision. Only the bite of needle into flesh stayed the same, the slow spread of shining silver-blue.

He could hear Conall's whispers, now, even over the whir of the machine. His warped senses felt the words, they caressed him as sweetly and as lovingly as a hot tongue. Not English, but what Conall had called *Faen*, the Fae language. Words that hovered just at the edge of Josh's understanding. Not a prayer, because the Fae had no gods, he'd said; and not a spell, because channeling magick wasn't like casting a spell; yet it felt like both.

…spára m'anam-sciar ó rochar. Spára a'n'tinn, impi mé lat.

...spare my soul-share from harm. Spare his mind, I beg you.

Jesus. Conall was pleading with the magick.

If the magick heard, though, it gave no sign of it. Josh could feel it now, in some strange way, with a sense he'd never had before today; it rushed through him, a silent torrent that battered his mind, poured into his art and beyond it, and left him dizzy and disoriented in its wake. Except there was never a wake, never a time when the surge had passed, just more of the energy. Almost as if it were being pulled, drawn.

One link left. A flicker of movement caught Josh's attention; he looked up, the needle poised a hair's breadth above his skin.

Conall was slumped against the padded table. He

was clearly visible, yet translucent; Josh could see the table through him. He wore a pair of jeans, a little too large for him, and nothing else. The Fae trembled, and his breathing was shallow and rapid.

"D'orant..."

Conall turned, and the alarm in his vivid green gaze cut through the haze shrouding Josh's thoughts. *"Dar'cion*, you have to stop." The Fae's voice was thin, almost inaudible. "I can see the magick, and you can't channel this much of it. No human could. Hell, most *Fae* couldn't. Only me."

"That makes sense, since I got your magick. And you need me to finish. Simple as that." Josh blotted sweat off his forehead with a forearm, and twitched as he felt the dragon scramble to get out of the way. *Thank God I'm wearing a shirt, the hawk on my chest probably thinks it's hooded. I hope.*

"Not at the cost of your life." Conall's eyes actually glowed, seeming more real than anything could possibly be. "And this will kill you."

God, he's beautiful. "I have to disagree with you." Josh held Conall's gaze with an effort; he had to work to keep his voice even, to keep it from catching in his throat. "But if you don't shut up and let me work, baby, we're going to have our first fight. And right now is a bad time for one."

"Josh, *damn* it—"

"I will do anything for you. Anything except let you die."

Something wrenched in Josh as he looked away. Turned his back. There was no other way to do what he had to do, because if Conall asked him again, he wasn't sure he'd be able to refuse him. Those eyes...

Once more, needles bit flesh, and gleaming metal followed their progress. There was a roaring in his ears now, a crescendo matching the flood of the magick welling up in him. The only parts of him that weren't trembling were the hand holding the machine and the wrist he inked. Those, he held still by sheer force of will. Closer... closer... one more pass of the needles.

SHIT. His vision whited out, a sleet storm of something like static blinding him.

His hand, though, continued to move. Sure, confident. Guided by the magick.

And then the magick was gone.

Silence really can be deafening, was his first dazed thought. After the thunder of a moment before, the sudden quiet felt like someone had taken his head and stuffed it in a sack. And buried the sack.

There was a soft moan behind him.

The machine clattered to the table as Josh lurched to his feet. His muscles protested—how long had he been sitting in the same position in that chair? Who cared? He staggered as he turned, and caught himself on the edge of the table.

Everything stopped. Conall stood before him, holding on to the table for support, his cleanly-muscled chest heaving as he fought for breath. Red-gold hair darkened to near auburn with sweat was plastered to his face and forehead, and his arms quivered with the effort of holding himself upright. And his eyes still glowed, smoldering like verdant coals.

"*Dar'cion...*"

225

Chapter Twenty-Five

The word—*dar'cion*—was barely out of Conall's mouth before Josh was catching him up in his arms and kissing him hard. Conall's eyes went wide, startled, but then he returned the kiss with equal fervor, one arm going around Josh's waist and the other around his neck as their bodies melded together.

One kiss turned into a whole host of them, Josh apparently needing to use his mouth to prove to himself that Conall was corporeal. The Fae's head fell back, too heavy to hold up, or so it seemed, and his human's hungry mouth traveled down his throat like flame licking at wood. He was still having trouble standing, and it was a pleasure to let Josh take most of his weight as he leaned into the human's larger, stronger body. It felt like forever since he'd been able to hold him, and his hands couldn't get enough of the solid warmth in his arms.

"Am I doing this right?" Conall manage at last to raise his head, and pulled back a little, only enough to let him see better. He laughed up at Josh, gently nipping at his chin. "I haven't had much practice at reunions, I'm afraid."

"Quit worrying about whether you're doing it

right. You're perfect." Josh's hands slid down and cupped Conall's ass, pulling him in tight. Conall groaned as his body responded, hardness growing quickly, heat building.

Without warning, Josh staggered. "What the hell?"

"Oh, fuck." Conall used the word with a careful and vehement precision, moving to brace his lover until Josh found his feet again. "It's me. It's my fault." *Magick and arousal... arousal and channeling.*

"No." Josh cut off Conall's attempt to protest with another kiss. It was impossible for Conall to think, with his lover's erection grinding into his belly, the scent of their need for each other hanging in the air like a heavy mist. "Not your fault," the human growled, before taking his mouth again.

Conall wrenched away with a groan, curses *as'Faein* tumbling over themselves in his head. "It *is* my fault. Because I want you. But my magick is still blocked." The Fae's hands slid down Josh's body to his hips, rested there as he marveled at the lean hardness of the muscles. "We have to finish the SoulShare bond."

"Explain to me why this is a problem." Josh's erection strained at the zipper of his jeans, the head already peeking out from the tight waistband. Conall looked down at it, and then slowly back up at Josh, and groaned as he saw the human watching the same thing with an expression that was, if anything, even hungrier than his own was.

"It's a problem because arousal anywhere other than in a dream makes me channel. If I let this happen, I'm not going to be able to help it. I might not even be able to hold off until I come. And it's all going to go straight through you. Like it just did." Conall ached as he looked up at Josh, a real physical ache that amazed him. *Fae aren't supposed to feel like this. Ever.* And yet… the thought of putting Josh through more of the struggle he'd been helpless to do anything but watch as he slowly took form was acutely painful. "I don't know if you can take that. You've already been through too much."

"I have to, *d'orant*. I can't keep going like this." Josh hung his head, almost as if he was ashamed of his words. "I need you to take the magick back." A jaw muscle jumped, his grip on Conall's arms tightened. "I'm sorry."

Conall's time sharing Josh's body had taught him so much, in such a short time, so much about being human, and so much about Josh himself. The male's generosity of spirit was astounding, his willingness to carry the burdens of others nearly incomprehensible. How hard those words must have been for him.

"You have nothing to be sorry for." Conall touched Josh's chin, tilted his head up. "You didn't ask for this." *I have to do this. I have to finish the bond. But I can't harm him in doing it.* Hesitantly, he touched his lips to Josh's, then with more assurance, when the kiss was returned. Josh's tongue slipped into his mouth, searched it, twined with his; Josh's hands closed around his upper arms, drawing him in.

Conall took a deep breath, caught Josh's lower lip between his teeth, worried at it. *I'm the one who's supposed to know what the hell's going on here, I have to be the one to make it work.* "Touch me as much as you can, *dar'cion*. I'll try to draw off some of the energy."

"Now there's a fucking hardship." Josh laughed softly. His hand dropped to the button of Conall's jeans, and the light caught the impossible chain around his wrist, gleaming off metal that couldn't possibly be there.

Then the hand undid the button, and Conall forget all about tattoos, impossible or otherwise, as Josh reached inside and closed his hand around his semi-hard shaft. His hips jerked, and Josh unzipped the jeans and let them fall to the floor, always keeping the other hand curled around him.

"Damn." The dragon curled around Josh's forearm blinked at Conall's lengthening cock, its gaze inscrutable. *It's a good thing we aren't trying this at the nexus itself.* The thought of what would likely happen to Josh's amazing images if the human were forced to channel right at the source of the magickal energy drew a grimace from him, one that went unseen against Josh's shoulder. Josh stroked him, murmuring softly, without words, and Conall groaned.

And when Conall groaned, a shudder rippled through Josh. Conall's head jolted up; his heart raced. *"Dar'cion?"*

Josh shook his head. "It's all right—oh, fuck."

No need to ask what Josh was cursing at, not when Conall could feel his shaft softening in the human's grip, and when he knew the reason for it. His own fear. "I can't, *m'dar'cion*. Not knowing that it harms you."

For a very long moment, all was still. Then Josh stepped back—not far, maybe half a pace, leaning back against the padded wooden table—and looked him up and down, slowly and intently. In that gaze Conall saw heat, confusion... and laughter?

"Yeah, that's probably part of it." Yes, that was definitely laughter, of a quiet, rueful sort. "But that's not all there is to it." He shook his head. "You've just been through probably the most terrifying experience of your life, am I right? Being trapped?" He waited for Conall's nod. "You haven't had a body for most of the last twenty-four hours, you've been stomped on by a fucking golem, and we both know how much you enjoyed the train ride up here."

Conall blushed. He'd hoped that Josh had forgotten about those moments of total panic when they boarded the Acela. "Your point?"

Josh reached for Conall's hand, held it gently. "You finally have your body back. And all of a sudden, you're expected to lose your virginity—and hurry up about it, there are two lives on the line here, get with the program! Wham, bam, thank'ee, sir. Right here in a tattoo parlor, which is sexy as all hell."

"You're lucky I've figured out human sarcasm." Conall was smiling too, now, but the smile faded. Still holding Josh's hand, he met the human's gaze. "You're right. About all of it. But I would be very pleased to complete our SoulShare here." He stepped closer, letting the human draw him in. "This is your place—this is *you*." Even when Josh hadn't been able to see him, he'd been able to see perfectly well, himself; the joy in his *lanan*'s eyes, his face, joy shining through even when Josh's mind was overwhelmed by the magickal energy flowing along the purely human channels that were never meant to carry it. It was a sweet echo of the delight he'd seen in those eyes in the shower, as Josh had succumbed to the power of the awakening bond.

The delight in Josh's eyes now told Conall that he'd managed to say the right thing. "Can we try this again?" Josh murmured, just before his free hand came up to cup the back of Conall's head and hold him still for a long, slow kiss. "To hell with what we *have* to do. I've wanted this since I first saw you. Just to hold you like this."

No Fae would ever say anything like that. Conall's eyes closed as Josh's kisses wandered from his lips to his cheekbones to the line of his jaw. No Fae would be content just to hold someone, no Fae would be satisfied with anything less than a partner's careful attention to his or her pleasure. That was what one chose a partner for. The dance of pleasure. Never for whatever this was. Intimacy.

There wasn't even a word, *as'Faein*, for the way Josh was making him feel. *Reverence* was also a word foreign to the Fae, one he'd learned in the human world. One Josh was teaching him the meaning of now, caressing his restored body, coaxing it to a kind of life it had never known. And no word for the yearning he felt, the need to give back.

"God, you're beautiful. There's just no other way to say it." Josh's voice was tight, his breathing irregular. His hands explored Conall's body as if they'd never touched before, as if the human had to learn his body all over again.

Conall's eyes snapped open at this. "*I'm* beautiful? Have you never looked in a mirror, *m'dar'cion*?"

"The ink is a gift, a talent, it's not—"

"Fuck the ink." Now it was his turn to reach, to touch, to caress. To try to figure out this strange business of cherishing, as he traced the planes of

Josh's face with his fingertips, and felt the rush of arousal that flooded him as Josh's eyes widened, darkened. Soul was calling to soul, and the bond abhorred the space that still separated them. "*You* are beautiful. And I want to take you. No, I *need* to."

After centuries of desperate self-denial, how strange it felt to speak those words. But they were true, and they only became truer as Josh nodded, bent to browse kisses along his cheekbones. He could feel Josh's hands moving, at his own waist, making short work of button and zipper, and somewhat longer work of getting out of his much tighter jeans. Terry's had been loose enough on Conall to fall; in the end, he had to help Josh out of his, groaning softly as his hands slid back up hard-muscled thighs to curve around the human's taut, firm ass.

"Do you have any idea how sexy that is?" Conall felt Josh's lips moving against his ear, and then the tug of teeth in the curve of it. "Knowing how touching me does that to you?"

Conall's nostrils flared as he drew in a deep breath. His cock was stirring again, growing, hardening, pressing against the crease of Josh's thigh. Something else was stirring, too, something deep in the half-soul the Pattern had left him with. Something was seeking the rest of itself. "Am I hurting you?"

He didn't really want the answer to his question, because if he was harming Josh, there was no way he could continue. And he needed more. He needed his *scair-anam*. Not for the sake of getting his magick back, not to experience the pleasure he had already given Josh but had never felt himself, but to be whole.

I was broken before I ever went through the

Pattern. He shivered as Josh's tongue circled his ear. *I never dared to let anyone come this close. I had no idea how broken I was.*

"You're not hurting me." Josh's hips moved against him, in a slow, steady, demanding rhythm; soft lips and a hot tongue ran down his throat to his shoulder. "I can tell you're aroused. I can feel it."

"I should hope so." Conall barely kept from groaning from the sensation of his hard cock trapped between his body and his lover's by Josh's insistence.

"Smartass." Dark eyes glinted at him, laughing, as Josh raised his head. "I can feel the ley energy. The magick. But when it gets to be too much, I just look at you. Like this." Josh took Conall's chin between two fingers, held it, his own parted lips just a breath away.

"Then keep looking at me." His lips teased at Josh's, his tongue flicked out and traced around their tantalizing fullness. "Don't stop. Though I had such plans…"

"Oh, really?" The palm of Josh's other hand flattened against Conall's lower back, warm, possessive. "Such as?"

"You made it sound so real, in our shared dream, when you talked about taking me." Conall was fully erect, now, and he could feel wet warmth trickling down the side of his cock; he glanced down, and the sight of his proud organ pressed between his body and Josh's inked abs made him clench his teeth against a groan. "I wanted to do that. Turn you around, bend you over this table, and do my best to make you teach me some new curse words."

"Once the bond's completed, I promise I'll let you have your way with me, baby." Josh's slow smile heated Conall all the way to his suddenly curled toes. "But I know what I want to give you this time. Exactly what you gave me."

Conall needed the support of the table again. "Fuck," he whispered.

Josh nodded. "Just lean back and enjoy, lover." He kissed the Fae once, hard, his lips parting Conall's and his tongue sweeping through like hot velvet; he groaned into the kiss, though, and shuddered, and quickly pulled back, his gaze locking with Conall's again. "I am so going to enjoy being able to kiss you like I mean it," he growled.

"I'm going to need to be sitting down."

"Sitting, hell, you're going to be horizontal and spread for me." The human's smile held more promises than the Fae had ever seen in one place. "Now be quiet and let me work."

Feeling suddenly weak in the knees, Conall leaned back and braced his arms against the padded table. Those arms started trembling as Josh mouthed his way down his throat, his chest. By the time the human reached his hard and well-defined abs, he was fighting to keep from gasping for every breath. He wanted to hold still. Wanted to savor this. Josh was right. *To hell with what we* have *to do.* He needed this male, who was going slowly and gracefully to his knees in front of him. And Josh wanted his pleasure, in a way no one ever had before.

"My senses are still fucked up." Josh's lips moved against the sensitive skin of Conall's groin, just above his thatch of red-gold hair; Conall felt the heat of his breath, and his cock jumped, twitched, scattering clear drops. "And it's amazing." The human's tongue curled out, barely missing the base of Conall's shaft and playing in his curls. "I can't describe it. The taste of you is like running silk between my fingers. Or letting it fall over my cock. So gentle, but so strong."

"I want to do that for you." Conall couldn't make his voice rise above a whisper. "Play with you that way." *So many things I've never been able to do. I want them all.*

"Anything you want." Josh's voice was almost a purr. Then his mouth found Conall's shaft, and if there was any more purring, Conall couldn't hear it over his own moans.

He wanted to tip his head back, close his eyes, to focus on the tongue and lips exploring his cock. But Josh needed him to watch, so watch he would.

Fuck. This is going to last about ten more seconds. Conall clenched his teeth as Josh ran the flat of his tongue up the underside of his curved-hard shaft, cupping his balls with one hand. Then a gasp was followed by a string of sibilant curses *as 'Faein*, most of which Conall had once been sure he would never have occasion to use, as one fingertip lightly stroked behind his balls.

Josh's smile was wickedness personified. "You like the taint. Good to know. Next time we'll see if you like it licked."

Conall reached down and worked his fingers into Josh's hair, fisting it as tightly as he could. "*Scílim g'fua lom tú, dar'cion.*"

"And that means?"

"I think I hate you. *Dar'cion.*"

Josh laughed. The laughter rippled down Conall's spine; his cock throbbed, wept, ached. His breath caught hard. He had felt an echo of this sensation before. In the shower. When he had been the one kneeling before a lover, trying everything he could think of to pleasure him. Josh's moans, his cries, had been equal parts passion and delight, and that joy had reached out to draw a Fae into its embrace.

I wonder if it has to be this way. Finding the bond the same way, both of us. Hesitantly, Conall urged Josh closer with the hand in his thick dark hair, even as he clutched more desperately at the table with his other hand. "Please."

"What a beautiful sound." Josh swirled his tongue around the head of Conall's cock, kissed it gently, licked away the clear beads that formed one after another. Conall watched, entranced, as Josh let himself be pushed, took Conall's length in his mouth, teased the nerves below the head with his tongue as he sucked hard, his cheeks hollowing.

Josh's eyes drifted closed, his expression blissful; instantly he jerked, groaned, shuddered, and his eyes opened wide again. Immediately, his gaze went to Conall's; his hand curled around the Fae's long shaft as his mouth released it with a soft pop. "Oh, no you don't, *d'orant*."

"I don't what?"

"Shut down because I forgot myself for a second." Two fingers, now, stroked between Conall's balls and his tight entrance. "You're so close you're shaking. I'm not letting you go this time."

Conall nodded tightly. Easing his legs farther apart to give Josh better access, he groaned harshly as his *scair-anam* accepted the invitation with a finger plunged deep into virgin darkness.

Yes, he was shaking. But not with need. Or not with need alone. He couldn't get his breath, his knees nearly buckled as Josh's hot mouth took him deep one last time.

Joy. A bliss so intense he thought his bones might melt from it. His hand clenched tight in Josh's hair, and a cry was ripped from his throat as he curved and went iron-hard and then pulsed and shot thick jets down his lover's open and eager throat.

Conall felt Josh's mouth, moving on him. His tongue, soft yet demanding. The suction drawing the last of his seed from him, but not the last of his pleasure. The dizzy ecstasy was unlike anything he'd ever even known how to imagine, and he was beginning to think Josh was never going to let it stop.

A hand stroked the inside of his thigh. Josh was still trying to find new ways to pleasure him. Even after... hell. Even after a heart-stopping climax, and soul-searing joy, his *scair-anam* wanted to give him more.

"Are you all right?" Conall's words sounded flat, pedantic, after the rapture that had gone before them. But he had to know. Getting his magick back would be wonderful. But Josh's freedom would be *beyond* wonderful.

What kind of Fae was he, now, to be putting a human's needs before his own?

A SoulShared Fae.

Josh sat back on his heels, looking up at Conall. "Jesus. Did it feel like that for you, when you did that for me in the shower?" The human's eyes were glazed, unfocused; then he shook his head, and laughed softly. "Shit."

Conall stroked Josh's hair, gently, but possessively. *My* scair-anam. *Mine.* "If it felt almost as good for you as it did for me, then yes. But what I meant was, are you still channeling?"

Instead of answering, Josh staggered to his feet, and held out his hands. The dragon on his left arm was quiet; the chain around his right wrist, while beautifully detailed, no longer gleamed with the sheen of metal. "I think things are back to normal." His gaze caught Conall's, his eyes dark and inviting and intelligent. "As close to normal as they're ever likely to get again, anyway."

Conall's breath caught in his throat. No pretending he didn't know what Josh meant. *He's talking about a lifetime.* "You're going to need to teach me everything." He took the hands that were being held out to him, gripped them firmly. "Fae suck at relationships." *And how am I saying this, when I've never even said I love him? When I'm not even sure I can?*

Josh grinned. "Well, I'm obviously already teaching you vocabulary."

"Seriously." Conall tightened his grip on Josh's hands. "Not to mention the fact that I've been so fucking alone for so long, I don't know how to be with anyone. Human, Fae, or houseplant."

Note to self: keep making my lanan *laugh.* Josh was still chuckling as his mouth settled over Conall's, and the Fae was startled to discover a kiss could in fact taste like laughter.

Until the phone rang. No, until the *motherfucking* phone rang. At least, Conall was reasonably sure it was the phone. He couldn't think of any other reason why Josh's discarded jeans would suddenly be informing him that they were too sexy for their shirt.

"Fuck, it's Tiernan." Josh released Conall and snatched up his jeans, digging the phone out of the pocket and putting it to his ear, his arm slipping back around Conall's waist as he did so. "Don't take this the wrong way, Tiernan, but I hope this is an emergency."

"You might say that." The preternatural hearing of an Air Fae had no difficulty hearing the other end of the conversation. "Where are you?"

"In the tattoo parlor."

"Have you and your boyfriend managed to finish your bond yet?"

Conall's eyebrow shot up; Josh's arm tightened around him. "Yes. All's right with the world. Why?"

"No, it isn't." The other Fae's voice sounded strained. "I'm assuming he's there with you. Ask him what Demesne he is—no, shit, ask him if he can channel."

Gently, Conall took the phone from Josh, and put it to his own ear, in careful imitation of the human. "This is Conall Dary. Of the Demesne of Air, and exiled from the Realm for refusing to turn the greatest channeling power since the Sundering to serve a Noble's petty desire for revenge. What do *you* need?"

There was a moment's silence. "Fuck me. Ask, and ye shall receive."

"I don't understand."

"You don't need to. Just get the hell downstairs, and bring Josh with you. Whatever you did in New York sent a surge of magickal energy down the ley lines to the nexus here, and I just found out that it fried every ward I had around the place."

"This is my problem why, exactly?"

A snarl carried perfectly over the phone. "Because I can't get mine back up. And unless you want the *Marfach* figuring out how to torture your *scair-anam* until you surrender to him, I strongly suggest you haul ass down here and figure out a way to keep it off the premises."

Chapter Twenty-Six

Just keep putting one foot in front of the other, Meat.

"Not like I have a whole lot of fucking choice, is it?" To hell with worrying about being overheard, no one was on the streets at the ass crack of dawn. Speaking aloud kept the monster distracted, gave him space for the thoughts that could get him killed. No, probably not killed, not yet, but seriously wishing he was dead.

Motherfucker doesn't care if it kills me. The *Marfach* had woken him after only a few hours of sleep, and forced him back down into the tunnels. Because he'd dropped the fucking knife. The one he'd stolen from Kevin Almstead, on the last night of his life. His old life. The stairs, the tunnel wouldn't have been much, back then. Now? When he could barely feel his feet and kept crashing into walls when his goddamned passenger got distracted? At least he'd been able to find an access stair he could use right after he got the fucking knife back, this time. Kicking down a door had been a walk in the park, next to that hike through the tunnels. Once he offed Guaire, he never wanted to set foot underground again.

Choice? Laughter. *None at all.*

The male was too damned cheerful. Janek tried to force what was left of his mind away from the pleasant image of throttling the horny son of a bitch, but it didn't really want to go. "So what happens when we get there? We just walk in?"

If you move your ass instead of wasting time talking, yes, we should get there just before the club closes at four. Guaire should still be there. He's not trusting enough to let anyone else close up for him.

"And he's just going to let us walk in there and kill him?"

The silence in his head said it all. *Once I have done what I need to do, he will have very little choice in the matter,* the bitch finally replied.

You're lying through your teeth. But that's all right. Things aren't necessarily going to go the way you think they will.

Janek nearly fell as his feet stopped moving. He was back where he'd started, just a couple of steps away from the recessed doorway leading down into the Metro maintenance tunnels, the one where he'd slept those precious few hours. Someone else rested there now, a grizzled derelict, probably sleeping it off after getting shitfaced at one of the dive bars around the corner.

You're early. You need to hide.

Janek felt his body being turned toward the doorway. Yeah, the old fucker was sleeping it off, he had DTs and the scent of the cheap booze on him was strong enough even Janek's mostly dead nose was curling up from the stink. "Find me someplace else."

Here. The tone was cool, the bitch's "don't dick with me or I'll feed you your balls without breaking a sweat" voice.

242

Janek shrugged. Drawing the knife out of its makeshift belt sheath, he bent and drove it up under the drunk's ribcage, working it around until he was sure he'd found the heart. Once he was satisfied, he sat down heavily on the opposite side of the doorway, wiping the blade on his jeans.

Was that really necessary?

"Just getting warmed up."

Chapter Twenty-Seven

Josh took the stairs down to Purgatory two at a time, weaving between customers who were on their way out. Conall was right behind him, cursing softly in an interesting mix of *Faen* and English and something Josh had to assume he'd picked up on community access television.

The club was nearly deserted; the bar was closed down, the lights were down on the dance floor and up in the cock pit, and Lucien the bouncer was rounding up the last few straggling customers, notable for their lack of both sobriety and clothing. Josh looked around, expecting to see Tiernan in the doorway to his office. Instead, he spotted him at one end of the bar, standing next to a door that Josh assumed led to a storeroom.

"That's him?" Conall murmured, stepping around to stand beside him.

His lover's carefully neutral expression surprised Josh. "Yes, that's Tiernan. Is something wrong?"

"Hopefully not."

Conall fell silent as Tiernan gestured to them. As they crossed to the bar, Josh noticed Tiernan's expression was almost a mirror image of Conall's—

alert, wary, and in a lot of ways reminding Josh of a guard dog keeping a close eye on a masked stranger.

"Your Grace."

Tiernan's eyes narrowed as Conall spoke. "How the fuck did you know?"

"I felt the elemental wards you left in the apartment in New York. And yes, by the way, I *am* Conall Dary, a pleasure to meet you too, and thanks so much for asking me to save your ass from evil incarnate."

Josh's mouth dropped open slightly. *Who are you, and what have you done with Conall?* he nearly blurted.

"I don't like to be called that." Tiernan almost looked embarrassed, except that Josh couldn't imagine anything embarrassing him, not considering the goings-on down here on a more or less nightly basis. "Bad memories. I'm just Tiernan, this side of the Pattern."

Without waiting for either Conall or Josh to respond, Tiernan turned on his heel and walked through the door, gesturing for them to follow.

Josh fell in immediately behind him, then glanced back when Conall was slow to follow. His *scair-anam* was staring through the open door, one hand half-raised as if to shield his eyes. "Something wrong, *d'orant*?"

"It's so bright."

Josh blinked, puzzled, but had to turn to follow Tiernan down a flight of steps into near-darkness before the other Fae disappeared around a corner at the bottom. Conall followed after him, his bare feet nearly soundless on the stairs; the lower they went, the more Josh felt the hair rising on his forearms, and on the back of his neck. *I guess I can still feel the magick, a little, even now. Either that or I'm freaking myself out.*

The storeroom was small, and crowded, and dimly-lit; Tiernan was already unlocking another door in the far corner of it by the time Conall came down the stairs, using both a touch-pad and an elaborate key. The door swung wide, and Josh caught a glimpse of an even smaller room, with a black leather chaise in the middle of it, before his attention was drawn away from it as Conall flinched.

"You mind if I do something about that?" Conall was obviously speaking to Tiernan, even though he wasn't looking directly at the other Fae, who was framed in the doorway to the other room.

"Just don't short it out like you did the other one. We need this one."

"Fucking Nobles," Conall muttered. Then he closed his eyes; drawing himself up, he took a deep breath, and gestured.

For an instant, Josh's vision blurred, but the moment was past so quickly he almost didn't have time to notice it. And when Conall's eyes opened again, his relief was obvious. "That'll do for now."

"I can barely see the lines." Tiernan was leaning into the smaller room, staring at the floor. "You sure you didn't fuck something up?"

"Bite me, your Grace."

This is going to get ugly. Josh moved closer to Conall, reached for his hand.

Tiernan grunted, then stepped aside and motioned for Josh and Conall to enter the smaller room. There wasn't much more to be seen on the inside than there had been from the outside; just the black leather chaise, which on closer examination looked to be from the same set as the sofas and loveseats and chairs in the cock pit upstairs. And which, strangely enough, had what looked like large iron staples set into the head and the foot. No, not looked like, were. And there were padded cuffs hanging from them. *Shit.*

Conall was looking at them too, his lower lip caught briefly between his teeth. He turned to Tiernan, still holding Josh's hand. "This is how you ready yourself to tap the ley energy?"

One corner of the other Fae's mouth quirked up in an incredibly sexy smirk. "That's one use for them."

Conall turned back to Josh, and the sudden flare of heat in the Fae's verdant gaze brought a flush to Josh's cheeks and sudden, vehement life back to his cock. "Will you do that for me?" Conall's whisper was hoarse, and his grip on Josh's hand tightened. "If I need it?"

"Christ on a crutch." It was cool, down here below ground, maybe the only place in Washington that was cool right now, yet sweat prickled Josh's forehead and gleamed on the intense colors of his inked chest. "Whatever you need."

Tiernan cleared his throat. "I wasn't aware that great and powerful mages labored under the same magickal restrictions as the rest of us."

"Bite me someplace else, and if you need a picture or directions I'll be glad to oblige." Pointedly ignoring the other Fae, Conall studied the floor. "If I want to tap into this kind of power, I have to be just as careful as any other Fae." He drew the toes of one bare foot carefully along the floor, as if tracing—or skirting—a line Josh couldn't see. "I take it the nexus itself is directly under the chaise?"

"You take correctly, though we can shift the furniture if we have to. And it's aligned along the Earth line, since that's what I use. I try not to tap into the raw energy except in cases of dire emergency." Tiernan's crystal hand clenched briefly into a fist.

"An unexpected level of wisdom, from a Noble." Conall sounded distracted; his gaze went from Tiernan's hand to the walls, the ceiling, back to the floor. "You had this warded with Earth? I can still sense traces of it."

"You *must* be the greatest mage since the Sundering. You're certainly the most fuck-all irritating. Of course I warded with Earth, I can't do shit with living magick unless I'm in a total panic."

"Does the *Marfach* know this nexus is here?"

"It came from there, that's where it's been living for most of the last two thousand years."

Conall's head tilted as he regarded the other Fae with a cool curiosity totally at odds with his disheveled appearance—there hadn't been time for much in the way of tidying up after Tiernan's phone call, just throwing on jeans and racing down the stairs. "But this energy isn't living magick."

"No shit, Sherlock. The *Marfach* is pissed to the wide after living two millennia on the equivalent of sawdust and water." Tiernan grimaced, and to Josh he appeared almost embarrassed. "And before you shove a stick up my ass again, it got out because I tapped into the ley energy to boost my powers when a defective dickhead who used to be a bouncer here tried to kill my *scair-anam*, and I accidentally turned half his head to living Stone when I drilled through his eye socket with the stuff while I was supercharged."

"That was a piece of—" Conall's mouth closed

firmly on whatever it was he'd been about to say, and his eyes met Josh's. "No. No, it wasn't. You did what you had to do, with your *scair-anam* at risk." His hand turned in Josh's, his grip tightening. "And it could be worse, I suppose. If it's confined in so little living magick, it's not at full strength. Which is why you're still alive, I'm sure."

Tiernan snorted. "Nice save, you were in danger of not being a total asshole there for a second."

"For someone who needs me to cover his ass, you're not exactly going out of your way to make me feel welcome."

"For someone directly responsible for trashing the wards in the first place, you're not—"

Josh cleared his throat. "Could the two of you possibly save the pissing match for later? I think we have other things we need to be doing."

Conall, at least, looked slightly abashed; Tiernan merely smirked and crossed his arms. "Do I get to watch?"

"For the third time, bite me, Noble." Conall jerked his head toward the door. "You want me to clean up your mess, get out of here and let me do it."

Tiernan shrugged. "I'm just going to go up and make sure everything's cleared out upstairs. A minimum number of explanations later would be nice. And I'll wait for Kevin. I called him after I called the two of you." He stepped through the door, and moments later Josh heard feet going up the stairs.

Conall sat down on the chaise with a sigh of what sounded like relief. "That could have been worse."

"Oh, really?" Josh quirked a brow. "Do all Fae get along that well?"

"This side of the Pattern? I have no idea. But the reason I'm here at all is because I was betrayed by a Noble lady who was pissed I wouldn't play her little game of *a'gár'doltas*. Vendetta, I suppose you'd say." Conall looked up as Josh sat down beside him, the sharp set of his jaw softening somewhat. "I did warn you that I suck at relationships. And a big part of that is a near total inability to work and play well with others."

As casual as the words were, there was still a note of sadness in Conall's voice that tore at Josh. *Fae don't love.* Conall's words on the train echoed in him. Did the Fae still believe that? Even after what had happened upstairs?

Could it be true?

Fuck, no. "None of those others were your SoulShare." Josh took Conall's hand in both of his. "We'll make this work. Hell, I haven't waited this long to be able to touch you only to walk away."

Slowly, a light came into Conall's eyes, a light Josh remembered from shared dreams, and from perfect moments of mutual mind-blowing delight. "Help me put up this ward, *dar'cion*. And then…" Conall reached out a hand, ran the backs of his fingers over Josh's stubbled cheeks. "You have a great deal to teach me."

Josh caught at the hand that caressed him, clasped it tight. Looking over the Fae's shoulder, he spotted the padded leather cuffs, dangling from short and sturdy-looking chains. "You said you might want those? The cuffs?"

He felt a shiver run through the Fae. *He feels so delicate. But when he was inside me—I've never known anyone that strong. Never imagined anyone could be that powerful.*

"I think I would feel safer that way. Free. To let go." Conall coughed, softly. "You know I've never really been able to. And to channel the kind of energy that's under this floor, I'm going to need to be aroused well beyond anything I've ever let myself feel before." He smiled, finally, a small and secret smile. "I need you to take me where I can't imagine going, *lanan*."

"I would have to be three days dead to turn down a request like that." Just Conall's smile was making Josh's jeans uncomfortable. He needed to kiss those lips, so he did, leaning into the Fae and bearing him back to lie on the chaise, pinned under him.

Opening Conall's mouth with his own, he searched the Fae's mouth with his tongue. Conall moaned, and turned the search into a duel, as eager to explore as Josh was himself. That eagerness almost made Josh forget what he was supposed to be doing. Almost, but not quite. One hand slid down Conall's arm, catching his wrist and drawing the arm up over his head, never breaking the kiss. Conall obligingly left it there as Josh groped for the cuff on that side, found that it was open.

Oh, shit. Keys?

As if reading Josh's mind, Conall laughed. The sound was like nothing human. It was wild, ephemeral; it stung, it sparkled. Magick. And it was erotic as all fuck.

"I can get out, *m'dar'cion*." Teeth nipped Josh's earlobe. "No keys necessary. Any Fae could. Either Tiernan allows himself to be bound, or the bonds are a gift for his human."

Josh groaned in blissful pain as his cock informed him it wanted out, *now*. Clenching his teeth, he managed to open the cuff one-handed, guided Conall's wrist into it, and felt the clasp click home.

Conall tugged, experimentally, at the bound wrist, as Josh did the same with the other cuff. "I like this already." He rose up, straining at the bonds, for another hot kiss; then Josh started sliding down his body, and he let his head fall back with a groan.

The Fae's brick-red shaft was already halfway out of the slack waistband of his jeans by the time Josh reached it. Josh took the head into his mouth, swirled his tongue around it as he undid the button and the zipper of Terry's borrowed jeans, and was rewarded with a throbbing, a taste like musk and honey at the back of his throat. Reluctantly, he released the already-rigid organ and moved back to pull Conall's jeans the rest of the way off.

"Take yours off too." Conall's gaze was fevered, glittering. "I want to see."

Damn, he's almost there already. "Is this what they call topping from the bottom?" It came out a lazy drawl, but Josh's heart was racing. "Maybe I should make you wait."

Josh ran his tongue up the inside of Conall's thigh, broad and flat, doing his best to ignore the Fae's anguished groan. *I have no idea what I'm doing, I'm no fucking Dom.* He traced with his tongue the sensitive crease where hip met thigh, licked his way down until his tongue skimmed the Fae's heavy globes.

"Please." He could barely hear Conall's whisper. "You promised."

Josh looked up at this, past the weeping cock that strained up in front of him. And smiled, slowly. *I know what he wants.* "Beg me, *d'orant*."

"Shit." The chains rattled, Conall's hips jerked, clear drops scattered from the head to fall on the Fae's heaving abs. "That's perfect... more. More."

"That's not begging." Nice, long, slow lollipop lick, all the way up, that sweet honey-musk trickling down onto his tongue.

Conall grunted and yanked against at the chains. "Almost there..." The words were distorted, and spoken with a thick accent Josh remembered from the first hours after Conall's arrival. "Please, *dar'cion*."

The sight of his lover drew an involuntary groan from Josh. Sweat shone on Conall's brow, trickled down his temples, darkening the hair there to a shade almost auburn. Arm muscles bunched as he struggled against the restraints; his perfectly chiseled abs heaved with each gasp for breath.

"*Please*." There was a ragged edge to the Fae's voice now. "I'm so close. Much more, I won't be able to channel... *too* good."

Josh nodded, and slowly kissed and licked his way down Conall's shaft, all the way down to the soft skin behind his balls. Gently, almost delicately, he lapped at the Fae's taint, the exquisitely sensitive skin between the base of his cock and his tight entrance. The volume of cursing increased, and Conall's whole body shook as he struggled to stay still. Holding his breath, Josh parted his lover's thighs, and breached the puckered rosette with the tip of his tongue.

Everything happened at once. Conall bucked, arched, like a wild horse trying to throw a rider. He choked out a word or two, in the Fae language.

And Josh hit the cold concrete floor, jerking in the throes of a seizure. The dragon on his arm hissed, the hawk on his chest dug claws into his skin and shrieked.

It stopped as suddenly as it had started. Josh slumped to the floor, like a puppet with its strings cut, trying to remember how to breathe. In, out. In. Resting his forehead against the concrete. Yeah, that felt good. Cool.

"Josh!"

Gradually, the repetition of his name got through to him. He raised his head, blinked up at his panicked lover, staggered to his feet, and half-fell onto the chaise beside Conall. "I'm all right."

"Like fuck you are." Conall's voice was tight, controlled. "It's too much power, even I can't channel it all and when I lose it the backlash hits you. I don't even dare try to Fade, this close to the nexus."

Shouts from outside the door cut off whatever reply Josh might have made. Before he could get to his feet, the door crashed open. Janek O'Halloran half-shoved, half-carried Kevin into the nexus chamber, a gleaming silver blade at his throat, a red trickle already staining the collar of the lawyer's dress shirt. Close enough to dance with them came Tiernan, pure murder in his eyes, but helpless to do anything about it without risking having his SoulShare's throat slit.

Half of O'Halloran's head was made of crystal, and it glowed, a sinister, throbbing, infected red. The former bouncer laughed, a thick, clotted sound, as his one-eyed gaze came to rest on Conall.

"Wish to die, mage, while you still can. Soon even the power to wish will be denied you."

Chapter Twenty-Eight

"Conall! *Damn* it, Conall!"

Josh's voice was like icy water, shocking him. Conall wrenched his gaze away from the livid pulsing madness trying to draw him in — madness, yes, a Fae who looked too long on the distorted evil that was the *Marfach* went mad beyond hope of healing.

He recognized the human held at knife's point, from the sketches in the book he'd found in the apartment and from his conversation with Josh on the train; this must be Tiernan's *scair-anam.* Kevin. Which explained the low, feral snarl coming from the other Fae.

"Let go of him, *bodlag.*" Tiernan's voice promised death, as did his stance. Conall had watched enough *scian-damsai,* knife-dances, to know a master of the art when he saw one. Not that a blade-master stood a chance, unarmed, against pure evil. But Tiernan looked entirely ready to risk himself, even sacrifice himself, for the sake of the dark-haired, dark-eyed human.

Josh shifted where he sat, moving to put himself more squarely between Conall's shackled, naked body and the *Marfach*-golem. Conall shook his head. "Don't take the chance," he murmured. "You can't stop it. I don't think you can even slow it down."

"Do I look like I give a fuck?" Josh's voice was just as soft, and even more vehement. "It's not getting you."

For the moment, at least, all the man-monster's attention appeared to be on Tiernan. "I don't know what the fuck you just called me." This voice was nothing like the one that had first spoken to Conall; this was a hoarse, hate-filled human snarl. "And I don't give a shit. I've been waiting to kill you since you put this monster in my head and left me for dead. And if you don't swear to me you won't do that fading shit you do until I put this knife in you, I'm going to hand you your sugar daddy's head while it's still screaming."

"I think…" Kevin's voice rasped, not surprising given the angle at which the behemoth had his head wrenched back. "Getting a lobotomy… enhanced your creativity."

"*Misnach g'demin*," Conall murmured. Courage indeed, and rewarded by a jerk of the knife, and a fresh spill of red that stained the human's shirt collar.

The air around Tiernan warped, twisted, a slow, lethal swirl of magick. Elemental magick. Earth magick was used mostly for protection, but the ruin that had once been the tall human's face proclaimed the other use to which it could be put. The blue of Tiernan's eyes flared like burning ice from the center of the growing storm; even though the other Fae dared not look directly at the *Marfach*, that gaze promised death just the same. "No more warnings. Let him go."

"What'll you do if I don't, dickhead? Kill me?"

The behemoth laughed. "You did that once already, and you fucked it up."

"Give me another chance, then. I promise to get it right."

A shudder wracked Kevin's captor; the hand that held the knife wavered, then steadied. ***"You will do nothing, your Grace. Your little magicks can do nothing against me, and you are unprepared to use the ley energy."*** This had to be the *Marfach* speaking. This voice could drive Fae, or even human, to pure gibbering insanity, a voice full of red hot pokers twisted in clinging guts, the eyeless stares of crab-cleaned corpses.

"You're awfully confident for a brain-rotted zombie." Sweat beaded on Tiernan's upper lip, but he gave no other sign that the hideous voice affected him.

The Marfach's lips curled back in a snarl. ***"You remember this blade my dear friend Janek holds to your* scair-anam's *throat, yes?"*** It laughed harshly as Tiernan blanched. ***"I see you do. The blade that ended your brother's life, magicked keen enough to sever a head from a body. Or a soul from its other half."***

Rage and despair rolled off the other Fae in waves that were almost palpable. To a Fae's heightened senses, the scent of blood was thick in the air of the tiny room. *What would I be doing, if that blood were Josh's?* Conall had to close his eyes, fight for calm in the face of the fury that threatened to consume him at the thought.

"But you are irrelevant, your Grace."

Conall's eyes startled open again; the *Marfach*'s human host, Janek, had turned back to face him. Once again, Conall had to look away, or risk madness.

"The mage is my prize, my victory, my vengeance."

Shit. I canNOT let it have me. Before the Sundering, the *Marfach* had inhabited living magick, magick made physical, and warped and twisted it to an evil only hinted at in the few surviving histories of that time. Living magick like the substance of Conall's being. And if it took him…

Only one Fae now living could have unmade the Pattern from within the Realm. Could he be forced to do it from without?

"Put down the knife and back away."

Shocked by the sound of Josh's voice, Conall groaned as his SoulShare got to his feet, stepped directly between him and the *Marfach*'s tool. "*Dar'cion*, don't."

The creature's laughter was every bit as stomach-turning as its speech. *"I have no use for humans, except to see how interestingly you can be made to die. This one—"* Kevin's head was jerked up and back, in sadistic punctuation. *"He remembers very well how I go about that."*

The magick below the floor was whispering, singing, a soft seductive sound. Conall almost reached out to take it in; with this kind of energy source, he might stand a chance of being able to channel enough magick to do something against the *Marfach*. But no— any channeling that great would catch Josh up as well, burn him out from within, and cast him aside.

"No use?" Josh spoke calmly, reasonably. But one hand was behind his back, the one with the tattooed chain around the wrist, and it clenched into a trembling fist, a lightning rod for his *scair-anam*'s tension. "Not even for the human who carries you everywhere?"

Conall held his breath as Janek growled, let it out slowly as the enormous male shuffled around to face Tiernan again. "You promised." Somehow, Conall didn't think the *Marfach*'s host was talking to the other Fae. "You promised me Guaire. You don't get shit until he's dead."

Conall still couldn't look directly at the *Marfach*, and Josh was between him and Kevin now, but Tiernan's face told him all there was to know about what the monster was doing to the human. "Let him go, dick-boil." Tiernan's words were gritted through clenched teeth. "You want my word I won't Fade? You have it, and trust me when I say you'll be begging me to Fade long before I'm done with you."

Fade.

Oh, shit. Conall found himself staring at the tattoo around his SoulShare's wrist, the beautiful silver chain that had brought him back into existence. *I have one chance to stop the monster. Maybe.*

Holding his breath, Conall Faded to incorporeality, refusing to give himself time to remember the terror of being a living ghost, trapped without physical form. And if there were gods, as so many humans apparently insisted, surely they smiled on reckless mages, because the Fading didn't send a lethal jolt of ley energy through his *scair-anam*. His hands slipped through the locked cuffs like smoke; cursing at the slowness of his movement, he rose from the chaise.

"You are defying me, Meat?"

Son of a bitch. With what felt like agonizing

slowness, Conall pushed himself into Josh's body. *Don't move, lover—I just need a few more seconds.*

Conall felt Josh start to reply, and then choke back the words. *Don't say anything. Just put your arm out in front of you where I can see it. The one with the chain.*

"I'm going to make sure you deliver what you promised me." The knife in Janek's hand bit into Kevin's throat again; by now the collar of the human's shirt was soaked with crimson on the side kissed by the blade, and his face was as pale as paper. "Guaire can't possibly feel enough pain to make me happy, but I'm sure as shit going to enjoy making him try."

Josh's arm came into Conall's field of view, and he aligned his own with it. *Once I start to channel... once your body channels, the chain should come alive. It should bind me within you again.*

"So you can stop this thing. Hell, yes." Josh's lips barely moved. "Do it, *d'orant*. Use me."

Use me. Those two quiet words stopped everything. Ever since he'd come into his birthright of power, everyone and everything in Conall's life had been trying to use him. Every minute of his life since that moment had been a battle *not* to be used, a struggle to keep his distance. From anyone who might arouse him, and the magick within him, yes, but more than that. From anyone who wanted to turn him to his or her own ends. Which meant, everyone.

He'd been missing so much more than half his soul, even before he went through the Pattern. And he'd been resisting the male who was trying to give it back to him. Even when he needed Josh's touch to drive away the pain of transition... even when he finally admitted his desire, his need... something in him had kept his distance. For Josh's safety, that's what he'd told himself.

There was a human word for this. They called it bullshit.

Use you? Fear gripped Conall, genuine fear for Josh, this time. *I didn't think this through. You might not survive this.* He could barely make himself think the words. *The energy I'm going to have to channel to have any chance of stopping the* Marfach — *the channeling could kill you.*

"I won't let it. You need me."

Josh's calm, total determination stunned Conall. Tiernan's fury at the threat to his human was at least something comprehensible to a Fae; Fae might not love, but threaten to deprive one of them of a prized possession, and the one doing the threatening would discover the true meaning of suffering. But the quiet strength Josh radiated was something totally alien, a gift of everything the human was, presented without fanfare.

No denying it. Not any longer. Not to himself, and not to the other half of his soul.

S'vrá lom tú, m'anam-sciar. No other gift was great enough to match what Josh offered. *Though the love of a Fae is undoubtedly a mixed blessing.*

"Idiot." Conall felt Josh's smile within himself. "Get this done, lover."

With the SoulShare bond completed, Conall could reach the magick within himself once again, and that would be enough to let him begin, without the ley energy. Conall let the magick well up in him, fill him, and nearly cried out with the sheer relief of it, the caress of the power within him after believing it out of his reach forever. The chain inked around Josh's wrist leapt to gleaming life, real, solid truesilver binding him into his lover's body.

Janek finally seemed to notice something amiss as Josh, at Conall's urging, raised his chained arm, palm out toward the monster and its human hostage. "Where the fuck did the twink go?" Janek shifted his grip on Kevin, moved the knife to put its point under Kevin's chin, denting the skin, piercing it. His grip on the silk-wrapped hilt went white-knuckled; blood trickled down the cruelly sharp blade.

Tiernan lunged—

Power surged through Conall; the air swirled, seemed to go solid. Tiernan froze in the middle of a suicidal charge; the pulse pounding in Kevin's throat stilled; a glistening bead of blood clung, poised, to the razor's edge of the knife.

"What the hell?" Josh's gaze went from Janek to Kevin to Tiernan, and back again. "What did you do?"

Time is stopped, for everyone but us. Conall tried to flinch away when Josh looked at the malevolent red crystal scar that was most of Janek's face, but was startled to discover there was no need. Whether it was because he was seeing through Josh's eyes, or because of the timestop, he could bear the sight of his race's ancient enemy. Not that he wanted to look any longer than he had to. *We don't have much time. The longer I hold this, the worse the snapback is going to be when I let it go.*

"You can stop time, without breaking a sweat?"

If I had a body, I'd be sweating. Not true, but the awe in his lover's voice bothered Conall, and he wanted it to stop.

"What are you going to do?"

Conall could feel Josh's heart racing as if it were his own. Which, at the moment, it was. *I need you to help me channel the ley energy. Even I can't handle that much unless I'm prepared.*

Josh's laugh was slightly breathless. "Aroused, you mean? Damn. Here I thought getting you to lose your virginity upstairs was awkward. At least there I could touch you. And we weren't staring at something Chuck Norris would check under the bed for before going to sleep."

Close your eyes, then, Ianan. *And imagine what you'd do to me, if we were anywhere other than here, any time other than now.*

"Oh, sweet fuck." Josh's eyes closed, and he drew in a deep, unsteady breath. "I'd start with kisses—"

Don't use words, lover. No time. Show me.

Josh groaned. So did Conall, as his human's imagination came to vivid life and he saw himself, back upstairs in the tattoo studio, being shoved—no, thrown—against the padded table, bent over it, his feet kicked apart. Josh's hand fisted in his hair, twisted his head back to receive a kiss that should have left his lips smoking. And there was a fucking brand trying to find its slick hard way into his ass.

For a moment, Conall was lost in his lover's fantasy. He felt the thick blunt head he'd taken so eagerly into his mouth in the shower breach the tight ring of muscle at his entrance, felt the burn of it, the breathtaking invasion he'd only known in dreams. He bent over, clutched the far side of the table so hard his knuckles went white as the bone beneath them, and tried to spread himself wider.

I would let you do this. And more. A whole lifetime, so empty, so hungry to be touched and never realizing it. Forced to starvation, because sating his hunger could have destroyed a world. *No, I WILL let you do this.*

"Christ, this hurts." Josh sucked in a breath through clenched teeth, reached down to adjust himself in jeans with no room left in them for the attempt. Apparently, his human was sharing in Conall's steel-hard, weeping erection.

It's time. Conall shuddered, from anticipation as much as arousal, opening eyes he hadn't realized he'd closed to find himself staring at the horror that was the *Marfach* and its human host. What was left of Janek's human face was twisted into a snarl, the white of his single eye blood-red; what had probably once been the black and red of the tattoos covering his shaved head were faded to a leprous gray and a strange brownish red that looked like liver.

But all of this was merely a frame for the mass of crystal harboring the malevolent red glow that was the *Marfach*. The living Stone had taken the exact shape of what had been left of the human's face after Tiernan had destroyed it; shattered bone and mangled flesh and what looked like part of an eye, a deflated, gelatinous orb with a strange crescent-shaped piece carved out of it, with a smooth clean path bored through all the carnage. And there was a glow within the crystal, a shade of red that Conall suspected fire would be, if fire could rot.

Ill met, for thee, Destroyer. The words of the ancient challenge welled up in Conall, the salutation tradition said had been spoken by Dúlánc Loremaster before the last battle with the *Marfach* in the Realm. Then, it had taken all the Loremasters in the Realm to banish the malevolent force from the heart of magick. Here, now, there was only Conall's power, and that of the ley lines the monster had so imprudently vacated. But the *Marfach* was weakened, and Conall's magick was limited only by his capacity to channel. His and his SoulShare's.

"Need a little help, *d'orant*?" Josh laughed, softly, and the image that formed in his mind left Conall breathless and aching with need. And wondering why a pleasure-loving race such as the Fae had never come up with anal beads.

You and I need to talk. About quite a few things. But for now… hold on tight, dar'cion. There was no avoiding his task any longer. He could feel time beginning to strain at the bonds he'd put on it, and the joy of the SoulShare bond was rising in him along with his arousal. The joy that let him tame the untameable magick.

Closing his eyes, he felt Josh's strength wrap around him, the way his lover's brilliantly-colored arms had wrapped around him from behind when he was in the throes of a transition nightmare. He needed no more than that.

The magick seethed beneath Conall's feet, and he called to it; it roared into him, into Josh, buffeting them both. He felt Josh's struggle to brace himself against an invisible wind, a gale that threatened to rip the breath from the human's lungs. Conall's eyes snapped open; he raised both hands and let the magick stream out through him, into the tiny room.

Their shared body staggered, nearly fell, as the

timestop released. He dared not fall, though, dared not even blink. His focus now was the knife in Janek's fist; he heard Tiernan's hoarse shout, and threw up a shield of solid Air an instant before the other Fae would have slammed into Janek's knife arm.

I'm almost sorry, human. There was no way to do what he needed to do while most of Janek's body held so little magick, and there was no way to put the necessary magick there without causing the enormous human enough pain to drop a charging rhinoceros. *Almost.*

The human's body jerked as the magick thundered into him. Kevin staggered away as Janek screamed and clutched at his head, the instantly-forgotten knife in his hand slicing off most of an ear and sending a spray of brownish-red gore splattering against the nearby wall. Another trickle of blood spilled from one corner of Janek's mouth, as the scream went on.

"Any chance of being able to cover my ears?" Josh's voice was inaudible over the never-ending howl; he nodded slightly toward Kevin, who was doing just that, flattened hands pressed to the sides of his head.

None. Just a little longer. Conall risked a look at the *Marfach*. Magick contorted the air near Janek's face in a way that fascinated and repelled; Conall's stomach wrenched as he watched it, and raised Josh's hands to shield himself from the sight. If he tried a banishing now, the monster would probably be able to fight him off. Cripple it with Janek's agony, though, and the impossible might be made to happen.

Conall felt Josh's eyes go wide, and his own

joined them an instant later. The beautiful dragon on Josh's left forearm launched itself into the air, flew a tight circle around the Fae and the humans, and hovered over Janek, wings bating, a tiny stream of white-hot fire hissing from its jaws to crisp the faded ink on his scalp. And the black-headed hawk tore itself from Josh's chest with a screech; the ceiling was far too low for the raptor to stoop properly, but its talons tore strips from graying flesh, sank deep into the human's back.

The steady stream of curses coming from Tiernan paused. "Fuck me backwards. That can't be a *savac-dui*."

"*It can be, and it is, your Grace*." Josh's body was starting to tremble, on the brink of being overwhelmed by the torrent of magick only Conall's presence enabled him to bear at all. "*Now, kindly find something else to do with that mouth while I focus*."

Now. It has to be now. Before his lover's all too willing body gave out under the strain of the magick. Conall turned inward, groping for control over the maelstrom threatening to scour him away to nothing from within. He never had occasion to wonder whether his capacity to channel magick exceeded his ability to bend it to his will. *Hell of a time to be finding out.*

One of the channelings bound into the Pattern at its creation was a banishing. It was nothing innate to the Demesne of Air, and nothing Conall had ever learned. But his body remembered it, remembered being seized by it and forced by it through the keen wire-blades of the Pattern. Only days ago? *Shit.* The form of it was still there, within him; he drew in more of the ley energy, breathing it in, willing it in until his soul felt tight and drawn with it and Josh's body was quivering like a plucked harpstring.

A soundless blast threw Josh backward, and Conall with him, over the chaise, to land headfirst and hard on the concrete floor behind it. Pure evil, hot like the wind out of a crematorium. Josh's sight grayed, threatened to go black. Conall fought to keep them both conscious. *Stay with me*, dar'cion—

Conall's gut wrenched, heaved as laughter forced its way out through Janek's raw and bleeding throat. ***"You hide from my sight, mage, but no matter."*** The human coughed, gagged, but his discomfort meant nothing to the monster that was using his voice. ***"The strength of your magick makes the very air a weapon for me to turn against you. And against your pet."***

Josh choked, convulsed. Conall felt the air go solid in his *scair-anam*'s lungs, the same trick that had been used against him by the Lady Liadan. And then the air began to burn within the human.

Pure, cold rage seized Conall. Josh's chained hand clutched at the chaise, drew their shared body up. Tiernan was staring at Josh in shock, leaning against the ward Conall had put up; Kevin was slumped against a wall, as far from Janek as he could get in the small space, one hand to his throat and red trickling between his fingers. And Janek himself...

The human's contorted and bleeding body was glowing, a dull, mottled red. Smoke and the smell of burned flesh hung in the air like a pall as the dragon continued to do its work, and the hawk clung to one of Janek's arms, talons buried in his shoulder. Where flesh gave way to living Stone, a vortex swirled, red and black and opening onto a vision of flames.

"Come to me. Or your human dies, and I will take you while you are bound within his corpse."

"Don't, *d'orant*." Josh had no voice left, but he needed none. "If it kills me... the chain will just be ink. You'll be free." The words were brave, the human's inner voice even.

But Josh was staring into the vortex as he spoke, and for a moment the human's self-control slipped. For an instant only, Conall shared his *scair-anam*'s thoughts as much as his vision, felt the terror brought on by supernatural evil and almost-human gore. *Josh —*

The glimpse was gone. "Do it. I told you. Use me."

Yet his SoulShare trembled.

Fury opened Conall as wide to the magick as arousal had. He gestured, simply, and the gesture became a whirlwind. Tiernan and Kevin both hit the floor, covering their heads with their arms. Conall pointed, using Josh's hand. The wind whipped at Janek, tore at him, flayed him. Ate him away, ribbons of flesh and shards of bone vanishing. Until all that remained was the furious red Stone. Conall snarled, and tapped deeper into the primal force beneath the floor.

The Stone, and the *Marfach* with it, vanished.

Chapter Twenty-Nine

"Where the fuck did it go?" Tiernan was leaning on—pushing on—what looked like a pane of glass. Except that there wasn't anything in front of him.

"*Beats the hell out of me.*" Josh was almost accustomed to Conall speaking through him. At the moment, though, Josh was gasping for breath, trying to reassure himself his lungs hadn't just been seared medium rare, and managing that and speaking someone else's words at the same time was a little tricky. "*And you might want to go shield your* scair-anam, *I'm not finished yet and I'm sure you don't want him ending up like the sorry son of a bitch who just left us.*"

"Care to let the wall down first?"

"*Ah, gratitude.*" Josh felt power surge through himself—no, through Conall, he was just a conduit—and Tiernan fell forward, whatever had been holding him up evidently gone.

As the other Fae staggered to Kevin's side, taking him into his arms for a brief intense embrace before pulling back to check the wounds in his throat, Josh turned inward. Hesitantly. Did he even *know* the male he was sharing his body with? He closed his eyes, but that wasn't anywhere near enough to block out the memory of watching Janek's body bloodlessly shredding before his eyes. Or the memory of Conall's utter determination to make it happen. "Conall?" His lips moved without sound, and he turned his back to the couple huddled against the wall.

Are you all right, dar'cion?

The voice Josh heard in his head was so different from the one that had spoken through him moments before, he could almost believe there were two different speakers. Except *that* would make him even crazier than he already was. Which was really saying something, since at the moment his whole body was vibrating with the same energy that had ripped apart a would-be murderer, his dragon and hawk tattoos were perched on the head of the chaise blinking down at him, and he still had a hard-on that might kill a Clydesdale. "Ask me again when the walls stop screaming, okay?"

Shit.

So strange. He could still feel Conall inside him, but at the same time it felt exactly like there were arms around him. "You're funny when you curse. You're so precise about it."

Words matter. Any words. In his mind, he could see Conall shaking his head. *How do I fix this, lover? There's one more thing I have to do, and I can't do it without you. But I can't force you.* The Conall he saw stopped, caught himself. *That's not true. I could. But I won't.*

"After what I've just seen, I have no doubt that you could." Soft murmurs came from the other side of the little room; apparently, Conall wasn't the only Fae who could be gentle when his SoulShare needed him to be. "You sure as hell aren't what you look like."

271

No. So much sadness, so much regret in one word. *Too much...*

The inner voice went still. Josh wanted a shoulder to shake, an ear to whisper into. "Too much what?"

Too much power. Josh caught a glimpse of the image in his lover's mind; a man forever young, yet old beyond human imagining, standing outside a window by night, firelight flickering on his face, not daring even to go close enough to peer through the window for a glimpse of the hearth within. *Let me use you, just once more. And then I will leave you in peace.*

"What the *hell* are you talking about?" Josh's left hand wrapped around the chain around his right wrist, as if to bind it—and Conall — more tightly to himself. "What do you mean, leave me?" The words stuck in his throat, choked him.

I can feel what you feel, m'dar'cion. *What you felt. Your fear of the monster. And of me.* Conall felt... hollow, somehow, within him. Empty, even though filled with unimaginable power. *Fear of what I did, what I can do. What I will do, someday.*

"Oh, no, you don't." A low rumble started deep in Josh's chest. "Am I afraid? Fuck, yes, I'd have to be insane not to be, with what I've seen in the last five minutes. And I haven't understood one single thing that's happened to me since Sunday afternoon. But I would do all of it again. A hundred times, if I had to. If *you* needed me to." He gripped the chain tighter, feeling the links press into his flesh. One more unreal bit of reality. "You do *not* get to walk away from me for my own good."

Conall was silent, but the feeling of loneliness, the memory of isolation persisted.

But what if I—

"Unless you sent that motherfucker to the other side of the world, you might want to think about getting a ward set up before it figures out how to get back here." Tiernan's irascible growl was strangely muffled; Josh craned his neck, and saw that the Fae's arms were around Kevin, his head resting on his husband's shoulder.

"Tiernan, God damn it, we're—"

No. He's right. Josh could have sworn he felt fingertips brush his cheek. *We have to make this place safe.*

"If you think this means we're not having this conversation, you can think again, *d'orant.*" Josh hauled himself up onto his knees, rested his forearms on the black leather chaise. "I can get all the way up if you need me to, but it might take a minute."

No, this will do.

Josh felt the energy beginning to build again. Not that it had ever left him—his body still hummed with it, and his hawk and his dragon were still watching him, bright-eyed, from the back of the chaise—but he could tell that Conall was drawing in more of it.

"Shield your scair-anam, *your Grace. The strongest ward I know well starts from me and grows outward, and even benevolent magick doesn't sit well with a human body."*

Tiernan grimaced, but nodded; he closed his eyes, and a strange orb shimmered into existence around the Fae and the human. It was as if the air around them had become almost perfectly transparent crystal, yet left them free to move. "I take it we should cover our eyes, too?"

"Only if you want to be able to see after I'm done." *You should close your eyes too,* dar'cion, Conall added, no sarcasm in his inner voice. *If you want to see, I'll try to share my eyes with you, but elemental magick like Tiernan's shield interacting with pure magick like the channeling I'm about to do will put out enough light to burn out your retinas.*

"Thanks for the warning." Josh closed his eyes tightly, and ducked his head for good measure, resting his forehead against the smooth leather.

"*Tre...*"

The magickal pressure was building again; Josh shifted, his renewed arousal highly uncomfortable against the zipper of his jeans.

"*Dó...*"

Josh's body shook with the force of the magick contained within it. Yet there was none of the pain he'd known before Conall had joined with him. His SoulShare was carrying that part, and all Josh needed to do was trust him.

"*H'on...*"

"*I love you,*" Josh whispered.

Behind his closed eyelids, Josh saw light. A brilliant lattice of blue-white light, knots and strands like the design on Conall's back, only impossibly more intricate. Growing outward, from where he knelt beside the chaise, expanding in a perfect sphere around him. Sweeping out, passing through the circle of safety around Kevin and Tiernan and flaring even brighter when it did, filling the room. And Conall was still drawing in ley energy, so Josh figured it was still growing.

You're right, dar'cion. Conall's voice carried

tension, now. *I want to make it as big as I can and still have the energy to knot it off to make it permanent. This whole building, at least. I want your shop protected. The* Marfach *is never getting anywhere near you again.*

Not wanting to distract him, Josh just nodded. Using Conall's eyes, he watched in awe as the lattice around him hummed with something that was not quite life, but was very much like it. Impossible to be afraid of this. Probably impossible to understand it, too. But the world would be a very small, cold, and uninteresting place if it only contained what he could understand.

Conall whispered a word *as'Faein*, and a shiver raced across Josh's skin as the magick abruptly detached from him. Slowly, the light began to fade from the intricate pattern, leaving behind ghostly afterimages that lingered for a breath or two, and then disappeared.

Josh opened his eyes as the last of the light dissipated, just in time to see his hawk and his dragon launch themselves from their perches and soar to him. The dragon wrapped itself around his forearm and spread itself over his skin; the hawk landed beside him on the chaise, tilted its head and cocked an eye at him until he rose up and sat back on his heels, letting it find its home across his chest.

The chain around his wrist, too, faded back into ink and flesh, and he groaned at the unmistakable sensation of Conall leaving his body. "Don't you dare, *d'orant*. Don't you fucking *dare* run out on me."

Tiernan staggered to his feet, and helped a still-bleeding Kevin to his. "Given that there's no Water

Fae with healing abilities on offer, we're getting you to a doctor." Tiernan's arm was firmly around Kevin's waist, though it didn't appear to be needed for support; the lawyer, though, was still deathly pale and had a hand clamped firmly to his neck.

"What are you going to tell them, that I cut myself shaving?"

"Leave that to me."

As they reached the door, Tiernan turned back. "Lock up when you leave." Kevin dug an Armani-clad elbow into his ribs, and the Fae cleared his throat. "And thanks." Another elbow. "Fuck. All right. I owe you."

Josh barely heard the door close. He was too busy looking for something he knew his eyes could never find, not unless Conall chose to be found. He hadn't needed Josh's help to Fade, so chances were he wouldn't need it to stay Faded, if that was what he chose to do.

"Where are you?" Conall said that he couldn't move quickly when he was Faded, so he *had* to be here somewhere. But Josh's voice echoed off the concrete walls, just the way it would in a totally empty room.

"Conall. *D'orant*." Josh's hand wrapped around the tattooed chain on his wrist. "You felt me hesitate, didn't you? Felt my uncertainty. That's not fear. That's being human. Being unsure. Living with it, dealing with it. And going ahead anyway."

He paused, studying the leather cushion under his forearms, looking for just the right words. "I felt what you felt, too. Loneliness. Like you've never been able to be close to anyone. I suppose, with power like yours, you've never been able to tell who your friends are, and who's just out to use you for whatever they can get."

"I've had no friends."

Josh's head jerked up. Conall was standing by the door, his back to him, his head bowed.

"I told you Fae don't love. Fae do know friendship, though. Some do. I never have. I never dared to approach anyone, for fear of what might happen if we discovered we wanted one another sexually. And on the few occasions when someone else sought me out..." Conall's bare shoulders rose and fell with a sigh, his beautiful blue-silver ink gleaming in the dim light. "It was always to see what use they could make of me. Of my power."

Slowly, Josh got to his feet, feeling almost like a hunter, with prey easily spooked. "But you know I'm not doing that. You *know*."

Conall nodded, the barest movement of his head. "I do. But I made you a promise. I told you that you didn't always have to be the strong one." The ginger head came up; the Fae stared at the opposite wall, hands clenched into fists at his sides. "I promised you. And what did I do? I used you. I used you the way a smith uses a hammer or a tailor a needle. Like a tool."

Josh circled the chaise, came up behind Conall, and rested his hands on his lover's lean, hard shoulders. "No tool ever gave itself to be wielded. And I gave myself." His lips brushed the beautiful ink that covered Conall's upper back, ran up his neck, and disappeared into his hair. "You've made it very clear I don't always have to be the strong one." He laughed softly, nipped at the nape of Conall's neck. "When it comes to magick, lover, I'm nothing but a prop. And glad to be one."

Conall turned and looked up at Josh, his eyes glittering like cut gems with reflected light. "You are so much more than a prop." His voice dropped to the barest murmur, thick with the accent he had brought with him from his own world. "I need you. Not only for magick. Not only to drive the pain away. I'm not complete without you. And the thought I might frighten you away, because of what I am—"

"Never." Josh cupped the back of Conall's head in his hand, his palm tickled by short, soft hair; bent his head, and kissed him, hard and hungry. "Does that feel frightened to you?" He bit gently at Conall's lips, tugged, stroked with his tongue to soothe the bites. His arousal had been fueling Conall's magick for much too long. Now it was going to fuel something else entirely.

Conall merely moaned for answer, swaying into Josh, trapping his rising shaft between their bodies. Josh's free hand slid down Conall's back, cupped his ass, and pulled him in tight, groaning himself at the heat grinding against him.

"It's not going to take much to set me off, *d'orant*." Josh could feel the heat of Conall's panting breaths against his lips as he whispered, and the sensation just made everything worse. No, better. Definitely better.

"Wait until you're in me. Please." Conall worked his hips against Josh, stealing a bite or two of his own, nudging Josh none-too-subtly toward the chaise.

Startled, Josh let Conall urge him backward. "You want me to top?"

Conall nodded. He was trembling, but his grip on

Josh's arms and the little moans that rode every breath said clearly the trembling had nothing to do with fear, and everything to do with need. "If I'm ever going to understand what it is to be your lover, I think I need to learn to let you take your pleasure in me." The Fae smiled, a slow, heated smile, totally unhuman, and the fucking sexiest thing Josh had ever seen. "Use me?"

"Son of a *bitch*." Josh was on top of Conall before he even had time to think, and it was a good thing the Fae was already naked, because Josh was out of patience. And very nearly out of time, unless he did something drastic. Kneeling between Conall's parted thighs, he worked frantically at the button and zipper of his jeans, hissing as his cock pressed against the zipper teeth. "You're not helping," he growled, trying to work his jeans down his hips while Conall wrapped his hard-muscled legs around his thighs.

"You say that like it's a bad thing."

"God *damn*, I need you." Finally, he was free. He wrapped one hand around the base of his cock, snug up against his aching balls, and squeezed, as hard as he could, until he saw stars and couldn't get his breath. It helped, a little; at least he probably wasn't going to lose it before he could even accept the invitation Conall was straining to extend to him. But his cock was still streaming—he'd never seen it do that before, not like this. *Maybe it's having to wait so long that does it.*

Josh's next groan echoed off the walls, as Conall raised himself up on an elbow, reached down, moved his hand aside, and curled his hand around Josh's thick, blunt shaft. "I need more of your scent, give it to me." Green eyes teased him, taunted him; Conall's palm and fingers caressed him, and just when Josh was reaching to yank his hand away—because the only alternative to doing so he could see was a release that would be Fourth of July come early but wouldn't give Conall what he wanted and needed—Conall licked his own hand clean, a long, slow stroke. "And your taste."

"Fuck." The word exploded from Josh; he hooked one of Conall's legs over his arm, to open him wider, and positioned his head at the tight entrance his tongue had explored such a short time ago. "For a virgin, you are one hell of a tease."

Soft laughter reached into him, coaxing the fire that had been smoldering for the last hour or more into a blaze. "I'm a Fae."

Gritting his teeth, Josh tried to find purchase for his knees on the slippery leather surface and breached Conall's tight ring. Conall gasped, laughter giving way to shock, and then to arousal, and Josh had to close his eyes as he fought for another couple of inches. "So damn tight… am I hurting you?"

"No. Yes. Fuck if I know. But don't stop." Sweat shone on Conall's brow and slicked his hair to his forehead; his pupils were dilated wide, the intense gemmed green of his eyes just a ring around the darkness. He groaned as Josh went deeper, relaxing and then clamping down again, his back arching.

"Let go — Jesus, baby, let me in — oh, fuck." This last a reverent whisper, as Josh looked down and saw Conall's erection lying across his cut and heaving abs, scattering clear effervescent drops that evaporated almost as soon as they streaked his skin.

"You stopped—oh." Christ, that smile again. Conall's hand played over the glistening purple organ, looking small on the length of it. "Doing this feels so much better with you in me."

"Shit. That did it." Josh tried to hold back, but it was no good at all, his hips had a mind of their own and he took Conall as hard as he could, drilling deep, his hips rotating. Soft cries told him a Fae's pleasure spot was in the same place as a human's, and his whole body shook with his own pleasure as he found it again and again, as Conall's legs wrapped around him tighter and urged him even deeper.

And then it started. Joy. Building along with the orgasm he knew he wasn't going to be able to hold back any longer. And doubled, and tripled, then beyond all hope of counting, because he saw the same unbearable bliss in his lover's eyes, as Conall gripped and stroked and wrung himself. "Now—*d'orant*, now—"

Words stopped, thought stopped. And the brilliant, blinding light of magick was nothing at all next to the pure white-light joy as he released deep inside Conall's body, and felt spurts of Conall's heat welling up to coat his own chest and abs, and heard Conall's ecstatic cry. And, impossibly, felt Conall's pleasure, sweet burn and hot release.

Josh's next awareness was of being shaken, gently at first, but then with more force. "*Dar'cion*? Josh? I need air, lover."

Josh blinked, shook his head. He was lying on top of Conall, still inside him, but collapsed over him, as boneless as a cat in a sunbeam. "Sorry." He did his best to prop himself up on his fore- arms, managing to raise himself up at least enough to let Conall breathe. "Did you do that?—was that magick?"

The way Conall looked up at him sent a shiver of delight running down his spine to sizzle in his groin. "It might have been, a little. But only my own. I can't help that. It's going to happen every time from now on."

Josh lowered himself enough to brush his lips over Conall's in a warm, lingering kiss. "From now on? That doesn't sound like a male who's planning to leave me in peace." He tried not to look like he was holding his breath waiting for the answer.

"Hell, no." A hand cupped Josh's cheek, drew his head down until their foreheads touched. "I couldn't."

"Good. Because peace would be the last thing you'd leave me in."

Chapter Thirty

The worst part about waking up wasn't the fact that his face was ground into a mess of slivers of glass already slicked with brownish-red blood. The worst part was that his face felt a hell of a lot better than the rest of him did.

Get up, Meat.

"Fuck you." Shit, there was glass between his front teeth. It hurt like a son of a bitch. "I just got shredded. Nothing you can do to me is going to hurt worse than that."

Wrong twice, Meat. Your eye told you that you got ripped apart because what's left of your human mind couldn't process what was actually happening to you. Why did the male-monster sound so fucking cheerful? *And believe me, there are far more painful things than a simple banishing.*

With a great deal of concentration and effort, Janek was able to extend the middle fingers of both hands. "Where the hell are we?"

Raise your head and we'll both find out.

Janek snarled. His mostly numb hands scrabbled at what felt like a concrete floor until he thought he might be able to push himself onto his back. He took a deep breath and shoved.

Early morning sunlight slanted in through a window set high in a basement wall, nearly blinding Janek's one remaining eye. He lay with glass biting into his back, on a concrete floor next to the frame of a shattered mirror. He was surrounded by piles of cast-off junk, most of it knocked over, kicked in, or otherwise ruined.

A victim of your own temper tantrum. How appropriate.

Janek was fairly sure he'd never wanted to strangle the bitch more than he did in that moment. "Your tantrum. I just provided the muscle."

Details. The female laughed. *Hurry and regain your strength, Meat. We need to be away from here. The mage has revitalized me, with his gift of so much magickal energy, and our tool upstairs can watch this place well enough for us. I will know if he sees anything.*

"It wasn't a fucking gift as far as I'm concerned." Janek tried to grab the glass shard wedged between his front teeth, but all he managed to do was bloody his fingers. "And why don't you get Mr. Pain-in-the-Ass upstairs to come get me out of here?"

I would have to wipe his entire mind afterward, to make him forget you. You are quite the spectacle at the moment.

Janek stared at the cobwebbed ceiling, his hand falling back down to his side. *Fuck off and die.* Enough cutting himself just to score a few pissing-off points. *So let me lie here a while. It's not like there's anything urgent we have to be doing.*

Even as the thought occurred to him, though, he heard a rat nosing through the debris, somewhere off to his left. *Okay, so I need to get my shit together enough to fight off a rat. Still no rush.*

We need to be gone. The mage knows of this place, and might realize he has sent us here.

Big hairy fucking deal.

The *Marfach* was silent for so long Janek began to get suspicious. *It is a big fucking deal. That Dary twink didn't just get lucky, did he? He can take you on.*

Janek gagged, choked on a scream, as his spine arched like a fish on a barbed hook.

Regain your strength, Meat. We have much to do.

Epilogue

Conall let himself into Raging Art-On, closing the door behind himself against the chill October breeze. There were no customers in the front lobby, no surprise given the lateness of the hour. Josh's studio door stood open, but no light came from within; light came from the smaller rear studio, though, as did soft voices.

"...never going to be able to thank you enough, you know." Keen Fae hearing easily picked up Terrence Miller's voice. Josh's former lover had called, in tears, nearly a week after the battle with the *Marfach*. Bryce had thrown him out, he'd said. He was crashing on the sofa of one of the dancers in his ballet company, but that was only a temporary arrangement, and he hadn't known what he was going to do when it ended.

"There's nothing to thank me for, you did me a favor and we both know it." Conall was, as always, drawn to the sound of Josh's soft laughter. "I hadn't had anyone in this studio since Raoul moved out to Phoenix, six months ago. I was swamped."

Conall rapped softly on the doorframe, and both men turned, startled, to look at him. The room was more crowded than Conall remembered it; Josh was sitting on the table Terry used for piercings, while Terry stood behind a gleaming new tattoo machine, one hand running lovingly over the polished metal stand. It had only arrived two days ago, and Conall smiled, remembering Josh's delight when it came out of its crate. Even though it was to be Terry's, and not his own. His *lanan*, his partner, loved his art without reservation. "I'm sorry to intrude, but Josh, it's 9:30."

"Already?" Josh slid down from the table, his usual muscle tee doing nothing to conceal his broad chest and his six-pack, his jeans clinging as if he had inked them on. Conall was finding a great deal to enjoy about clothing styles, this side of the Pattern. "Terry, I'm sorry, can you close up for me? I have a date."

Terry grinned. "Get out of here. Make Red take you someplace that has tablecloths and more than one fork per place setting."

Josh reached into his own studio as he and Conall passed, catching up his jacket from a hook on the wall. He simply slung it over one beautifully inked shoulder, rather than putting it on, since they were only going downstairs.

"What was Terry talking about?" Conall shook his head, amused, as he followed Josh down the stairs into Purgatory. "Instant comprehension of the words only gets me so far, sometimes."

Josh reached back for Conall's hand; the Fae's transition pain had eased after the first month or so, but the two had yet to lose the habit of staying in physical contact whenever they could. Conall, for his part, hoped they never would; he was enjoying the ability to touch far too much. "He was telling you to take me someplace expensive to eat."

Conall was laughing as the two of them pushed through the black glass doors at the bottom of the stairs. Both men nodded to Lucien, and headed for the door to the storeroom, back behind the bar and around a corner, with Conall, at least, feeling as if he were physically pushing through the pounding music coming from the dance floor as well. He needed no key for the lock, not when a quiet word would do, though there were times he was amazed the lock could hear him.

Magickal light was, as usual, pouring out from under the door to the nexus chamber. It was visible only to Conall, though, and, to a lesser extent, Tiernan. Given that Nobles used the rarer elemental magick, they were less sensitive to the presence of the pure form. Conall whispered the word that relaxed the ward around the touchpad just long enough for him to enter the access code, then opened the door to allow Josh to enter head of him. And grabbed his human's ass as it went past, for the sheer enjoyment of it.

Josh growled softly, flinging his jacket aside, pinning Conall to the door almost before it was shut and kissing him hard. "Tease." He nipped at Conall's lip, sucked it into his mouth.

"Fae." The word was muffled, by Josh's mouth and by Conall's laughter.

"Same thing." Josh licked delicately at Conall's earlobe—it hadn't taken the Fae's *scair-anam* long to find out how wild that drove him. "Did you have a reason for asking me down here, or were you just wanting to make use of the cuffs?"

"You tempt me." Conall ran the flat of his tongue over Josh's chin, enjoying the rough rasp of a day's growth of beard. "Maybe after. But yes, I need to do something tonight."

"You know how I hate helping you out." Laughing, Josh drew Conall with him over to the black leather chaise. The two of them had added a few more comfortable touches to the spare concrete room over the last few months, since Conall needed to come down here more frequently than Tiernan did, to replenish his inner store of magick from its ley source. A fur rug on the floor, to keep the chill from bare feet; a music system, for Josh's dubstep and whatever new human music Conall was discovering at any particular time; a small table, holding a growing assortment of toys that had started with a string of anal beads. *Somehow, Fae magic never worked like this in the fairy tales I grew up with*, had been Josh's laconic comment when presented with the beads.

"Would you be willing to try something different, tonight?" Conall sat down beside Josh, resting a hand on his thigh, running it up and down the hard muscle and savoring the stirring he could already feel in his loins. Magick with Josh was joy, in so many ways.

"Anything for you, *d'orant*." Josh's arms settled around Conall; teeth worried gently at his throat.

Conall let his head fall back to give Josh more room to play. "Let me Fade, and enter into you. And then, when you touch yourself..." He smiled, at the shiver that raced through the body pressed to his. "You'll please us both."

"Oh, fuck." The word was almost reverent. "Voyeurism and exhibitionism at the same time." Josh stood, skinned out of his shirt, and tossed it aside.

"Humans seem to have a lot of —isms." Josh was

reaching for the button of his jeans, now, but Conall stopped him, wanting the pleasure of doing it himself. Slowly, so as to tease his lover even more, easing the button free of the fabric it strained against.

"And Fae don't?"

Conall shrugged. "We just are. We don't care so much about *how* we live, we just do it. And enjoy it." He nuzzled into the curly bush he was revealing, breathing deep, sighing with pleasure. A sigh that became a soft moan as Josh's fingers tangled in his hair, drew him closer. He had a lifetime of enjoyment foregone for the sake of magick to make up for, and how wonderful that Josh was so determined to help him do it.

"What do you need to do? And how fast can you do it? Because if you keep that up, I'm not going to make it till you Fade and get in me." The human's voice was a low rumble, almost a purr.

Conall laughed, breathlessly, as he worked Josh's jeans further down his thighs. "Tiernan and I decided I should try a Summoning. Call as many Fae as possible here. And maybe their *scair-anaim* as well, who knows? Half a Fae soul might hear it, even from within a human." He curled his hand around the base of Josh's shaft, traced a thick dark vein up the length of it with the tip off his tongue, and smiled as Josh groaned. "And you'll be glad to know that I've actually worked this channeling out ahead of time. So we won't have to stop before we're finished."

"You mean, it'll go off when we do?" Josh's chuckle turned to a moan when Conall took him into his mouth. Of all the delights they had explored together, these last months, it was the first one they had shared that proved to be the human's favorite.

"Exactly. Are you ready for me?"

"I always think I am." Josh's fingers tightened in Conall's hair, tilted his head so their eyes met; a tingle of anticipatory delight raced down Conall's spine and started his cock rising at sight of the light in his lover's eyes. "But it's always better than I remember."

"May it ever be thus." The closing line of the *ceangail* ritual, the binding of Royals, and as close as Fae ever came to wishing for forever.

Conall Faded, and rose from the chaise; he turned and backed into his lover, wrapping Josh's essence around him and sighing with pleasure. The need to share Josh's body to accomplish the greater channelings might have been born of necessity, and of his injury, but it was a blessing and he wouldn't give it up now even if he could.

Anytime, dar'cion.

The chain around Josh's wrist shimmered into all three dimensions of existence as the human reached down and cradled his shaft in the warmth of his palm. If Conall concentrated, he could feel it, soft loose skin over hardness. What a wonder, to feel his human's pleasure from within.

Josh sucked in a breath through clenched teeth and slowly stroked, tugging not quite gently at the loose skin. His cock grew darker, thicker as Conall watched, fascinated; beads of moisture welled up at the tip, trickled down to be spread along the length of the rigid organ.

More.

"As you wish." Josh made a tunnel of his hand, and his hips began to sway, to thrust; his free hand glided up his chest, gently twisting the nipple ring

Terry had put in for him, and Conall shivered at the delicious combination of sensations. "Do you want to know what I think of, when I'm doing this alone?"

You still have to do this alone? I'm doing something wrong.

Josh gave a short bark of laughter before letting Conall see what was in his imagination. Of course, it was Conall himself, kneeling before Josh, with the rush and splash of water all around and Josh's cock thrusting in and out of his mouth.

Let me make it good for you. Conall's plea, from the very beginning, repeated now in a husky whisper, as his own aching shaft found its place within Josh's rigid cock, being fondled, wrung, gripped. *Please. Use me.*

"Oh, sweet fuck."

Conall watched as Josh's free hand gripped wet hair darkened nearly to mahogany by the falling water and pulled the imagined Conall hard onto a shaft that jerked and curved. He felt the pull in his hair, and the hot mouth on his shaft, and his balls rising up and his cock stiffening. And the sheer blinding bliss of SoulShared climax.

Times two.

Blinded, deafened except to Josh's roar bouncing off the concrete walls, Conall barely felt the channeling release itself from his own substance. Once freed, it spread like ripples in water, driven by the power of that unimaginable shared pleasure, Summoning every Fae soul to come to Washington, to come to Purgatory, to the shelter of the wards. There was no knowing how long it would take to penetrate everywhere Fae or human SoulShare might be found, but at least it had started.

"Christ on a cracker." Josh staggered, nearly fell; he managed to make it back to the chaise before his knees gave out on him completely. Conall, of course, went with him, reluctant to give up the shared perceptions; all too quickly, though, the chain that bound him went back to being ink on skin, and dragon and hawk calmed and settled, and it was time to leave.

Slowly, reluctantly, Conall re-formed on the chaise, a forearm over his eyes to block out the dim light. "We might want to consider saving that for special occasions," he murmured.

"You think?" Josh turned to look down at Conall, one eyebrow going up and a corner of his mouth lifting in a smirk so sensual it could almost be Fae.

"Oh, and I suppose *you* can walk."

"The bike's parked back in the alley."

"I suddenly feel much better." It had dawned on Josh several months ago that given Conall's issues around cars of any kind, the best solution for those times when they needed to go somewhere together was a motorcycle. And riding pillion behind Josh had rapidly climbed Conall's list of favorite things to do.

"Thought you might." Josh grinned.

Quickly—amazingly quickly, really, considering that Conall, at least, had been seriously considering not moving for a week only moments before—Josh dressed, and the two of them exited the nexus chamber and ascended back into the club.

The Friday night floor show was in full swing by now, and Conall's attention was drawn to the pole set in a prominent place on the dance floor; as eager as he was to leave, and return to the apartment he shared with Josh, the man sinuously winding himself around the pole stopped him in his tracks. A curly mop of blond hair was, at the moment, upside down and spinning slowly toward the floor; a perfectly-chiseled body wrapped around the pole in ways that defied gravity, and the minuscule thong the performer wore did little to conceal a cock that sported a jaunty silver ring pierced through the flesh under the head.

Conall heard Josh chuckle beside him. "You like Garrett, hm? He's one of the few dancers left from the bad old days." Josh's hand found its way into Conall's, and Conall smiled. "A lot of the guys who work here come to me to get inked, or pierced, so I hear things. The bastard who owned this place before Tiernan didn't pay the dancers shit, didn't look after them at all. Tiernan's lucky Garrett stayed—he really packs the place."

"Human bodies can do the most amazing things." Conall shook his head in wonder, his gaze never leaving the dancer.

"And I want to show you a few more of them." Josh tugged at Conall's hand. "Come on. The bike's going to get you all nice and primed for me."

Laughing softly, Conall followed Josh up the stairs, and out into the darkness. The wards whispered to him as he passed their boundaries, and he nodded; the *Marfach* would be back, sooner or later, but surely it would be able to do nothing. Not against both of them.

Use me.
May it ever be thus.

Following is Chapter One of Deep Plunge,
SoulShares, Book Three

Chapter One

The Realm
2,327 years ago

If this is what a saved world looks like, deliver me from a fallen one.

Lochlann stumbled, went to one knee on the uneven, charred ground. He'd almost forgotten the luxury of riding, at this point. Of course, he'd been lucky to find a horse at all, when the three days of lightning and terror were ended and he'd emerged from his *dolmain* deep within the hollow hill and the world itself had been warped and twisted around him. The horse was luckier than he was, really; he'd left it at the last stream he'd forded before crossing the border formed by fire and storm and the spending of magick.

How many leagues he'd crossed on foot since then, he had no idea, but the length of silk he'd torn from his shirt to wrap around mouth and nose was black with soot, and he'd long since forgotten his last sight of anything green or growing. If not for the pull of the Summoning he followed, it would be simple to wander this blasted land in circles for a lifetime.

The dark-haired Fae staggered to his feet, brushed the soot off his leathers—though why he bothered was a mystery, their brown had long since gone black—and turned, shading his eyes with one hand and scanning the horizon. The channeling was drawing him toward a nearby rise. *Maybe I'll be able to see him from there. Or at least get some idea of what happened.*

As Lochlann approached the hill, instinct sent his magickal sense questing for energy to heal his rasping throat, his parched lungs. But the land around him was bereft of magick, and he was forced to turn within, drawing on the living magick of which he was formed. *Shit. Everything's drained. Everything.* He shuddered, suddenly cold. *Were they able to defeat it? Or am I being Summoned into a trap?*

The Fae sighed with relief as magick, unbound and unexpected, coursed through him. He breathed it in, let it fill throat and lungs and eyes and every other part of him, and then Shaped the magick into health. This was the gift of the Demesne of Water, the only Fae healing that could be accomplished without causing more pain than it eased.

He crested the rise, and stopped short with a whispered curse.

He stood, not at the top of a hill, but on the edge of a low cliff, overlooking a broad, flat valley. The skeletons of trees broke up the monotony of the landscape, and small eddies of blown soot chased each other across the barren ground.

And a few minutes' walk from the base of the cliff, a perfect circle was set into the ground, of a black so utter it both drew the gaze and repelled it. Around the circle were knots of muted color—

—Fae, clustered together, in clothing that might once have been finery. Some were wounded, and some of those were being tended to by others; some paced, arms wrapped tightly around themselves; some sat and stared, and even at this distance a Fae's keen senses could make out their stunned, dazed expressions.

I made it. But where's Cuinn?

Almost on the thought, the air stirred beside him, and an outline formed. A familiar outline, sandy blond hair, strong shoulders, lean hips, and pale green eyes gazing out sharply from the sketched-in face. Gradually, the rest of the figure filled in, and Lochlann could see that his one close friend was as battered and weary as any of the Fae gathered around the black circle.

"Did you win, or lose?"

Cuinn rolled his eyes. "If we'd lost, trust me, we wouldn't be having this conversation." He looked Lochlann up and down, his gaze measuring. "I take it the *dolmain* kept you adequately protected?"

Lochlann nodded. "It's an old one. It goes all the way back under the hill. But even so, I don't think it would have lasted through some of what I was hearing without the ward you put up." His body was going to remember the way the ground trembled all around him for a very long time. "Just out of curiosity, if my part in this is so important, why did you send me off alone, instead of letting me go with the four thousand Rovilin and Aine sheltered? You knew they'd be safe."

The shorter Fae opened his mouth to reply, then closed it again firmly, rubbing the back of his neck as if something there pained him. "They're safe. Yes. But they aren't what they were. And we need you the way you are."

"You lost me." Lochlann's gaze flickered to the black circle, and to the host of Fae around it. Some of them were growing restive; a few, the more mobile and the less patient, were wandering westward, looking off toward the horizon. "What happened to them?"

Cuinn raked a hand through his hair, apparently oblivious to the trails of soot he left through the length of it. "Living magick is going to be in short supply in the Realm. At least for a while."

"You told me that was going to happen, if you won." Every living thing in the Realm was formed of living magick, the energy that went into each channeling a Fae performed. But the source of that energy lay within the human world. And the battle that had just been fought had ended with the sundering of the two worlds, Fae and human, and the sealing away of everything in the human world. Along with the most ancient and evil enemy of the Fae race.

"Those of us who are left are going to have to make do with less, until we figure something out." Cuinn kicked at a stone, sent it tumbling down over the cliff, watched it fall. "We worked out a way to help the whole race use less living magick. What's left of the race, anyway." He stared out across the valley, nearly expressionless.

Lochlann knew the truth. Fae didn't love, not the way humans did. And while friendships—such as the

one he himself shared with the prickly Loremaster—
were not unheard of, most Fae considered altruism to
be a purely human pastime. But the Loremasters were
not most Fae; they knew the safety of the Fae race was
in their charge, and their failure to stop the *Marfach*
before it wreaked the devastation surrounding them
was bitter. Especially for Cuinn. "What did you do?"

Cuinn's features twisted in what could almost
have been a smirk, except Lochlann knew better.
"Kept them safe, as many as we could. Sent as many
Loremasters as we could spare from the fight off with
them. Rovilin and Aine put them all into a deep sleep,
and while they were sleeping, the two of them
completely remade what's left of the race." Cuinn, too,
was looking off westward, to where the sun burned
orange in a soot-laden sky. "Fortunately, they got it
done before we had to seal the portal, so they could tap
into the ley energy to do it."

"Remade how?"

Cuinn laughed, a short, harsh sound that was
almost a cough and definitely without humor. "The
Fae have Royals, now. And Nobles. The ones who can
channel elemental magick are going to wake up as
nobility, and they'll interbreed and keep their precious
bloodlines pure to keep their status. Elemental magick
doesn't drain the Realm. And the shapeshifting freaks
of nature who are the Fae Elementals are going to be
Royals. As long as they keep breeding, there will
always be more elemental magick."

"Would I have been a Noble?" Lochlann was
intrigued despite himself. The thought of Fae
accepting rulers would have made him laugh, if his
friend hadn't been so bitterly serious. Things were

going to be interesting in the Realm while the Fae got used to this new way of life. Not that it mattered to him.

"I doubt it." Cuinn's half-smile was the first Lochlann had seen on him since he'd Faded in. "Healing is the gift of the Demesne of Water, but you draw on pure magick to do it, not elemental. No, *chara*, you'd be a commoner—there they are!"

Cuinn was looking past him, off westward, to where two figures on horseback were sending up clouds of soot and dust all out of proportion to their size. "There who are?"

"Aine and Rovilin. Now we can start."

The Loremasters clustered around the black circle were stirring now, the wounded struggling to rise, pushing away the helping hands of their fellows. Even at this distance, Lochlann could feel the pain of the injured, the exhaustion of the more intact. A curse that went along with the gift of Water. Fae, as a general rule, were short on empathy, but healers were something of an exception. "Two more will make that much of a difference?" Shading his eyes, he studied the crowd around the circle. "There must be a thousand Loremasters down there."

"One thousand, two hundred and eight. If we haven't lost anyone since the battle ended. And we're going to need every one of them."

Cuinn's voice was tight, controlled; Lochlann turned back, and was astonished by the anger he saw on his friend's face. "What is it?" He rested a hand on the blond Fae's shoulder. "How many did you lose?"

"It's not that." Cuinn shook his head sharply. "Though we lost too damned many. Killed in battle, dead by their own hands to stop the *Marfach* from warping them, spent to nothingness banishing the bastard."

"Then what is it?"

"Every one of them is needed so desperately, and there are Fae down there clinging to life solely so they can let go of it where it will feed the last channeling." Cuinn spoke through clenched teeth, avoiding Lochlann's gaze. "They're all needed. Every one but me."

Lochlann's own chest was tight with Cuinn's unmistakable anger. An anger he didn't understand. "You told me you had your own part to play."

"I do." More anger, if anything. "And they won't tell me what it is." He glared down at the ink-black circle, as if it somehow collaborated with the Loremasters to hide the secret from him.

Lochlann followed the direction of Cuinn's gaze, focusing on the circle, rather than the Fae gathered around it. "What is that?"

"It's everywhere in the Realm."

He started to laugh, but Cuinn looked serious enough that he turned the laugh into a cough. Not difficult, given the soot and ash that hung in the air. "You lost me again."

Cuinn sighed, but Lochlann suspected he welcomed the distraction. "There's a very real sense in which space and time don't exist when you're dealing with pure magick."

"That much I follow." Magick was a paradox, both real and not, visible and invisible, permeating everything but with no form of its own. And any magick touched all other magick, in some way that

301

gave most Fae who weren't mages at or near the level of the Loremasters headaches to contemplate. That was how Fading worked, a thing Fae accomplished instinctively once they came into their birthright of power, moving from magick to magick, becoming magick themselves for the barest instant.

"That circle—" Cuinn gestured with a jerk of his chin—"is a barrier between magicks. Not just a ward. The magick on the far side of it can't touch the magick on this side of it."

Lochlann stared at the blackness. "I thought there wasn't any magick left on the far side of it." The preparation for the last battle with the *Marfach* had taken years, to hear Cuinn tell it, gathering together every remnant of living magick from the world humans and Fae had shared, to keep it away from the ancient enemy that inhabited that magick, fed on it, and twisted it into its own image of pure, unadulterated evil.

Cuinn coughed into his hand, "Damned soot." He rubbed at his eyes, reddened by smoke, their pale green even more vivid because of the blood hue. "The *Marfach* is there. And the energy in the ley lines. The ley power isn't living magick, strictly speaking, but no one wants to wager on the *Marfach* being unable to figure out how to use it somehow."

"I see your point." One look at the utter destruction around them was more than enough to remind him of the cost of that particular error. "So that thing is the only window between the two worlds?"

"It's not a window at all. It's a magickal representation of everyplace in the Realm. Every place where the *Marfach* could cross back. And that image, that representation, has been locked down, tempered, warded, sealed. Every protective channeling any of us knew." Cuinn's brows drew together again; the respite answering questions had given him was apparently over. "But it's still not going to be enough. Not until it's finished—oh, damn." Just that quickly, frustration yielded to a hushed sorrow. "They're starting."

Lochlann watched, fighting to breathe against a hollow sensation in his chest, as two critically injured Fae were carried out onto the gleaming black surface of the circle. If they were still injured, if they hadn't healed this long after the final battle with the *Marfach*, then their wounds were mortal. Yet they had refused to die.

"What are they going to do?"

"Watch." Cuinn's gaze was fixed on the circle, on the two Fae that lay there alone, their bearers having melted back into the onlooking throng.

Lochlann was about to reply, but bit back the words as spindles of silver-blue light rose up from the circle around each of the injured Loremasters. Spindles that bent, and wove themselves into intricate webs over each recumbent form, until the two were all but lost to sight, shrouded in dancing light. And then the webs started to tighten, to draw the two Fae down into the substance of the circle. As Lochlann stared, transfixed, they slowly gave up their substance to the light-sucking blackness of the circle.

"*Slántai a'váil*," Cuinn whispered. *Farewell*, as the webs gave back their light to the circle, silver-blue sparks chasing each other across the surface before being swallowed up in the darkness. That darkness was not entirely featureless, though; at the very limits

of his vision, Lochlann made out—or thought he did—
two fine lines of silver-blue, curving just under the
black surface. And the brilliant green of new grass
limned the circumference of the circle.

Before Lochlann could find his voice, two more
Loremasters were helped out onto the ebon surface.
These were able to sit, and did; the eyes of the male
were closed as he struggled with pain, but the female
saw, and gasped, as the light shot up around her.

His gift, or curse, of empathy allowed him to feel
her heart race with the touch of the net of lights; her
terror nearly overwhelmed him as the net began to pull
her down. Yet under the terror lay iron determination,
and she barely flinched as the first of her substance
disappeared.

"*Shit*—Lochlann, damn it, don't go with her!"

Cuinn's voice was like a dousing with cold water;
Lochlann gasped, shook himself, and tried to make his
eyes focus on his friend's face. "Where is she
going?—where are *they* going?"

Cuinn didn't seem to hear him. *"Eiscréid,* I
thought this would be far enough away that you
wouldn't be drawn in—"

"I don't have to be drawn in. I won't let myself."
Yet he had to fight to keep from looking back toward
the circle, to ignore the movement he could see at the
edge of his vision, to keep his attention on his agitated
friend. "What are they doing?"

"Two things. Neither of which we can afford to
have you caught up in." Cuinn took Lochlann by the
arm and firmly turned him away from the view below.
"Their souls are becoming a part of the portal. They'll
see to the protection of any Fae that passes through

into the human world, now that we've sealed the humans off from us, and hold the portal against the *Marfach*, if it tries to return here from the human world."

"That's one."

The blond Fae seemed to have trouble finding his voice. "They're giving the magick they're formed of back to the Realm," he managed at last.

Now Lochlann *had* to look. He turned on his heel, and saw two more Fae being assisted into the empty circle. Not quite empty; two more lines, finer than hairs and detectable only by their bluish-silver glow, arced through the blackness. And the green rim he had seen around the circle after the first two Fae departed was now a greensward extending maybe thirty paces from the circle's edge in all directions.

Resolutely, he kept his eyes on that swath of green, even when the flare of light told him the circle was about to claim two more wounded mages. This time, he saw the life suffuse the charred and barren ground, saw it go green from within, in an ever-widening circle under the feet of the Loremasters who awaited their turn in the black.

"You *want* to do what they're doing?" Lochlann risked a look back at Cuinn, who was watching the scene below with a predatory intensity, unhampered by Lochlann's gift.

Cuinn nodded tightly. "I know how badly they need magick, and souls, to make this work. But they won't let me be a part of it. Other than to seal the channeling off when the last of them go into the Pattern." A muscle jumped in the sensual male's jaw — and even burned and exhausted and black with

305

grime, 'sensual' was one of the first words anyone would use to describe him. "Do they really expect me to be content with that?"

"At least you'll be there to help me, when it's my turn." There were four Fae, now, two males, two females, taking their places on the circle; Lochlann carefully kept his gaze fixed on the empty center of the circle and focused on not sensing the emotions swirling around the black expanse. "After seeing this..." He shook his head slowly. "I could never do what you asked of me alone."

"You could if you had to. But I'll help you."

The two Fae fell silent, watching the dance that went on below them. It *was* a dance, slow and stately and possessed of a terrible beauty. Four by four, now, the Loremasters came, kneeling on the hard black surface, the females surrounded by swirls of skirts blackened with smoke, the males by cloaks rent and stained with blood. Lochlann saw faces he knew, males and females he had shared a night with, sometimes more, and in those moments he had to look away. Four by four the nets of light took them, and the life they poured into the land pushed back the devastation. Silver-blue tracing slowly filled the darkness, bright points of light racing along arcs and whorls that grew more and more intricate with every vanished Fae.

The sun sank, and the moon rose, and by the time the last few Loremasters entered the circle, it was almost as if they knelt on a piece of the night sky itself. Cuinn cleared his throat and turned to Lochlann. "Do you think you can be close to them and not be drawn in?—I should say good-bye, but you don't have to come with me if it would put you at risk."

"I can manage." Lochlann's own voice, unused for hours, was gruff and choked. "Hurry, before the lights take them."

Cuinn nodded, and Faded; Lochlann followed, taking form at the very edge of the black circle beside his friend.

This close, the beauty of the portal took his breath. Midnight blackness was set with icy silver-blue light, a magnificently complex net of glittering diamond. The four Fae who knelt in the midst of it were equally beautiful, though each bore scars from the battle they had endured. Only one of the four was known to Lochlann, and that by reputation only—Dúlánc, the leader of the Loremasters, the strongest of them, and nearly a thousand years old. So ancient that his age had begun to show, his black hair was frosted with white. And from him, Lochlann sensed no fear at all; apprehension, yes, but it was nearly lost in fierce excitement.

"We will be enough." Dúlánc's deep voice seemed to come from the very depths of exhaustion as he addressed Cuinn, yet it trembled with that same excitement. "If you seal the Pattern well behind us, we will be enough to hold the portal against anything less than one of our own, wielding the magick of a whole world."

"I won't fail you." Cuinn stood, feet shoulders'-width apart and arms crossed, his jaw set in what might have been determination and might have been anger. Both, probably. "But I should be with you."

Dúlánc sighed. "One had to remain behind. And none of us are capable of doing what you will one day do."

"Do I get to know what that is?" If anything, his friend grew even more pugnacious in the face of the senior Loremaster's formality.

"Not yet." The hint of a smile touched the elderly Fae's lips. "One of the things you have to do is figure it out."

"I would feel better about that if I didn't know for a fact you don't actually know everything."

Now Dúlánc laughed outright. "Fortunately for all of us, stubbornness is essential to your task."

The older Loremaster was still smiling as he turned to Lochlann. "Brother of Water, I should have thanked you before now, but believe me when I say that we are grateful for what you are about to do. This work—" Dúlánc's gesture took in the whole of the circle—"is far from finished. And without you, it could never *be* finished."

"I don't understand." Lochlann felt his cheeks warm, at being addressed as 'brother' by a male already a legend. "But I'll do as Cuinn's explained to me."

"We can ask no more." The smile, the laughter in the eyes faded. "From tonight, you will no longer be Lochlann, but Lochlann Doran." Lochlann the Stranger, Lochlann the Exile. "Until you find the one destined for you on the other side."

"What about me?" Cuinn put in, one eyebrow nearly disappearing into the sandy blond locks that fell over his forehead. "Am I to be renamed as well?"

"Oh, yes." Dúlánc chuckled dryly. "Several of your fellow Loremasters had suggestions for a new name. I chose to ignore them. From now on, you will be Cuinn an Dearmad. Wisdom of the Forgotten. For

308

forgotten we will all surely be. None of the four thousand were told the truth of the portal, and they will wake to a world without Loremasters."

"Dúlánc." The woman who knelt behind the elder mage spoke softly. "The Pattern remains unfinished until we enter it."

"Thank you, Aine." Dúlánc took a deep, cleansing breath. "Cuinn, Lochlann, you might want to step back."

Lochlann obeyed, and as a precaution averted his eyes. But even looking off into the magickally restored forest bordering the portal site, he saw the light. Saw it build, saw it flare. And heard his *chara*'s long, unsteady sigh when darkness returned.

"Cuinn, I'm sorry—"

"Stand back." Cuinn's eyes were a sharp green glint in the darkness, reflecting Pattern-light. "All the magick for this is going to have to come from me—I don't want to drain you accidentally."

Again Lochlann gave way, but this time he watched. Cuinn closed his eyes, bowed his head. His hands clenched into fists, then relaxed. And he began to glow. At first, it was as if his skin was suffused with fire, the way a child's hand looked clutching a light-orb crafted by a doting parent. The light swiftly brightened, though, and in a matter of moments his friend was engulfed in white and green fire, subtly patterned. *Yes, he told me, his father was Air and his mother was Earth.*

He closed his eyes, briefly, to let the searing after-images clear.

When he opened them again, Cuinn still blazed as brightly, but knelt beside the circle, reaching for the matte-black surface. The green and the white raced out from where he touched it, like oil touched with a spark, or like frost etching itself on glass; the circle flared up brilliantly, then faded once again to blackness. This was a different sort of blackness, though. The circle now gave back the starlight like a mirror, and when Lochlann edged closer to look, he saw the brilliant silver-blue tracery faded to the thinness of a hair, nearly invisible.

"Are you ready?" Cuinn spoke quietly, from behind him.

So soon? Lochlann's heart raced as he turned. But, then, why wait? "If the portal's ready, yes."

The magickal glow hadn't faded entirely from Cuinn yet, and Lochlann caught his breath at his friend's beauty, his features edged in shifting light. He had never bedded Cuinn—their sort of friendship was a rarity among the Fae, and would never have survived the kind of sexual collision he knew the Loremaster favored—but it was easy to see why males and females alike vied, and sometimes even dueled, for his attention.

"It's ready, though I'll probably have to help you through. One of my first jobs come morning is to trigger the wards the others crafted for this place, and figure a way to open the portal when necessary without me having to spend magick to do it directly." Cuinn shifted his weight uncomfortably. "Do me a favor? Be careful, once you're over there. If things went as we planned, nothing physical can harm you. Look around, find out what the Sundering has done to the human world. And then when you find the human with the other half of your soul, you shouldn't need the invulnerability any more, because with his help you'll be able to tap directly into the raw magick that's left on that side."

"Slow down, *chara*. Breathe." Lochlann managed a smile. "You told me most of this already." Cuinn had first approached him, tentatively, several years ago, not long after the Loremasters had started their planning. "And I agreed to do it. I'm a volunteer, remember?"

"I know." Cuinn took a deep breath, and let it out in a sigh. "I'd feel better if we were able to be more certain. We tried to control as much as we could, but there are aspects of this that are beyond anyone's ability to foresee or control. And no one has been able to test the system."

"That's my job. And I trust you." Words rarer even than 'I love you' among the Fae, and never spoken lightly.

"Maybe you shouldn't." The gaze Cuinn turned on him was haunted, his emotional aura that of a male pushed to his limits and past them, and facing a task that demanded everything he had left.

Lochlann shook his head. "Send me through, *chara*."

Cuinn stared at him a moment longer, then nodded. "All right. Go."

Lochlann stepped tentatively onto the circle, not sure what sort of surface would greet him. It was solid, and as smooth as it looked; he moved out to the center, the small space of darkness in the tracery of light, and knelt as he had seen so many other Fae do in the course of the endless day just past. He looked down at the gleaming surface, and fought down dizzying vertigo. The silver-blue Pattern gleamed in the circle below him, its lines finer than spun silk. And past the lines, he saw a sky full of stars. "*Cho'hálan*," he whispered. *So beautiful.*

One swirl of light, directly in front of him, caught his attention.

Dúlánc, it said, in the curves and angles of *d'aos'Faein* shaping. Beside it, another skein of lines shaped *Aine*. There were other names as well, all subtly shifting, rearranging themselves. As if their bearers were trying to find their places in a new reality.

Cuinn gestured, whispered, and the mirrored surface vanished.

The brilliant glory of the lines revived, and for an instant longer Lochlann was enthralled by beauty.

But the lines were blades, keener than any knife. Lochlann fell through them, between them, the blades cutting deep and bloodless.

But not deep enough.

He dropped through the Pattern to the bottom of the cage of his ribs, before he stuck. He tried to lunge for Cuinn, sought his hand, nearly blinded by the pain. His wordless screams rent the night air, one after another. *It's gone wrong, no one could survive this!*

Cuinn, as pale as his own revenant, stared at what was left of Lochlann in shock. Then he gestured, and a whirlwind sprang up around him. He pointed at the center of the circle.

The merciless wind hammered at Lochlann the Exile like a great fist. His scream went ahead of him, opening the way into his new world.

Glossary

The following is a glossary of the *Faen* words and phrases found in *Hard as Stone* and *Gale Force*. The reader should be advised that, as in the Celtic languages descended from it, spelling in *Faen* is as highly eccentric as the one doing the spelling.

(A few quick pronunciation rules — bearing in mind that most Fae detest rules — single vowels are generally 'pure', as in ah, ey, ee, oh, oo for a, e, i, o, u. An accent over a vowel means that vowel is held a little longer than its unaccented cousins. "ao" is generally "ee", but otherwise dipthongs are pretty much what you'd expect. Consonants are a pain. "ch" is hard, as in the modern Scottish "loch". "S", if preceded by "i" or "a", is usually "sh". "F" is usually silent, unless it's the first letter in a word, and if the word starts with "fh", then the "f" and the "h" are *both* silent. "Th" is likewise usually silent, as is "dh", although if "dh" is at the beginning of a word, it tries to choke on itself and ends up sounding something like a "strangled" French "r". Oh, and "mh" is "v", "bh" is "w", "c" is always hard, and don't forget to roll your "r"s!)

Ach but
a'gár'doltas vendetta (lit. "smiling-murder")
amad'n fool, idiot
asling dream
beag little, slight
bod penis (vulgar)

bodlag limp dick (much greater insult than a human might suppose)

bragan toy (see phrase)

briste broken

buchal alann beautiful boy

ceangal Royal soul-bonding ceremony in the Realm (common alt. spelling *ceangail*)

cein fa? Why?

céle general way of referring to two people

le céle together

a céle one another, each other

coladh sleep

cónai live

cugat to you

dar'cion brilliantly colored. Conall's pillow-name for Josh.

dóchais hope (n.)

d'orant impossible. Josh's pillow-name for Conall.

dre'fiur beloved sister

dre'thair beloved brother

dubh black, dark

Faen the Fae language. *Laurm Faen* — I speak Fae.

as'Faein in the Fae language. *Laur lom as'Faein* — I speak in the Fae language.

fan wait (imp.)

fior true

gan general negative — no, not, without, less

g'féalaidh may you (pl.) live (see phrases)

g'fua hate (v.)

g'demin true, real

fada long (can reference time or distance)

impi I beg

lae day

lanan lover. Tiernan's pillow name for Kevin, and vice versa

laurha spoken (see phrases)

related words — *laurm*, I speak; *laur lom*, I am speaking, I speak (in) a language

lofa rotten

Marfach, the the Slow Death. Deadliest foe of the Fae race.

marú kill

minn oath

mo mhinn my oath

misnach courage

ollúnta solemn

orm at me

pian pain

rochar harm (n.)

savac-dui black-headed hawk, Conall's House-guardian

scair'anam SoulShare (pl. *scair-anaim*)

m'anam-sciar my SoulShare

scair'aine'e the act of SoulSharing

scian-damsai knife-dances. An extremely lethal type of formalized combat.

scílim I think, I believe

sibh you (pl.)

s'ocan peace, be at peace

spára spare

spára'se spare him

sule-d'ainmi lit. "animal-eyes", dark brown eyes

s'vra lom I love (lit. "I have love on me")

ta'sair I'm free (exclam.)

tre three

Tre... dó... h'on... Three.... two... one...

tseo this, this is (see phrases)

uiscebai strong liquor found in the Realm, similar to whiskey

veissin knockout drug found in the Realm, causes headaches

viant desired one. A Fae endearment.

Useful phrases:

...tseo mo mhinn ollúnta. This is my solemn oath.

G'féalaidh sibh i do cónai fada le céle, gan a marú a céle.

"May you live long together, and not kill one another." A Fae blessing, sometimes bestowed upon those Fae foolhardy enough to undertake some form of exclusive relationship. Definite "uh huh, good luck with that" overtones.

bragan a lae "toy of the day". The plaything of a highly distractable Fae.

Fai dara tú pian beag. Ach tú a sabail dom ó pian i bhad nís mo.

You cause a slight pain. But you are the healing of more.

Cein fa buil tu ag'eachan' orm ar-seo? Why do you look at me this way?

Dóchais laurha, dóchais briste. Hope spoken is hope broken.

Bod lofa dubh. Lit. "black rotted dick". Not a polite phrase.

Scílim g'fua lom tú. I think I hate you.

S'vra lom tú. I love you

About the Author

Rory Ni Coileain majored in creative writing, back when Respectable Colleges didn't offer such a major. She had to design it herself, at a university which boasted one professor willing to teach creative writing: a British surrealist who went nuts over students writing dancing bananas in the snow but did not take well to high fantasy. Graduating Phi Beta Kappa at the age of nineteen, she sent off her first short story to an anthology that was being assembled by an author she idolized, and received one of those rejection letters that puts therapists' kids through college. For the next thirty years or so she found other things to do, such as going to law school, ballet dancing (at more or less the same time), volunteering as a lawyer with Gay Men's Health Crisis, and nightclub singing, until her stories started whispering to her. Now she's a lawyer and a legal editor; the proud mother of a proud Brony and budding filmmaker; and is busily wedding her love of myth and legend to her passion for m/m romance. She is a three-time Rainbow Award finalist.

Made in the USA
Monee, IL
03 August 2020

37520863R00177